ANXIETY

ANXIETY : A SMOKE & MIRRORS BOOK - 1

ANXIETY

A SMOKE & MIRRORS BOOK

1

A Tale of Murder, Mystery and Romance

H. D. THOMSON

Fear of self is the greatest of all terrors, the deepest of all dread, the commonest of all mistakes. From it grows failure. Because of it, life is a mockery. Out of it comes despair.
— David Seabury

CHAPTER ONE

MARGOT DAVENPORT SHOULD never have opened the front door. She should have just kept on getting slowly and thoroughly drunk that night. But the pounding on the door went on and on, reverberating throughout the house and inside her skull. Stumbling from the couch in the living room, Margot knocked over her glass and an empty wine bottle, and grabbed onto her throbbing head with a hand.

"Damn it!"

In the hall, she tripped over her fur ball of a cat, Marmaduke, who streaked past her and up the stairs. She swore again. The banging continued. The crazy fool outside had given up on the doorbell long ago.

"John! Come on. Open up! It's me, Jake!"

At the mention of Johnny's name, Margot's stomach twisted and rolled with sudden nausea. "Okay! Okay! Give me a second."

She groped for the light switch to the hall. Nothing happened.

"Damn, stupid thing!" That's what she got for not replacing the house's ancient wiring.

"John, I'm freezing my ass off!"

"What do you expect," Margot muttered, wondering if this guy was playing some sick joke at her expense.

Margot hit the outside light switch and peered through the glass panel beside the door. A man stood on the front porch. She didn't recognize him, but then again, the sheet of snow and the light's glare against the night backdrop didn't help matters.

A gun or pepper spray for protection sounded pretty nice right now, but Margot hated guns and had never expected the need, living on the outskirts of Greyson, Arizona. It wasn't like this town up in the White Mountains was loaded with crime. The worst incident had been a case of disorderly conduct last winter, and that had been from a drunken tourist.

"Who is it?"

A pause on the other side followed—almost as if she'd surprised him.

"Margot? Is that you? It's Jake Preston."

Though muffled, his words were clear enough to make out. The name sounded familiar, but she couldn't recall what Johnny had said about him.

Margot frowned and winced as pain cut across her temple, brow and the base of her skull. She should have stopped at one glass of wine. "How do you know Johnny?"

"I worked with him at Miltronics for several years on the outskirts of Boston."

Margot debated about turning this Jake away as she watched him stamp his feet against the porch. He must be freezing—what with the wind and snow.

"I know it's late, but I need to talk to John. Please. If you could just get him, you'll see I'm harmless."

The urgency in his voice made her decide. He obviously didn't know about her brother. She sighed heavily. What she had to tell him wasn't going to be easy.

Margot unlatched the lock and opened the door.

An angry gust of wind burst into the house, tearing the knob from her grasp. The door flew wide and crashed against the wall. Gasping, she reeled back as snow flew in, stabbing her face with icy spikes.

"Here, let me." He stepped inside and shoved the door closed with his shoulder. He turned his back against the light from the kitchen, casting his face in shadow. His baseball cap further shielded his features—along with sunglasses of all things.

How very odd. Sudden apprehension curled up her spine as Margot stepped away from Jake and the doorway. Topping a good six-feet, he appeared far larger than when he'd stood behind a locked door.

"What are the sunglasses for?" she asked.

"The light."

"What?"

"My eyes. They're sensitive to light. I injured both corneas as a child."

"Oh." She must have been staring at him like an idiot, but something about him made her uneasy. And it wasn't just the glasses and pale complexion.

He must have sensed her disquiet, because he explained further, "It's called *traumatic iritis*. It's something I've had to live with for as long as I can remember." He shrugged a large canvas backpack from his shoulder and placed it on the floor. "Can you get John for me?"

"He's dead."

Margot never intended the words to come out so abrupt and final, but...it hurt. Balling her hands into fists, she fought against the sudden tears that burned the back of her eyes. *Please no. Not now.* She couldn't fall apart in front of this stranger.

"He can't be. That's impossible."

"His—" Margot cleared her throat. "His funeral was today."

He flinched, stumbled, and hit a shoulder against the front door. A muscle in his square jaw clenched and unclenched, and his ragged breathing magnified the tension filling the foyer. He said something under his breath she didn't catch.

Goose bumps crawled along her spine. She needed another drink. Seeing how her brother's death ate at this man was like witnessing her own pain.

"How did he die?" Jake finally asked.

Outside, a metallic crash resounded as a gust of wind hit the house. They both jumped, and Margot swallowed a scream. A faint clang immediately followed. Then nothing but the howling wind.

"I think that was a trash can," she said and tried to form her thoughts into something coherent. Then she realized her lack of manners and how she couldn't thrust him back out in the storm without explaining more about Johnny, but she wasn't about to bring him back into the living room and broadcast her drinking with an empty wine bottle and glass on the floor. "Why don't you put your coat on the post behind you, then we can talk in the den."

After he took off his down jacket, he removed his hat to reveal very dark, almost black, shoulder-length hair, a shade lighter than her own. He had a blunt nose, square jaw, and a strong, stubborn looking face. She wondered about his eyes, and if they were just as inflexible, but she saw only her face reflected in his lenses.

Margot led him across the hall and was about to hit the switch by the door of the den when Jake caught her wrist, his gloved fingers cool and smooth against her skin. "Don't."

At the harshness of his voice, her breath hissed into her lungs and her heart jerked inside her chest. He stood directly behind, so close the warmth of his breath whispered across the nape of her neck.

Only when she pulled away from the light switch did he release her wrist. "It looks like there's a lamp on your desk," he said in a smooth, warm baritone. "I'll get it instead. It might be too bright otherwise."

She exhaled, feeling a fool. There'd been no reason to act the neurotic. He'd just been concerned with his vision. Nodding, she folded her arms across her middle and followed him into the darkened room. He reached the desk and turned on the brass lamp, throwing the room into muted shadows.

Looking around, he slowly walked the length of the large room. "You must like to read."

"I do, but not as much as it appears." Books from ceiling to floor lined two walls. Along the third wall, more books filled every available space in the cherry wood shelves on either side of a deep red, brick fireplace. Other than the two chairs and sofa grouped to one side of the room, the only real relief, her desk, a Chippendale replica, sat facing a huge bay window bracketed by thick, forest green velvet drapes. Margot loved this room, the bold, rich colors, the faint musty smell of old books, the feeling of being surrounded by so much knowledge. "It's my business—selling rare books over the Internet. At least it has been since I left the corporate world, but now with everything going electronic I've been forced to start looking into doing e-book conversions for authors."

"John mentioned you had a store."

Margot's arms tightened around her middle. She didn't know if she was up to discussing her brother with this stranger without cracking. Johnny's death was still too fresh, too painful.

"Did you want a drink?" she asked. "I'm having wine."

"Just water."

Margot escaped into the kitchen. After she poured Jake's water, she fixed herself a fresh glass of Merlot. She took a deep drink, savoring how the liquid, warm and full-bodied, slid over her tongue and down her throat. Oh, how it eased the pain and dulled the senses.

Finally gaining some control of her ragged emotions, Margot squared her shoulders and returned to the den to find Jake had moved to a book-lined wall.

"Here's your water."

"Thanks." He took his drink, his black-gloved fingers flexing over the etched glass. The leather looked supple as it molded over the knuckles and tendons of his hand. Strange. But if he wanted to hide his hands, it was no business of hers. Still, she did wonder.

His hands might be scarred and ugly, but the rest of him looked anything but. A thick black belt wrapped around a pair of narrow hips encased in faded jeans. The material molded over his long, lean legs, while a long-sleeved, black turtleneck hugged his tight, muscular chest and stomach. Not many men could get away with such a shirt, but he could.

So he had a nice body. That didn't mean she had to stare as if she hadn't seen one in a long while.

"Please. Tell me more about John. How did he die?"

She walked over to the high-backed, wing chair in forest green velvet, but couldn't bear to sit down. Instead, she moved to the window and turned away from the night sky and falling snow to find him facing her. The desk lamp behind Jake thrust him in deep shadow while his glasses, more effective than any imaginable shield, masked his expression.

She swallowed down the sudden tightness in her throat. "It was a car accident. It looked like he didn't have the car under control when he hit the turn. He was going way too fast and couldn't make it. The railing gave and he fell into the ravine. He didn't stand a chance."

"Do they know why the car went out of control?"

"No."

"Did you talk to him that day? Did he seem upset?"

Clenching the glass to her chest, she raised her chin and straightened. "It wasn't suicide."

"Of course not," Jake quickly assured. "He wasn't the type."

The stiffness in her fingers and spine eased. "Some people thought differently."

"Then they didn't know John." The corners of his mouth dipped downward as he rested a hand against a bookshelf. "So he didn't act odd before the accident?"

"I don't know. I never got a chance to see him. He must have been on his way here. He was only a couple of miles from home when his car went off the road. Why do you want to know?"

"No reason in particular. Just thought he must have had his mind on something. He was a damn good driver."

She stilled. Something in his tone didn't ring true. He'd been asking a lot of questions. People asked questions for reasons, not out of a sense of politeness.

"John talked a lot about you."

Heat fired into her cheeks. "Really? That doesn't sound like Johnny." What the hell had he told this—Jake?

"Yeah. I even have a photo of the two of you." He pulled his wallet from his jeans pocket. After some difficulty, he slipped out a crinkled paper, walked over and showed her a picture.

She glanced down at it and tensed. The photo had been taken over three years ago in Boston on her twenty-fifth birthday. Just before her divorce. She stood between Johnny and Malcolm, an arm around each. She looked happy. What a lie. She'd been anything but. That morning she'd had her last fight with Malcolm before moving out.

She polished off the rest of her wine and walked over to the fireplace to set her glass down on the mantel with a surprisingly steady hand. "Why the photo?"

"It's not just the photo. He also gave me this." Jake pulled something else from his pocket. Gold glittered against the lamplight. A necklace with a large circular medallion.

Margot sucked in a lungful of air. Not just any necklace. Johnny's. A gift she'd given him on his birthday. She raised a trembling hand, and Jake draped the chain across her palm. She lifted the medallion of a bull, signifying Taurus, John's zodiac sign. She turned it over and read the inscription on the back. "To the hero in the family. Love, Margot."

A deep wave of emotion caught against Margot's chest as she squeezed the medallion. "I..." She cleared her throat. "Where did you get this?"

Once again, shadows deepened around Jake as he stepped away from the light and Margot. He tucked the picture and wallet back into his rear pocket. "John gave it to me. He said that if I ever needed time to myself or needed a place to stay, I'd be welcome here. That I could rent a room for a while. He thought that if you couldn't reach him for some reason, the picture and medallion would assure you I was legitimate."

Questions, doubts swirled inside her head. She blinked as a fresh wave of pain pounded into her skull.

What did it mean? Was Johnny's car accident something more? Impossible. Too crazy to even contemplate. No, for Johnny to give Jake his medallion told her just how much he trusted this man.

Unless Johnny didn't give it to Jake. She frowned. Which

didn't make any sense. Why would this man show up at her door with a stolen medallion? She had nothing to offer, no money, no fame...

"What about the motels in town?" she asked, stalling.

"I tried the two, but they're both booked solid because of ski season."

Margot opened her mouth to say something, then shut it. She didn't like this. Didn't like it a bit. What had Johnny been thinking? He knew she liked her solitude, that she'd come back home to get her life back together after the divorce, that she'd claimed the house as her own, even going as far as getting the paperwork together to buy out Johnny's share. He'd never really been interested in the place. Other than the lab outside in the barn, which Johnny had built a couple of years before he'd joined Miltronics, everything else was pretty much her own.

When it came down to it, she could see Johnny making the offer. He'd always been the type to get caught up in someone else's troubles. Now Johnny was gone, and it was just her. She could tell Jake no and it would be the end of it, but part of her wanted to say yes. After all, he'd known another side of Johnny. A side Margot never had the opportunity to see. Johnny's work had been so important to him at Miltronics, yet he'd been so reticent on the subject.

"How long would you be staying? That is if I decide to rent you a room."

"One week. Two max."

She rubbed the back of her neck. Two weeks. Not very long. At least she tried to tell herself that. She'd do one last favor for Johnny. Yes, and she'd also get a chance to add a few more precious memories of him. "I have a room on the ground floor in the back by the stairs. It's not very big."

"It doesn't matter."

"Fine. It'll be a hundred twenty-five a week plus meals."

He nodded and placed his glass on the desk. "I'll get my things."

Margot led Jake into the hall. In the foyer, he hunched down on one knee by his canvas backpack and swore.

"What's wrong?"

"I must have left a zipper partially opened. It looks like some snow seeped inside. Can you show me the room? I need to check if my laptop's okay."

"Sure."

As he followed her to the back room, she grew conscious of him directly behind, of his heavier steps, of his much larger frame, but most importantly, of his masculinity. Other than Johnny and the men at the gathering after the funeral today, it had been ages since she'd been alone with a man.

She was about to turn on the room light by the door, then thought better of it. Being touched once tonight by Jake was enough. She stepped away from the threshold to give him plenty of space to enter. "Here it is. If you need anything..."

"Thanks," was all he said as he walked inside. Not bothering with the light, he closed the door, leaving her in the hall to wonder how he could see inside there without bumping his shins on everything in his path.

Shrugging, she turned away and went back for her glass. She also picked up Jake's untouched water. In the kitchen, she refilled her glass with wine and went upstairs to her room. She closed her door but didn't bolt it. She couldn't. For some stupid reason, this room didn't have a lock, and she'd never bothered installing one.

Well, she wasn't going to act paranoid and put a chair under the knob. After all, one of the reasons she'd moved back here was because of the lack of crime in the area. Her brother had always been a good judge of character, so if he had befriended Jake, it was good enough for her.

Margot quickly undressed, changed into her nightgown and slipped under the down comforter. In the dark, she sat up against the headboard and sipped her wine.

She thought of Jake directly below. What was he doing? Was he also lying in bed unable to sleep? What had driven him from the Boston area to come here of all places? Was he running from something or someone? A woman, maybe? She'd sensed his pain even though he'd hidden it well. Eventually, exhaustion and alcohol numbed her thoughts and pulled her lids closed.

ANXIETY

~~*~~

Margot jerked awake. She lay there, heart pounding, mind struggling for a reason why. Then she heard it. From outside. A high, piercing cry. It sent goose flesh up her arms and legs and chilled her soul. Another cry ripped through the night, sounding more terrifying than the first. Such pain. So much pain in that one cry...

Silence followed. Thick and suffocating. Then it hit her. Marmaduke!

Margot had completely lost track of her cat. So focused on Jake, she could have easily missed Marmaduke slipping outside.

Snapping on the bedside light, she glanced over to the chair where Marmaduke slept at night and found it empty. Heart ricocheting against her ribs, Margot flung back the covers. Vivid memories of when she was a child drove her from the room.

At the age of ten, she'd stood frozen in the front yard, unable to stop the neighbor's Doberman from killing her cat, Sassy, unable to close her eyes against the terror or her ears against the screams—screams similar to the ones she'd just heard.

There were coyotes out there, animals just as savage as any Doberman.

When Margot couldn't find Marmaduke on either floor, she thrust her bare feet into a pair of boots and grabbed her jacket and a flashlight.

The second she stepped outside and closed the door, an angry, frigid wind slapped at her exposed face and hands and tore the breath from her lungs. She brushed at her hair as it whipped into her face, while snow pelted her from an impenetrable, black sky.

How could she possibly find Marmaduke in this mess? The outside light barely penetrated past the porch. Granted, she knew the property and how the front yard sloped downward to an outcropping of aspen intermixed with pine. If anything, Marmaduke would venture there or the barn to the left.

With the flashlight in one hand, Margot grabbed the shovel butted up against the wall for protection with the other hand. She paused at the bottom of the porch stairs and peered into the darkness. The idea of finding Marmaduke's remains turned her stomach, but the fear of leaving him out in the cold, possibly wounded or even dying, urged her through the snow and past the porch's illumination.

The cry of the wind, high and mournful, swept through the trees as Margot snapped on the flashlight. She aimed its beam down the driveway, where snow darted and whirled across the ground, and swept the light to the left.

That's when she noticed another light, faint but distinct. It penetrated through the falling snow and barren trees from the barn window.

Someone was in the lab.

CHAPTER 2

WHIMPERING, JAKE LAY naked on the linoleum floor in John's lab. A million vicious talons pierced through his flesh and into the marrow of his bones. He wanted to die, to cave into the pressure. Another tidal wave of pain roared through his veins. He gasped and pulled himself into a fetal position.

The seizure had hit him just as he'd opened the door to the lab and turned on the light. He'd barely managed to get inside and shut the door before falling to his knees.

This attack was far worse than the other two. They'd hit him unexpectedly and with such savage intensity that they'd completely incapacitated him. Yet, they were gone after several minutes, as if he'd hallucinated each episode.

If only he'd kept his nose out of it, done his job, he wouldn't be paralyzed on a cold, hard floor, in some lab in the middle of nowhere. But hell. His morals had interfered. Now he was paying for it. If only, if... Shit.

He would have done it all over again.

Over the pain, he heard the rattle of the doorknob.

Margot.

He couldn't be found out. Not now. He'd left the light on. So damn stupid. He lay right, smack in the middle of the room. He'd be impossible to miss. She was going to ask questions, get suspicious. He couldn't afford that. Not when she'd been married to Malcolm.

Jake focused on the space beneath the desk. Raking in a lung full of air, he dug his fingers into the linoleum and crawled across the floor. Every muscle screamed a protest. Sweat broke out on his brow.

Just as he pulled himself under the desk, another pain, more violent than the last, slammed into him. The unexpectedness of it tore the breath from him.

And in that instant, nothing mattered. Margot. Being discovered. Nothing but the pain and the knowledge that he was dying.

~~*~~

Margot paused on the outside of the lab door. She thought she'd locked the barn. But then...maybe she hadn't. God, she didn't know. Ever since Johnny's death, she hadn't been able to wrap her mind around a coherent thought.

She should call Carl, Greyson's deputy, and get him out here, but Margot balked at the idea. Carl would just use it as another opportunity to make one of his lame passes. Then he'd give her that look of his and tell her to stop acting paranoid and lay off the alcohol. After all, nothing happened around here. Plus, who could possibly be interested in anything in the lab?

Unless Jake— Well, he had another thing coming if he thought he could waltz in here without getting her permission.

Curiosity, more powerful than any fear, eventually got the best of her. Inhaling a breath of courage, Margot shoved her flashlight into her coat pocket and opened the door. Lifting the shovel in both hands, she paused on the threshold and listened. She could have sworn she'd heard something. But the only sounds were her breathing and the hum of the refrigerator in the corner. Icy, winter air swept into the lab. She stepped inside and closed the door quietly. Nothing looked disturbed. Which didn't explain the office light in the far back of the building.

"Is anyone here?"

Margot didn't receive an answer, but then, she hadn't expected one. If a thief was hiding somewhere, it was highly unlikely he'd come out and introduce himself.

Palming the shovel's handle, she moved cautiously across the floor. The light from the office threw the far corners of the main room into grotesque shadows. The computers, vials, microscopes and other equipment cluttering the countertops that ran against the walls on either side suddenly appeared menacing and unfamiliar. On those same counters, cages once holding mice sat empty. A number of stools butted up to the counters, while in the middle of the room sat a metal desk and a large table with three computers, all now silent. The chrome refrigerator in the far corner continued to hum back at her. She dreaded the idea of going through its shelves, knowing she wouldn't be able to make sense of anything inside.

Johnny had always kept this part of his life private from her—at least near the end. He'd probably given up explaining the validity of one of his hypothesis or some other theory after getting tired of seeing her eyes glaze over too many times. She'd never been able to grasp his conversations. They were like a foreign language and in school she'd been terrible with Spanish or French.

Tension cut across her shoulders as she stepped into the office in the back of the building. "Marmaduke, are you in here?"

No cat. No person. Completely empty.

She exhaled a shaky but relieved breath, turned off the office light and used her flashlight to retrace her steps back to the front door. Maybe all that wine had gone to her head after all. Maybe, just maybe, it had been an owl or a coyote and not Marmaduke, she reasoned, as she stepped outside and closed the door. The cat was probably safely asleep somewhere in the house, and she'd just missed him. Just in case, she'd double check the lab tomorrow in the light of day. Right now, she found the place too creepy.

As to the light, Margot hadn't a clue. Maybe she just hadn't noticed it on until tonight. God knows, for the longest time she hadn't been interested in anything around her other than her books. Setting the shovel against the barn wall, Margot drew the lapels of her coat closer around her neck. She shuffled through the snow toward the house, all the while arcing the flashlight's beam back and forth for signs of Marmaduke, but she didn't find him anywhere.

Once inside the house, she replaced her boots and jacket for a robe and walked into the kitchen where—of all things—Marmaduke sat regally by his empty, water dish.

"Why you little monster!" She crossed the room and eyed the cat with a mixture of relief and disgust. "You really don't deserve any water. Not after scaring the pants off of me like that."

But she picked up his dish and filled it with water anyway. Over the sound of the faucet, a noise, faint but distinct, echoed through the house. A door closing. She snapped off the water and looked at the doorway leading to the hall.

"Who's there?" she whispered. "Jake?"

Only the tick of the kitchen clock answered her. Then Margot noticed the cat. Tall switching in clear agitation, Marmaduke, sat hunched low on all fours.

"You heard it too, didn't you?"

Uneasiness pricking the back of her neck, Margot moved across the kitchen and bent down to place the water dish on the ground by Marmaduke. Suddenly, the cat sprang, bounding from the kitchen and disappearing into the hall.

Margot jerked, sloshing water over the bowl as she placed it on the floor. Cautiously, she walked to the doorway and peered around the corner. She found the hall empty. The door to Jake's room stood closed.

She laughed self-consciously as she stepped into the hall. Her nerves were obviously shot. And Marmaduke sure as hell wasn't helping matters.

Suddenly, the air stirred about her, teasing her hair and seeping into the fabric of her housecoat.

Someone was in the hall with her.

Pivoting, Margot searched the shadows around her. Her bare toe hit something on the hall mat. She looked down. A set of her keys to the lab. She swallowed, her throat suddenly dry. She picked them up. They were warm to the touch.

"Hello?"

Her whisper washed over the hall and died into silence.

Unable to shake the feeling that someone was watching, Margot backed out of the hall and into in the kitchen. With a shaky hand, she put the keys back on the empty hook on the wall beside the doorway to the laundry room.

No. It couldn't be. They'd only been childhood stories, made up scary tales between Johnny and her during long boring days stuck in the house as kids. There were no ghosts. Never had been. Still, her hand wouldn't stop trembling. After all...Johnny was dead. Which could mean it might be him who— No. Impossible.

To hell with her headache. Margot needed a drink, something with a kick, anything to calm the wild beat of her pulse. She uncorked the bottle on the counter and drank the first glass without pause. The second, she savored. At the sink, she stood until tension eased from her limbs. Her pulse slowed and a numbness settled over her mind and body.

Suddenly, Margot was exhausted. The funeral, the cries in the night, her fear for Marmaduke's safety, and Johnny's co-worker in the other room. And, of course, her overactive imagination. Ghosts. Really. She rested both hands against the kitchen counter and bowed her head.

"Are you all right?"

Margot whipped around, her robe billowing around her, and stumbled. She caught the counter with a steadying hand and found Jake in the doorway, the hall's shadows clinging to his large frame. He still wore the same clothes he had on earlier. "Ah—yes. Of course. I just couldn't sleep."

"The same. Do you mind company?"

She cleared her throat, trying to appear unfazed. "No. I can light a fire in the den. It won't be so chilly in there."

The fire wasn't such a good idea, Margot soon realized as she stood back and watched the flames put an intimate cast to the room. She glanced over at Jake beneath her lashes. Something about him fascinated her. Some inner energy or magnetism. She couldn't even begin to explain to herself never mind anyone else as to the reason why.

He sat with a leg crossed over the knee in one of the high-backed chairs. The black clothing accented his lean frame and pallor. Maybe he was recovering from some surgery, an accident or a broken heart. He turned and caught her stare. Flushing, she swung around and sank down onto a matching chair. Already she disliked those sunglasses. Because of them, she had yet to read his expression.

"So tell me, how long have you—did you know Johnny?"

"Almost four years."

"Mmmm. What was he like to work with?" She leaned forward.

~~*~~

Jake glanced at the place where her robe gapped open, revealing the shadowy curve of her breasts. He could see why Malcolm had married her. She was gorgeous. All the right curves, and a face that would make even a dead man's heart race. More than anything, she was completely unaware, or uncaring of her appeal.

He smiled sadly. "He had a quirky sense of humor. You might say he was the optimist in the department. But he pulled his weight. Out of everyone, I knew I could count on him. He was very much a team player. I can't think of anyone who disliked him."

Before Margot turned to shield her face with the thick wall of her ebony hair, he caught sight of her expression. The anguish, the despair. Sudden affinity caught at his insides.

"I'm glad he was well liked," she whispered. "Malcolm showed up at the funeral. He was the only one from Miltronics. Then again, I wasn't really expecting anyone. Northern Arizona's quite a ways from Massachusetts. But I am surprised you hadn't heard of the funeral."

Damn. She didn't know. How could she not know about the fire, the dozen people who died? What did it mean? Was she so out of touch with the world around her? He decided to keep the news to himself, and, instead, cleared his throat. "I don't work there anymore."

She swiveled in her chair to look at him. She had beautiful, bold, brown eyes with thick winged brows that accented their rich color. She looked innocent. But could she really be, having been married to Malcolm? Jake wished to hell he knew.

"You must have known Malcolm then. My ex-husband." The alcohol had thickened and added a roll to the end of her words, giving her voice an oddly sexy intonation. But even the wine didn't relax the tightness to her lips.

"Somewhat. I was in a different division." Which was a damn lie. "I know he wasn't the most popular person around." Which wasn't.

She leaned back against the high-backed chair, exposing the long column of her throat to the fire's glow. "I can believe it. He's a very stubborn man. Too much at times. But so very smart and logical. And ambitious."

He tried to keep the bitterness from his voice. "I'll grant him that."

As she turned the wine glass in her hand, the flames from the fireplace flickered through the crystal. As she stared at it, her expression turned thoughtful. She bit down on her lower lip. "You didn't happen to hear anything earlier tonight, did you?"

He shifted in his chair. "No. Why?"

She shrugged. "I thought...I guess I must have just heard a coyote."

The sigh of the gas fire in the hearth enveloped the room. He watched as she sank deeper into her chair and laid a cheek against a brocade throw cushion.

When she yawned behind the back of her hand, he rose from his chair. "I'll let you get some rest."

She sent him a rueful, sleepy smile. "I'll try."

Jake went to his own room to sleep, but after an hour of battling with his sheets and a racing mind, he gave up and slipped from his room. Light from the den illuminated the hall in a soft, yellow glow. He entered the room. Gas flames still danced around the ceramic logs in the fireplace, their light revealing Margot asleep in the chair where he'd left her. Somehow, she'd retained a grasp on her wine glass without spilling its contests.

He walked over to her. Bending, he eased the partially filled glass gently from her fingers and placed it on the end table. She shifted but didn't wake.

Jake noticed she'd downed far too much alcohol tonight. Could it be because of a guilty conscience? Or something more? Yet the reason might be simply because she'd just buried her brother.

None of the wine had spilled onto her robe, part of which had slipped from one creamy shoulder to reveal a red satin nightgown. Her skin looked as silken as the gown shimmering against the firelight.

His chest tightened.

Unable to stop the impulse, he reached down and curled a finger around a lock of her satiny hair. She stirred. The ebony strand slipped through his fingers to curve against her cheek, and her lips parted. They were wide and bow shaped. So damn kissable.

But was Margot really delicate? Was she like her brother, John, whom he'd trusted and respected? Or did that face hide something hard and unfeeling? Something just as ruthless as Malcolm? After all, she'd married Malcolm. At some point she'd been attracted to him.

He sighed. Who was he to judge? He was far from anyone's Prince Charming. And what did it matter? Either way, she was unattainable.

He pulled a crocheted blanket from a basket by the chair and draped her in its warm folds. For one long moment, he watched her as yearning and loneliness sank and pooled deep in his gut. Then he slipped silently from the room.

CHAPTER 3

S O WHAT'S HE like?"

"Who?" Margot acted dumb as she hid behind the evening paper and pretended to read the business section. She didn't particularly like being reminded of how she'd let alcohol and her bad judgment convince her to rent a room to Johnny's co-worker.

Joyce Hoffman grunted. "Your house guest, renter, whatever you want to call him."

"He's okay. Did you know the Dow lost 120 points yesterday?"

Pressing down on the newspaper between Margot's two hands, Joyce crumpled it against the restaurant's table. "Just 'Okay'?"

Margot eyed her friend with amusement. Joyce's short, platinum hair swept back from a face chiseled with smooth precision. She might look the cool blonde, but Margot knew better. Joyce could lose her temper with the best of them. And she cared. Always had. From as far back as grade school.

"Yes. 'Okay'."

"Oh, come off it, Margot!" She grabbed the newspaper and flung it into the adjacent chair. "Give me a break, will you? You're not even reading the thing!"

"Oh, all right. I'll stop. And can you keep it down? We *are* in a restaurant. I don't want everyone in town knowing my business.

It's bad enough as it is." She sat up in her chair and glanced around the room decorated in a definite country flavor with stenciled cows edging the doors and ceiling. Even though only a few locals dotted the room, the place was packed. Ski season was in full swing. Many a person from the Phoenix area escaped the desert to Greyson and the surrounding mountains for a bit of snow and clean air. "And as for Jake. There's really nothing to tell. He's been renting a room for almost a week now. Not enough time to see much of him, other than in the evening. He seems pretty busy and keeps to himself, which is just fine."

"Is he cute?"

"I never noticed." Margot laughed. "Oh, okay. Just stop rolling your eyes like that. I guess he's kind of attractive. I haven't really gotten a good look at him." Margot sank back against her chair.

"Well, why not?"

"I don't know." She picked up a pepper shaker and twirled it in her hand. "I've only seen him in the evening."

"Oh, I seeee..."

Exasperated, Margot plopped the shaker on the light blue tablecloth, leaned forward and whispered, "No, you don't. I'm not sleeping with him."

"Now calm down. It was just a little wishful thinking on my part. Anyway, it's about time you hooked up with someone and had some fun. We all know Malcolm didn't do you any favors." Both elbows on the table, Joyce leaned toward Margot. "I can understand wanting to come back here for a while to lick your wounds after the divorce, but you're still here."

"I like it here."

"That's something I'll never understand. If I'd been you, I would never have come back. And if I had, I'd have left so fast your head would have been spinning."

"Then why are you still here?" Margot asked, surprised at the bitterness in Joyce's voice.

"It's called money." Joyce drummed her fingers by her plate. "I was stupid not to try for a degree or move out when I had a chance."

"You still can."

Joyce grunted and arched a blonde brow. "Yeah, right. My brother can't function on his own. Plus, I inherited the grocery store from our folks. It takes all my time, and trying to unload it to some local or crazy tourist hasn't worked."

Margot really didn't know what to say to that, and thank goodness the arrival of their dinner saved her from having to reply

"Hey, ladies. Having a night out on the town?" Mark, owner and tonight helping out as waiter and cook, placed two steaming plates on the table.

"I was getting a little claustrophobic in the house," Margot said as the meal's aroma wafted to her nose, tempting her that second to sink her teeth into a thick battered shrimp. From past experience, she knew they tasted as heavenly as they smelled. To hell with calories. People didn't come to Mark's Hideaway for something light. Grease was his trademark. From thick wedged French fries to shrimp and monstrous hamburgers.

Mark stuck a pencil behind an ear. "Hey, Margot. I've been wanting to ask you if you've got any cookbooks."

"Oh, just a couple hundred. Anything in particular?"

"Got anything from England? I wanted to try something different. Maybe some fish and chips they wrap in newspaper over there. Or maybe I'll go way out and try my hand at something real sick and sweet like buttered tarts."

"I might. I'll see what I can find and give you a ring later tonight. I know I had this recipe for dumplings and stew. The dumplings were to die for. Johnny loved them. Every time he came to visit he'd talk me into making them."

To her horror, tears welled in her eyes. Oh, please not now. She couldn't lose it here. She thought she'd be able to say her brother's name aloud without crumbling. The strained silence and Mark and Joyce's pitying glances worsened the ache in her chest.

Mark clumped her on the back. "We all miss him. You did good on the funeral. All those flowers, the speech...."

She blinked rapidly. "Yes, I...thank you, Mark."

He cleared his throat. "Well, got work to do. I can't stand around here jawing all day."

After eating, Margot cut the evening short, left the Hideaway and Joyce, and drove home. She wasn't up to acting jovial, and she didn't want to drag Joyce's mood down with hers.

Time. Margot tightened her grip on the steering wheel. People told her that was the only thing that really helped after the death of a loved one. But she didn't care about time or tomorrow. She hadn't for a while.

Granted, she liked her job, her Internet bookstore and converting books to electronic formats and everything that went with it. She'd never go back to being a corporate lawyer. The competition, the grueling hours and everything it entailed had chewed her up and spat her out until she no longer had anything to give.

Margot turned off the main highway, guided the car along a narrow paved road and up a long, crooked driveway. Her large, two-story, red brick house, draped in deep shadow sat on top of the hill. Its Queen Anne-styled tower jutted fiercely up into the night sky, while windows, black, empty, and lifeless, stared back at her. Not exactly the most welcoming sight, but it was home and had been off and on for the last twenty-eight years. And now with Johnny gone, every inch of it was all hers—from the wrap-around porch and gingerbread trim to the high-pitched roof.

Two years ago, she'd returned to this place for good. She'd come here to get her life back together again after losing her job and divorcing her husband. Some might say she came here to hide, but Margot would be quick to argue.

The moment Margot stepped into the house, closed and locked the front door, the hairs on the back of her neck stood on end. In the foyer, she could almost feel the physical touch of someone's eyes on her from the darkness, so strong was the sensation. Heartbeat breaking into a gallop, Margot reached for the switch to the hall light, but paused and swore under her breath. The stupid thing didn't work.

Awareness still prickled against her skin. Frozen, yet poised for flight, she peered down the hall. Nothing separated from the thick shadows, while the only sound was that of her short, ragged breathing.

No. Not again. She couldn't handle this feeling of being watched.

"Jake?" she called, even knowing he wouldn't answer. He was out for the evening. The reason why she'd left the house in the first place, unable to remain inside with only herself for company.

No one was there. At least no one human, Margot decided as she ventured further into the house. The heels of her boots echoed against the wood floor.

"Johnny? Is that you?" Then she realized the craziness of the question and mentally shook herself. "Enough."

She squared her shoulders, pulled her boots off, and hung her jacket in the closet. "Ghosts, Margot? Now really. You're losing it."

Needing a drink, Margot strode into the kitchen and turned on the light. She hated the tremble in her hand as she pulled a new bottle of red wine from the small wine rack on top of the counter. She'd had water at dinner, knowing how much Joyce would protest if she'd gotten anything stronger. After she took several deep swallows of wine, the shaking eased somewhat. Only when she refilled her glass, corked the bottle and slid it across the counter to butt up against the wall, did she dare look back out into the hall.

Empty.

What had she expected? Or should she say *who*? Johnny? Margot laughed shakily. "You're becoming one of those hysterical females. The type you loathe in those old horror movies."

Talking aloud didn't calm her nerves much. Not even the wine helped tonight. Work. Maybe that would do the job. Glass in hand, Margot hurried into the den and turned on the MP3 player to the soothing strains of Jewel—anything to keep the house's suffocating silence at bay.

Then she remembered Mark and the cookbook. She walked over to the shelf along the room's far corner and ran a finger across the microwave books, past copies of *Betty Crocker*, *Jewish American* and *Old Settlers* cookbooks. She frowned, unable to find the volume or remember the exact title. All she recalled was the blue and white cover. Damn! She couldn't lose it now. Not just because of Mark, but because the book contained Johnny's favorite recipe. Any token memory of her brother was better than none.

It didn't help that the books were in a hodgepodge order. Strange. Margot could have sworn she'd gone through this room and alphabetized everything for year-end inventory, cross-referencing each title with her database.

She'd have to give Mark a call and let him know. Margot went to her desk for the telephone book and opened the drawer. As she peered inside, her grip on the handle tightened. The stapler sat turned over in the far corner. The stack of fresh, yellow sticky, notepads had fallen, fanning across half the length of the drawer. Pens and pencils, usually neatly arranged inside the holder against the front were scattered over the telephone book.

Someone had been in her desk drawer.

~~*~~

Jake stared at the mirror in his room and hated the reflection that looked back at him. He barely recognized himself. He tugged at the dark brown wig. Before leaving Boston, he'd thought of dying his hair instead, but he'd decided the wig a better option. But he hadn't counted on it being itchy as hell, and he should have at least picked a better color, something that didn't leach the color from his face.

The room's bright light threw his features into a grotesque caricature. Nothing helped. Without the disguise, he'd always be some sick freak. Disgusted, he turned away and glanced at the dresser where a syringe rested on top of a small black case. He'd been about to give himself an injection when he'd heard Margot's unexpected arrival. Damn, but he'd had a close call.

Sighing deeply, he slipped on his gloves. It would have to wait now, he conceded as he put on his glasses, turned off the light and left the room. Hearing a noise from the den, he walked down the hall and stopped in the doorway.

Margot stood leaning over the desk, muttering something

under her breath. Reassured at the low lighting, he ventured further into the room.

She glanced up and turned, her lips parting in surprise. Her black hair swayed with the movement and draped over a shoulder in a smooth glossy wave. The black corduroy jeans and red silk blouse clothed a body he hadn't been able to keep his eyes off since he'd first stepped through her front door. The full breasts, tiny waist and flare of hips shouted sex. Thank God, Margot hadn't a clue as to the effect she had on him, and he intended to keep it that way.

Until the ability to attract a woman was stolen from him, he'd never realized how much he'd loved everything about them. It was far too long since he'd tasted a woman's lips or breathed in her scent, caressed the soft skin of a rounded breast, and held the firm, naked flesh of a woman's hips in his hands as he buried himself into her body.

He noticed her narrowed eyed gaze and asked, "Is something the matter?"

"Were you going through my things?"

He flexed his fingers. Obviously, the wrong question to ask her. Stay calm, he told himself. Don't antagonize. He just might talk himself out of this. As long as he remembered to play it cool and keep it as close to the truth as possible. He'd learned quickly these last couple of months. Had to in order to survive. A good lie, a convincing lie always had some basis of truth.

"Yes." Think quick. He saw her hand on the drawer handle. "I needed to make a couple of calls and was looking for your phone book. I was having a hard time connecting to the Internet. Why? Did I make a mess of things?"

She shrugged and seemed to relax. "No. I was just wondering." She closed the drawer and leaned back against the desk. The action stretched the silk material across her full breasts, and his body reacted. Damn it. Where the hell was his self-control?

He focused on a safe topic. "Did you have a good evening?"

She shrugged again. "It was fine. I met a friend over at the Hideaway. Have you gotten a chance to try Mark's food?"

"No, not yet." Wondering suddenly of her *friend*, he glanced down at her left, ringless hand and over at her other hand, where she'd reached for her wine glass. He frowned. "John would hate..." He clamped down on his jaw. It was none of his business.

Her deep brown eyes softened. "Johnny, 'what'?"

"John would hate to see you like this." He nodded to the glass in her hand. "Alcohol'll just get you more screwed up."

Margot lifted her chin. The vulnerability and warmth in her face vanished. "So you're saying I'm screwed up?"

"I didn't mean it to come out that way." He flexed his fingers again. The leather around his hands had warmed and softened. "I'm just saying that John loved you. Talked a lot about you at work. He'd hate to see you drinking like this."

"Don't. Don't ever put your nose into my business. You're lucky I decided to let you stay here as a paying guest. It's only because of Johnny that you're under this roof. I can just as easily change my mind and tell you to leave." She drained her glass and banged it down on the corner of the desk. With the back of her hand, she wiped her mouth. Bitterness hardened her face. "If I want to get stinking drunk every night, that's my business. Got that? Not yours or anyone else's."

Hating her attitude, he couldn't stop even if he wanted to. "As long as you know what you're doing, lady. Every time I see you, you've got a glass in your hand. If you're not careful, you'll be walking around in a permanent, drunken stupor. Not an attractive sight by any imagination."

She pushed off the desk. "Don't patronize me. You have no right to stand there and judge. If I want to die from alcohol poisoning, if I want to—"

"What?" He advanced toward her, then, suddenly conscious of the lamp on the desk, turned so the room's shadows would cling and obscure his features. "Kill yourself? Is that what you're trying to do?"

"Of course not!"

Frustration burned in his gut. Oh, how he wanted to shake some sense into her. Didn't she realize that life was a gift? Not something to be trifled with? That it could all be taken away in an instant?

"Well, lady. You're going about it the right way. But why don't you make it faster? Get yourself a gun. That way you can hurry up and join your brother."

She hauled back a hand, but he caught it before it connected with his face. Tears glittered in her eyes and spilled down her cheeks. "L—leave Johnny out of it."

He forced her hand back to her side but retained his grip. She was panting, clearly agitated and so damn vulnerable. All because of him and his mouth. "Shhh..." He pulled her rigid body into his arms and whispered against her cheek. "I'm sorry. I shouldn't have said those things. But when you made it plain you didn't care about yourself or your life, something went off in me. Life's damn precious, Margot. And fragile. You must know that by losing Johnny."

She slumped against him. He heard her muffled crying against his shoulder and felt helpless. He cupped her head with a gentle hand and held her steady. He couldn't help her. Not when he couldn't even help himself.

"I don't care anymore," she murmured against his chest, her words barely audible. "It's like something in me died with Johnny."

"You'll feel better in time." Such stupid words. He lowered his hand to cradle the nape of her neck, tangling his fingers in the lustrous, ebony strands of her hair. As he brushed his lips across her brow and smelled the flowery scent of her shampoo, something in him cracked. He didn't want to care, didn't want to get involved.

"I don't think so. I was bad even before. But after Malcolm..."

Something in the tone of her voice when she mentioned Malcolm's name made Jake tense, but he managed to keep his voice calm. "He didn't hit you, did he?"

"...no he didn't."

Ah, but he did something, Jake thought. Something that couldn't be easily mended like a broken bone. The bastard. He'd get his. Jake would make sure of it.

Something between them changed. For a minute he thought it was his hormones and being without a woman for so long that gave him the mixed signal, but then he noticed a subtle differ-ence in her touch. The way her hand slid up his arm, the caress of her thumb along the junction between his shoulder and neck. Her lips brushed his cheek. Her breath lightly fanned his skin in little puffs. Closing his eyes, he drank in her scent, roses and another elusive fragrance he found dark and erotic.

"Kiss me." Her words whispered against his senses and flamed a hunger he rigidly kept in check.

He wanted to kiss her. He was going to kiss her.

Jake stiffened. He couldn't go there. Alcohol had to be fueling her to say and do things she normally wouldn't. Jake pushed her away, almost stumbling back in his hurry to escape the light and her gaze. She thought he'd rejected her. He could see it in her face. "It's not you. Don't think that. Don't ever think that."

~~*~~

Margot watched him rush from the room. She backed up against the desk and gripped its edge to steady legs that threat-ened to melt from under her. She might not have been able to see his eyes or their expression, but she'd heard the despera-tion and despair in his voice. For a moment, he'd made her feel wanted, made her want to believe in something.

The minute she walked out into the hall, she knew he'd left the house. The place felt empty. She'd completely lost track of time, but it didn't really matter. She was exhausted, tired enough to fall asleep without the help of alcohol.

In her bedroom, she stripped and stared at her naked reflec-tion in the dresser mirror. The lamp was kind, adding a smooth, even a satiny texture to her skin. A vision flashed in her mind's eyes, of Jake behind her cupping her breasts, bending her forward, holding her steady...

Sighing, she turned away from the mirror, but she couldn't so easily turn away from the sexual hunger burning into her skin. Having a virile man in the same house with her was exacerbat-ing the longing inside of her. She slipped on her nightgown and crawled under the covers. For the first time in a long while, the craving for alcohol had vanished. But in its place was something far worse. A craving for a man, not just in her bed, but in her life.

Closing her eyes, she let sleep pull her under.

~~*~~

The scream slapped her awake. She jackknifed up in the bed. Blood pounded in her ears as she sat and listened to the silence. Then she realized that this time the cry hadn't come from outside but downstairs. She scrambled from the bed and hit the cold wood floor running, almost banging into the side of her bedroom door on the way out. The night was black, illuminating nothing. With questing, outstretched hands, she found the stair's handrail and fumbled down the steps. Breathing deeply, she rounded the stair post and slammed into something warm and very human.

She opened her mouth to scream.

"It's me, Jake," he said from the darkness, holding onto her arms to steady her.

She let out a long, shaky breath. "What was that?" she asked in a hushed voice. "You must have heard it. It sounded so awful."

"It was your cat."

"Marmaduke?"

"Yeah."

"But I could have sworn it sounded more human than—"

"I stepped on his tail." He cleared his throat. "Scared the hell out of both of us. He took off somewhere. Sorry about getting you out of bed."

"I'm just glad I found out what it was. But what are you doing up?"

"I couldn't sleep."

Relaxing, she glanced up, only to be blinded by the night. Thick, black and total, it draped over Jake and everything around her. His hands, warm and strong, grasped her upper arms. She grew conscious of the coolness of the house, of the silk of her nightgown against her skin, but most importantly of Jake, of the deep woodsy scent of his after-shave and how his hands, minus the gloves, were now slowly sliding up and down her arms. Her toes curled beneath her. He smelled like what she envisioned a man should smell like. Desire lapped against her skin until it seeped through her flesh and took hold of her body.

He slid a hand up her arm and over a shoulder to cup her throat, while the other curled around her waist to press against the small of her back, inching her closer to the heat of his body. She met his lips halfway, opening her mouth beneath his. The kiss deepened, demanded and took. She raised a hand to feel his own against her throat. He had a long-fingered, strong hand, the skin smooth and flawless over the tendons and knuckles. She touched his face, his neck, his shoulders. Against her palms, his skin was satin over hard muscle. He was all male, all power.

He hauled her closer, pressing her sensitized breasts against his chest as his tongue mated with hers. His desire thrust against the shallow hollow of her hips. The thick, hardness of him scorched through the material of her gown to her belly and turned her legs to liquid. She slid her hands over the sleek texture of his naked back, over the muscles and tendons, down across the indentation along his spine and lower.

She froze.

He was entirely, absolutely, completely naked, every male inch of him. She whimpered as her breath came out in short, shallow pants, and desire slammed against her, painful in its intensity.

Margot stiffened. Oh, God. Had she completely lost it? Where was her sanity, her morals? She hardly knew this man.

"No!" She dragged in a lungful of air. "This is all wrong!"

Before it was too late, Margot ripped out of his arms, stumbled up the stairs to her room, and slammed the door closed.

~~*~~

Grabbing the banister, Jake stepped onto the stairs. Even the cold air against his bare skin couldn't douse his raging desire. He could run after her and take her. She'd been just as hot, just as hungry. It wouldn't take much to convince her to let him strip her naked, to touch, to stroke and kiss her until she was writhing and bucking beneath him, to make her come.

He stood under the cover of darkness, trembling, starving,

hurting. It had been too damned long. Her skin had been soft, smooth. She'd smelled like heaven. Jake flexed his fingers. He'd finally buried his bare hands into her hair. The strands had felt exactly like he'd envisioned. Like silken water. He'd wanted to bury his face in their waves and drink in their essence.

Jake let her go. This time.

CHAPTER 4

MARGOT FOUND THE house empty when she went downstairs the next morning. Not that she expected Jake. During the day, he went off to do his own thing, which was just as well. Mentally, she wasn't up to seeing him just yet.

"Meow."

The house wasn't completely empty after all. There was Marmaduke, Margot thought darkly to herself as he wrapped himself around her calf.

"You little monster." She scooped him up into her arms. "Because of you, I made a complete jackass out of myself."

Margot scratched behind the calico's ears and wandered over to the spare room where Jake stayed. She hesitated in front of the closed door, but only for a moment. So, she liked to snoop. Who was going to know, anyway? Shifting the cat onto one arm, she opened the door with her free hand and stepped past the threshold.

"Rraarr!"

Marmaduke dug his back claws into her wrist.

"Ouch!"

The cat leaped from her arms and raced down the hall.

Rubbing at the sting of claw marks on her wrist, Margot walked cautiously into the room. Nothing out of the ordinary. At least nothing to make the cat act so oddly. The bed lay empty, while the plaid, flannel sheets were rumpled and unmade, almost as if Jake had just stepped from them. Abruptly, she glanced away from the bed. It reminded her too much of last night and how she'd almost ended up there...with him.

She saw an odd, black case on the dresser. Still rubbing at her arm, she walked over to it. Sheer curiosity, nothing else, had her opening the box. Two empty vials rested inside curved, cloth holders. She slipped one from its bed and held it up to the morning light.

"Miracell."

Margot frowned. Strange. She'd never heard of it, but that didn't say much. Unlike her brother, she'd never had any interest in the medical field. She tipped it to the side. A few clear drops still remained. She raised it to her nose. Odorless.

How strange. Was it some type of penicillin? Maybe Jake had diabetes. Or did the vial have something to do with his sensitivity to light? He didn't strike her as a drug addict, especially after the way he'd reacted to her drinking. Johnny might have been able to tell her the vial's contents. Sighing, she carefully replaced the tube and closed the case. Only one person could tell her the truth.

Jake. Such a mystery. After almost a week, she didn't know anything more about him other than the fact he'd worked for the same company as Johnny. Miltronics. A company no one would talk about. A company where Malcolm, the most secretive of them all, still worked.

Something rustled behind her. Almost like a soft sigh. Quickly, she turned. No one was there. The cushioned chair in the corner sat empty; the thick rust drapes lay motionless. A stillness settled over the room. She shivered. Not again. She was *not* going to think of ghosts, or things going bump in the night or, in this case, the day.

Shaking off her wild imagination, she hurried out of the room, went into the kitchen, and then had a quick breakfast. Jake hadn't eaten. Usually, he'd leave his dishes neatly stacked by the sink or rinsed and in the dishwasher. He was a model tenant. Sometimes, it was almost as if he wasn't even here. A ghost. Silent and—

There she went again. She exhaled heavily. Ghosts. She

glanced at the bottle of Merlot on the counter. No, too early for a drink. Even for her. Maybe after lunch. Instead, she tied the garbage bag and hefted it to the front entrance. Setting it aside, she opened the door.

Malcolm stood in front of her, his hand raised to the doorbell.

"Malcolm!"

"Is that all you can say?" His lip curled up at one corner, but he stared back at her with remote, blue eyes.

"Go away." She stood in the middle of the entrance, having no intention of letting him past.

"Margot, really. Is that any way to welcome your husband?"

"That's ex, as in ex-husband."

"A technicality." He shrugged and offered her a large bouquet of mixed flowers, their fragrance teasing her nose. "Aren't you going to at least let me in?"

She ignored the flowers. "Why should I?"

"I want to talk."

He dropped the flowers back to his side and stepped toward her, pushing into her space, closer, even closer until she smelled the tang of coffee on his breath.

Lifting her chin, she didn't step back. "We don't have anything to talk about anymore. Why can't you just go and leave well enough alone?"

Something flickered in the back of his eyes. She'd annoyed him. "But I've missed you."

Margot laughed harshly. The flowers and the smile didn't fool her. Malcolm's clean-cut, tanned, boyish looks might have blinded her years ago but no longer. His light brown, almost sandy hair, cut close to his head, suited his clean, almost beautiful features. Little crinkles at the sides of his light blue eyes and tiny brackets at his mouth were the only lines that marred his smooth complexion. His Armani suit accented his tall, lean form, while the padding in the shoulders masked his narrow body. Even though Malcolm was thin, she'd learned all too quickly how much strength his frame held.

He might look picture perfect and have the money to compete with Midas, but four years with him had cured her of ever wanting him again. Malcolm was incapable of having an intimate relationship with anyone. Female or male. It just wasn't in him. Malcolm cared for Malcolm and only Malcolm, and that about summed it up.

"You miss me?" Margot lifted her chin. "I find that hard to believe."

"Well, believe it." He shoved past her and into the foyer, then tossed the flowers on the hall table. "After all, you're the one who left me."

Tension cut along her shoulders and neck, and she curled her fingers into fists at her sides. She hated Malcolm's head games. "As if you gave me an option."

He stepped toward her, lifted a hand and rubbed a knuckle against her cheek. Then he dropped his hand to his side, but on the way down his fingers grazed the side of her breast. Margot didn't flinch, didn't do anything but stare back. She damned well knew him touching her like that was no accident. Oh, how she wanted to lash out at him, but memories of past encounters stilled the urge. Malcolm was strong, vicious, and quick to lose his temper.

"Don't you miss me a little?" he asked.

"No."

He pressed forward, giving Margot no choice but to back up. Unless, that is, she wanted him touching her again. She swallowed hard. The last time he'd put a hand on her, he'd hurt her badly. All too clearly, she remembered that day when he'd come home from Miltronics in a near temper. She'd made the mistake of doggedly asking questions about what they were working on after several times he'd told her to stop. He'd flown at her then, rage changing his face to something ugly and frightening. That night her arm had almost snapped as he pulled it behind her back and twisted until the pain forced her to her knees.

Crossing her arm, she cupped the elbow where she'd been injured. She'd never gone to the hospital. Call it fear or stupidity or just being young and insecure. Even now, when the humidity climbed, twinges of pain would slice through the tendons of her arm.

Walking further into the hall, Malcolm looked around. "How can you stand it? You've become a real hermit." He shook his head. "Who would have thought? Poor Margot. Has life been that bad that you have to hide out in this hellhole? Or maybe I've got it all wrong and you're getting all nice and cozy with some guy?" His smile looked far more threatening than friendly. "Getting it on the side and not telling anyone about it?"

For some crazy reason Jake came to mind. "It's none of your business who I see."

"Oh, so you are seeing someone."

"I didn't say that. Why are you so interested in my personal life all of a sudden?"

Shrugging, he walked past her.

"Where are you going?" she asked, quickly following him as he strode down the hall.

He didn't respond, but peered into the den, then entered the living room. She walked around the tanned leather couch and trailed a hand along its top, all the while controlling her growing anger. Experience had long ago taught her that the only way to win any type of battle with Malcolm was to be cool, rational, and above all, fearless.

"You haven't had anyone come by from Miltronics, have you?

Her hand stilled on the leather. She thought of Jake again. "No."

He narrowed his eyes. "You're lying."

"Why in the world would I lie? I've nothing to hide." She arched her brows in disbelief. "Really, Malcolm. You're way off base."

Margot didn't know if he'd bought it as he strode from the room. With growing suspicion, she followed him into the hall and watched him glance into the kitchen. Something was going on, something she couldn't even begin to guess at.

Suddenly, he rounded on her and smiled. "You're looking good, Margot." Slowly, so very slowly, he trailed a finger along her neck. "You know, I think I want you back in my bed. You were always pretty damned hot. Always so eager to please."

When his index finger slipped past the scooped neckline of her sweater, she grasped his wrist and pushed vainly at his hand. He leaned into her, pressing up against her until she found herself shoved up against the wall.

"What's wrong?" he asked. "Don't I turn you on anymore?"

"Don't."

Nausea burrowed into her stomach. She was not going to let him play with her head. She was done with being frightened and manipulated. Never. Ever again.

As Malcolm lowered his hand even further over her body, Margot pulled harder on his arm, trembling violently with the effort, but she couldn't match his strength or stop him when he covered her breast with his palm.

Margot sucked in a breath, raised her other hand and slammed her fist into Malcolm's face. His head jerked back. A mottled red flush crept up his neck and into his face. He lifted his hand from her breast and roughly slid it up to circle her neck. Using his body, he squeezed her harder up against the wall, digging his fingers around her throat. A black film seeped into the edge of her vision. Margot struggled for breath.

She'd done it. Pushed him over the edge.

CHAPTER 5

Pushed up against the wall, Margot stared back at Malcolm as the pressure of his hand against her throat tightened yet further. She was about to pass out and she didn't have the strength to fight back.

Corded veins stood out against Malcolm's reddened neck as he gritted out, "Don't ever—"

Suddenly, Malcolm flew backward. She caught his stunned expression as his body twisted in the air and tumbled to the ground. Malcolm slid across the floor and hit the back of his head against the wall with a loud whack.

Gasping in a lungful air, Margot stared back in shock. How? Who? Flattening both palms against the wall on either side of her, she glanced around, but no one else was in the room with them.

Fear etched across his face, Malcolm scrambled to his feet, touched the base of his head, and backed slowly down the hall to the front entrance.

There was no way she'd managed to shove Malcolm off like that. It was almost as if he'd had some type of crazy spasm or someone had grabbed him from behind and thrown him across the room. But that was ludicrous.

"What—what happened?" Margot asked in a voice gone harsh and raw.

Still touching his head with one hand, his face a sick, pasty white, Malcolm edged closer to the front door, caution in his every step and look. He sneered back at her. "You figure it out."

He disappeared out the door, leaving it open for a frosty breeze to blow into the house and brush against her skin. Shivering, she stepped around the forgotten garbage bag and closed the door after him. She leaned against the wood paneling, unable to stand properly without having her legs give out from under her.

"Is that you, Johnny?" she whispered.

She waited.

No answer.

But then, Margot never really expected one. For a moment, though, she'd hoped. Hoped? When was the last time she'd hoped for anything? After too many years of too many unanswered wishes.

It had to be her brother, though. How else could Malcolm suddenly fly through the air like that? But that was so crazy and so unlike Johnny. He'd been such a mild-mannered man. A man of science, a man who worked with his brain and not his hands. Then again, he'd been protecting her. Something she knew he wouldn't hesitate to act on.

She needed a drink. Bad. She pushed off the door and hurried into the kitchen. With fumbling fingers, she uncorked a fresh bottle of red wine and poured herself a healthy glass. Closing her eyes, she drank, drank until the shaking stopped, drank until a numbness settled over her body, drank until she didn't care about hope, about her ex threatening her, about her meaningless life...about ghosts.

Then Malcolm's words rang in her head.

You figure it out.

What could he mean? What was it that she needed to figure out? Obviously, it was something he thought she should know. Or maybe not. Maybe Malcolm was just being his usual snide self. But then why had he shown up today?

You figure it out. Something about her? Miltronics? Jake? Or maybe Johnny?

So many questions. And she didn't have an answer to any of them.

Grabbing the bottle and her glass, she sat down by the kitchen table and threw her feet up on an adjacent chair. After refilling her glass and recapping the bottle, she slouched further in her seat.

What did she need to figure out? She rubbed her brow. Pain throbbed between her eyes and against her temples. She didn't want to figure it out. Not now. Not when all this thinking was killing her head.

The doorbell sounded. She staggered from her chair. Shaking her head to clear it, she almost ran into the dark green, plastic bag filled with garbage she'd forgotten about in her hurry to get to the door. This time, she glanced through the side window and saw Joyce with her brother, Carl.

"Shit."

Margot didn't want company, especially Joyce's brother. Carl didn't miss an opportunity to hit on her. The only thing that had kept her from slapping him silly was her friendship with Joyce. But, oh, the temptation had been there to do some serious damage to that ego of his, especially since he'd always been a self-righteous chauvinist. Being one of only three deputies in the town and the surrounding area seemed to magnify his holier-than-thou attitude.

She swept her fingers through her hair to get the tangles out and took a couple of deep breaths, having the stupid hope that the added oxygen might clear her muddled head. It didn't work. She thought about not answering, but with her Cherokee parked outside, Joyce wasn't liable to leave without at least seeing Margot's face.

When she opened the door, Joyce took one look at her and rushed inside. Carl followed more sedately and closed the door.

"What happened?" Joyce demanded, frowning in great concern. "You look like hell."

"Malcolm was here and—"

"Shit." Carl's skin turned pallid. "He didn't hurt you, did he?"

Carl hefted his pants up and gave her a tough man look. The image of a strong deputy, with pressed uniform and shiny gun, riding into town was ruined by what looked like a grease stain on his potbelly, which Margot considered the biggest muscle on his body. From as far back as she could remember, he'd been more bulk than brawn.

"Of course he did," Joyce answered for her. "Why of all—"

"No, Joyce," Margot forestalled her. "He didn't get a chance to touch me. Something pulled him off me."

"What do you mean 'something pulled him off' you?" Joyce asked.

"Just that." God, the drink was loosening her tongue. She glanced at Carl, then took Joyce's elbow and led them further down the hall and out of his earshot. Carl loved gossip and ranked up there with the town's worst. Whoever said women loved to talk obviously hadn't been around a bunch of men for any length of time.

After letting go of her friend's arm, Margot massaged the bridge of her nose—anything to try to clear her head. "Malcolm had me up against the wall when something—don't ask me what—grabbed him and flung him into the air. He never saw the ground coming. I don't know what happened. It was almost like a ghost."

"You've got to be joking. A ghost?" The disbelief on Joyce's face was unmistakable.

"Yes, a ghost," Margot retorted in a hushed voice.

Joyce sniffed, and a look of reproof flashed in her eyes. "You've been drinking, haven't you? Now that I think of it, I can smell it on your breath."

"I had a glass or two after it happened," she admitted. "But that doesn't have anything to do with what just happened. Malcolm was there. He'd be the first to admit—"

"What's wrong?" Carl walked over to them.

Margot sent Joyce a fierce look and answered, "Nothing."

"I thought I heard you mention ghosts."

Margot bit back a snappy retort. She didn't need to antagonize the local law enforcement.

"Margot thinks a ghost attacked Malcolm," Joyce said.

She winced. It sounded far worse coming from someone else.

Carl hooked his thumbs over his waistband and rocked back on his heels. "A ghost, you say?"

"Yes," Joyce answered for her. "But she's been drinking. So..."

Margot disliked the conspiratorial look that passed between them.

"You need to lay off the bottle, Margot," Carl said. "It's not doing you any good. Next you'll be talking vampires." Exposing a set of big, white teeth, he deepened his voice. "I vaaant to suuuck your blooood."

He laughed at his lousy impression of Count Dracula, and Joyce joined in. Margot wanted to hit them both.

Still chuckling, Joyce flapped a hand. "Don't even start talking about vampires. She's got this guy who's renting a room from her, and he only shows up at night. Talk about weird. He could be some blood-sucking vampire for all we know."

"Thanks, guys."

Immediately, Joyce turned serious. "Oh, jeez, Margot. I'm sorry. That wasn't very nice. But really. It's hard to swallow. Ghosts. You told me that they were only stories. Maybe staying here by yourself isn't such a good idea after all."

"You don't understand. You weren't there."

"Why don't you just sleep it off," Carl urged. He kneaded her shoulder with a big, meaty hand, which she immediately shrugged off. "Maybe after you're sober—"

A loud crash reverberated through the hall. All three jumped and looked over to the wall where a picture had slipped from its mooring and fallen to the floor.

"See." Margot pointed. "That's exactly what I mean. Ever since Johnny—"

"Margot," Carl interrupted. "A picture fell. You're reading into something that ain't there."

She wanted to scream in frustration and get it through their heads that pictures didn't fall off walls by themselves. Instead, she changed the subject. "Why are the two of you here, anyway?"

Joyce smiled. "We were going to have lunch and thought you might want to get out for a bit. The forecast has another storm coming in, so you could be holed up here for a while. And actually, it was Carl's idea."

Margot could just bet. Sometimes Joyce could be as thick

skinned as her brother. Couldn't either one of them see she wasn't interested in Carl? She knew Joyce wanted her in the family, but Margot wasn't about to get involved with some self-important deputy with macaroni for brains. Not even for her best friend.

"Maybe another time," she said. "Right now, I'm way behind on inputting titles into my database."

"If you're sure..." Joyce tugged at her brother's elbow. "I'll call you later."

"Now, Margot. Ease up on the bottle." Carl gave her an important look before he allowed Joyce to lead him to the front door.

Margot only nodded and watched them leave. When the door closed soundly behind them, she slumped against the wood frame, looked up at the ceiling and groaned. "Tell me, is he annoying," she asked the empty hall, "or is it just me?"

The picture opposite from the one that had fallen, slipped from its hook and crashed to the floor. She didn't even jump this time.

"Johnny? At least, I think it's you." Stepping forward and slowly circling, she looked over the corners and shadows of the empty foyer and hall. "Thanks for the backup. But I think it's going to take a little more than falling pictures to get them to believe in ghosts."

Silence. Then again, had she really expected more?

CHAPTER 6

LATER THAT NIGHT, hunched over the computer in John's darkened lab, Jake stared at the monitor. Nothing rushed out at him. No stunning answer, no brilliant hypothesis. The equations blurred and melded into each other. He tried to swallow the panic, but it was still there. Ready. Waiting. He couldn't lose control. Not now. He rubbed at his brow with the heel of his hand.

Reaching over the keyboard for a breath mint, he tossed one into his mouth. Damn, but he was exhausted. He hadn't managed any decent sleep since fleeing Miltronics. When he finally rolled into bed, he'd lay awake, mind, and body unable to shut down. Sleep, as elusive as the formula he pursued, was imperative in rejuvenating his system. It troubled him, but not as much as the blood. He'd started spitting it up these last couple of days. Now that—that scared the hell out of him.

He wasn't ready to die. Not yet.

There were too many things he wanted to do. Nothing like climb Mount Everest, but he wanted a wife and children. His sister, Kim, had proven you could have a loving, normal relationship, something other than what he'd witnessed with his parents, a couple who lacked any real, deep affection for their children. To this day, he didn't know why they'd had kids.

At least Kim loved her husband and was ecstatic at the news

of being pregnant with her first child. The announcement had come days before Jake had run from Boston.

Damn it! He wanted to be around to hold the baby. He wanted to be an uncle, be able to watch the child grow and mature. He wanted— He stumbled from his chair. He wanted too many things, too many simple, unreachable things.

Moonlight pierced through the one window across from the desk, illuminating the tables, equipment and enough of the laboratory floor for him to cross the room without banging a foot or shin. At the window, he rested a hand against its edge as he peered outside. The night greeted him, the only time he felt comfortable since the explosion. He welcomed the shadows, which clung to the pines and rolling snow, camouflaging the mice, owls, and other small creatures he knew were out there.

A storm was due in tonight, but he didn't see any signs. Stars winked from above, and a stillness, a hushed sense of expectation washed over the night, or it could be his own imagination, his own hopes that he might find the key to unlocking the formula.

He glanced up at Margot's house. It sat on the hill, darker, thicker than the other shadows. Even though the sun had long since dipped behind the barren trees, the windows were absent of light. She was up there, though. Somewhere.

But what was she doing? Working? Drinking? Or staring off into some nameless space. He'd caught her doing that a number of times, thinking of God knew what as the house darkened around her. Was she remembering what had happened between them last night? She must have felt the same passion, the same hunger that still burned through his body. God, she'd been so soft and supple in his arms. The scent of her had driven him insane.

He'd been on her like a rutting dog and so damned close to going up those stairs after her. And he still wanted to, wanted to walk out of here and up the snow-covered hill to her house. He wanted her hot, whimpering for him.

He placed his brow against the glass. The chilled pane soothed his burning skin. From past experience, he knew he had a temperature. Even though mild, dangerous nonetheless.

Disgusted with his lack of self-control, he pushed away from the window. He had no time for sex. If he wanted to live long enough to have a good time in bed, he needed to get back to the computer and work. The answer had to be somewhere. He knew John had safeguarded a copy of the formula for him, but the question was where. It wasn't anywhere on John's computer or in the lab. Jake had made a thorough sweep, while he'd also searched every room in Margot's house. As for the idea of it being destroyed in the car crash with John—Jake didn't even want to think about it.

Sinking down in his chair, he focused on the numbers and equations in front of him. Concentration and determination were critical to unraveling Miracell. He'd get his answer or die trying. He laughed bitterly. That last thought came too damn close to the truth.

As he reached for another breath mint, a frigid breeze brushed against his skin. He stilled, his hand suspended in mid-air. The heater was on. He'd made sure, keeping the room regulated for the experiments he had to conduct. Shivering, he pushed away from the desk with a foot. The chair rolled and swiveled over the hard, linoleum floor as he turned.

A man in a bulky, down jacket stood in front of the laboratory's closed door. Malcolm. He'd slipped inside without Jake realizing.

"Hello, Jake."

The air locked in Jake's lungs for one, two...three seconds. Then he expelled it into one harsh sigh. He sat unmoving, as frozen and brittle as the trees outside.

Malcolm stepped further into the lab, and a beam of moonlight glittered off a gun. "Shocked? You shouldn't be. You knew I'd catch up to you."

He noted Malcolm wasn't holding a revolver but a semi-automatic. It was a gun that could rip through the lab in seconds, tearing through flesh and bone and anything within its path. Jake had no weapon, no form of defense other than himself. Granted, it might be enough, but there was also the chance of getting hit with one stray bullet. That one bullet would kill him.

"Have you come to kill me?" Jake asked from his chair, curling rigid fingers over the plastic armrests.

"Believe me, I'd like to. Would actually enjoy it after what you put me through. But, no." Malcolm nodded to the semi-automatic in his hand. "I thought it smart to bring it along. Call it self-preservation. Or a healthy dose of common sense. After all, I'm not dealing with a normal man."

"A gun? You think that's going to stop me? I'm not so easy to kill now, thanks to you." Bitterness hardened his voice. "If I wanted to, I could kill you right now."

"But not before I get a couple of bullets in you," Malcolm coolly replied. "Anyway, you won't. You had an opportunity back in Boston and didn't take it. You don't have the stomach for it, Jake. You never have. That's the difference between us. I'm not a coward."

"At least I'm not a murderer." Jake dug his fingers deeper into the plastic armrests. "Twelve people. All dead. And I was almost one of them."

The moonlight couldn't peal the shadows from Malcolm's expression, but Jake sensed a stillness, almost a weariness settle over the other man.

"Yes, well. That was an accident."

Jake's lips thinned. "Come off it, Malcolm. You left us for dead. The only reason I made it out alive was that I was in another wing of the building and you and your friends miscalculated how much it would take to level the place."

Malcolm sighed and shook his head. "You weren't supposed to die. You weren't supposed to even be there. You were far too important to the whole project."

"That's why you stabbed me with Miracell?"

"So I lost it. What do you expect? All I could think of was getting back at you when I walked in on you and found out you'd destroyed a critical portion of the formula. I saw the syringe and reacted."

"I get it now." Jake's voice thickened with sarcasm. "I was far more important than the others. So important that I deserved a slow and painful death."

"Oh, yes. I thought you had it coming. Then I realized injecting you with the formula was better than any plan I'd imagined. It was the best shot to ensure the formula's survival. Miracell's always been your brainchild, your baby. With any other scientist, it could take months, even years to get to where we were before the day of the blast. But with Miracell in your system, you have no choice but to reconstruct what's left of the formula and identify an antidote. That is if you ever hope to become a normal, functioning human being again."

Hatred twisted Jake's gut, hatred for everything he had once believed in, and hatred for Malcolm and everything he stood for. "And John? Was he supposed to die? That crash of his sure as hell was no accident. He started talking, didn't he? And you didn't like it. So you decided to shut him up for good—"

"Enough." Malcolm waved the gun in an arc. "I didn't come here to talk about John." Malcolm reached over and flipped the light switch with his free hand. He nodded to the computer at Jake's side. "It looks like you've started. Good. I want to know how far you've gotten."

Jake blinked at the sudden light that flared within the barn. "Turn it off. Margot'll see it and wonder what's going on."

"Ah, yes. My ex-wife." Malcolm's lip curled, but he turned the light off. "I hope you haven't been stupid enough to tell her about—"

"Of course not." Body tensed for any possibility, Jake watched Malcolm edge across the room. "How much does she know?"

"I don't know. I have a hard time reading her nowadays. Maybe nothing, maybe everything."

"But she was married to you, wasn't she? She must know something. She can't be completely in the dark."

"She knows only what I want her to know," Malcolm replied in a hard and ruthless voice. "However she's also John's sister. He could have told her everything that last week. And if he did, let's hope she's smart enough to keep her mouth shut. If she so much as breathes a word to the locals or someone in Boston, her life isn't worth one of her dime store books."

Rage launched Jake across the room. He slammed a shoulder into Malcolm. The semi-automatic tumbled from Malcolm's grasp and skidded across the floor without firing. He shoved Malcolm up against a table while digging his fingers into the flesh and muscle around his windpipe. Grunting, Malcolm bent backward over the table, struggling to pull Jake off him.

"Don't even think it," he hissed into Malcolm's ear. "I won't have it. I'll not have another death on my conscience. I swear if another person dies, I'll come after you. Do you understand? Do you?"

Realizing Malcolm couldn't answer because of his grip around his throat, Jake eased the pressure. "Do you *understand*?"

"Yeees—"

"Good. Because you can't hide. You know it. In the dead of night, before you know what's happened, before you even realize someone's crept up on you, I'll have both my hands around your throat, and I won't let go until I kill you."

In utter disgust, Jake flung him away. Malcolm tripped over his expensive wing-tipped shoes, awkwardly twisted at the waist and latched onto the edge of the table with one flailing hand to break his fall.

Brushing off his hands, weary and sickened, Jake watched Malcolm straighten. "Get out. Just get out."

Malcolm lurched sideways and snapped up the gun. With both hands affixed around the handle, he backed up to the door.

Jake froze. "Don't do something stupid."

"This isn't over," Malcolm said between long, shallow gasps. Semi-automatic thrust forward, Malcolm bumped his back up against the door. "That formula's mine. I've got too much money and time riding on it. One way or the other, I'm going to end up with it." He opened the door. Thick rays of moonlight rushed the room, highlighting everything in its path and the savageness of Malcolm's face. "You *will* find the answer."

Chin raised, jaw clenched, Jake bit out, "I don't have to do anything."

"True, if you want to stay the way you are—some sick freak."

Jake flinched. "Don't."

Having Malcolm say aloud what he'd come to think of himself was far more painful and self-effacing than Jake wanted to admit.

"Don't, 'what'? Tell it like it is?" Malcolm pressed on. "How happy can you be in the state you're in? Granted, you can do things you've always dreamed of, travel anywhere or any place you've ever wanted to go. But you can't be anyone. Not really. Maybe at night you can get away with it. But for all intents and purposes, you're dead. A freak of science. You don't exist."

Malcolm slammed out of the building.

Chest heaving, fists balled at his sides, Jake stared at the closed door. For several, long, agonizing moments as his heart pounded against his ribs, he stood transfixed. Malcolm's words reverberated inside his head. The truth in them ravaged him. A wave of impotence and frustration crashed over and around him. Only when his ragged breathing subsided, did he turn and shut down John's computer.

Then the thought rushed out at him and hit him full force. Malcolm. Margot. Malcolm was going up to the house to find out what she knew.

~~*~~

Margot sat slouched over the computer terminal in her den. Extending the right fingers of her hand, she stretched muscles stiff and cramped from inputting book descriptions into her database. She'd been at it all afternoon and evening. She picked up the last book, which she'd found in a little shop outside of Flagstaff, and trailed a finger across its spine. It was a first edition of *Nostromo* by Joseph Conrad in beautiful condition. The find had made her week.

With gentle hands, she placed it beside the stack of books by the keyboard. Books were her saviors, her escape. Within their pages, she could be the hero, invincible, able to slay dragons and fly to the outer limits of space. They'd helped her get through an awkward and troubling teenage period, a divorce and the loss of her job.

Now there was Johnny to cope with. Everyone had loved her brother. Even with only five years separating them, he'd been the one she'd run to as a child, the one she'd strove for approval while going through college, studying for the bar. Not her parents, never her parents. By the time she'd hit her teen years, she'd long since given up on proving herself to her mother and father. She wasn't the boy, the brilliant child, but a gangly, awkward, very average girl. Then she'd turned eighteen, it didn't really matter what her parents thought. They'd died in a boating accident off the coast of Baja, California that year.

Strange that she'd never been jealous, but Johnny was just that type of person. One could never stay angry with Johnny for long. And he'd always been there for her, championing her at every turn in her life.

To her deep regret, the one point of advice she'd never taken from her brother was Malcolm. Johnny had never liked him, but her brother, one to always have explanations grounded in fact, couldn't explain why, other than a gut reaction.

She fought back the sudden ache in her throat. She'd cried far too much already.

Sighing, she rose from her chair, all the while rubbing at the crick in the nape of her neck. The sun had long since slipped over the horizon, leaving the house in complete darkness.

She reached over to turn the desk lamp on when light from outside flashed between the curtains and disappeared. Frowning, Margot turned away from the untouched light and walked over to the large window. With some caution, she pulled the thick velvet drapes aside.

Someone was driving down the road, which wound through her property to highway 46. The car was unfamiliar, some type of recreational vehicle, but it had a longer, bulkier frame than Joyce's Land Cruiser. It couldn't be Jake. His vehicle was a small pickup, nothing like the one crawling over the snow-incrusted road. Headlights blinked through the trees, then vanished as the car turned onto the main road to the highway.

Strange that they hadn't come to the house. Unless, they were up to some mischief on her property, but Margot quickly discounted that. She wasn't living in a large metropolis anymore but a small town in the mountains with a fraction of the population. They were probably lost, she finally decided as she smoothed back the drape.

A noise, a metallic click of some sort, echoed faintly from the front of the house.

"Jake?"

She walked into the hall and found the front door closed along with the one to Jake's bedroom. He was still gone for the day.

"Johnny? Is that you?"

Silence.

"Are you trying to tell me something? Is that it? Are you here for a reason?" Slowly, she turned in a circle. No ghostly appearance made itself known. "I wish I knew what you wanted. Or why you're here."

She sighed in frustration before going into the kitchen and getting a glass of wine and something to eat. When she finished dinner, Jake still hadn't come back for the day.

She both dreaded and anticipated seeing him again. These last few days, she'd begun to look forward to his company, until, that is, she had slammed into his very male and very naked body last night. The feel of his skin against her hands still burned through her memory.

It had been so very long since she'd been held, kissed or caressed by a man. Her reaction could well be because she'd been celibate since Malcolm, and Jake had been that one match needed to set her system aflame. Then again, she was afraid it might be more than physical. She didn't like this sudden thirst for someone else's company. She'd finally become completely self-sufficient. She wasn't about to turn back now.

Jake's door remained shut. Curiosity tunneled into her system and pulled her down the hall to his room. After a moment of listening to her own breathing, she bit her lip, snapped on the hall light, then put her hand on the knob. The door opened silently inward. Light from the hall arrowed into the room.

She stepped inside, and, of course, found the place empty. The bed was neatly made. There were only a few signs of his occupancy. A comb on the dresser, a pair of jeans folded across the back of the cushioned chair. And his scent. A rich, masculine, wholesome aroma that curled around her.

On top of the low slung, bedroom dresser, a laptop computer further illuminated the room in a light blue, artificial glow. A screen saver of ocean wildlife shielded the monitor from view. She touched the mouse and row upon row of numbers and formulas lined the screen. Leaning forward, she peered at it but couldn't make any sense of it. She would have been better off trying to decipher a foreign language.

With a frustrated sigh, she backed away from the dresser and the computer. Her heel hit something hard. She glanced down and saw a dark object protruding from under the bed. Jake must have dropped it. She knelt down and reached out—

"Can I help you?"

She jerked up from her semi-crouched position and choked back the scream in her throat. Arms crossed, Jake stood with a shoulder pressed up against the doorjamb of the adjoining bathroom.

She slapped a palm against her chest. "God, you scared me. I didn't hear you."

"Are you looking for anything in particular?"

He didn't move away from his relaxed pose, but she sensed a tension, an energy animating from him. His sunglasses hid his gaze and any expression she might have gauged. Alone in the house with him, standing in the shadows of the same room with him, she found Jake suddenly threatening. His whipcord body beneath the dark jeans and long-sleeved T-shirt was hard, muscled and much stronger than her own. The black gloves over his hands made him appear even more sinister. What did she really know of him, other than what he'd told her?

She'd been caught red-handed, snooping where she didn't belong. "I thought you might need some fresh towels."

"I'm fine, but thanks."

He stood unmoving, not giving anything away.

Her explanation sounded far too lame. She gave up any

pretense and nodded to his computer. "I was just curious. Is it something you've been working on from your old job at Miltronics?"

"Yes."

"Do you mind me asking what?" She was growing more awkward by the second, and his non-committal answers weren't helping.

"Yes."

"Talking to you about Miltronics is like pulling teeth." She sighed. "You sound just like—"

"John?"

She rubbed her upper arms. "Yes."

His tone gentled. "Well, Miltronics has a way of keeping their employee's mouths shut."

"What do you mean by that?" She'd always wondered about Johnny's work, and maybe now was the time to find out.

He lifted his hand as if he wanted to rub his face but dropped it back to his side. "Maybe that didn't come out right. Much of their work is experimental and highly classified. The competition is fierce. They pay their people damn good, and because of that, they expect absolute loyalty and absolute silence."

"Are they associated with the government? Johnny wouldn't even tell me that."

"No. It's privately owned. They have a number of contributors. People with too much money and too much power." He pulled away from the doorjamb and walked into the room. "Enough about Miltronics. I don't work there anymore."

She took the hint and shut her mouth. He had every right to his privacy, but even knowing that didn't help her from feeling rebuffed. Turning to leave, she bumped her hip and knocked a section of newspaper off the dresser. She caught the folded newsprint in midair. About to put it back, she paused when the glow from the screen caught the word *Miltronics* in bold print across the newspaper. Frowning, she opened the paper and saw the caption on the front page of the Boston Globe.

"Twelve Dead in Explosion." Unable to read more because of the room's darkness, she reached over for the light switch.

"Don't!"

She jumped at the harsh urgency in his voice. She'd completely forgotten about his problem with bright light. The shock of seeing Johnny's company in the papers had blinded her to anything else around her.

"What is this? When did it happen? I have to know..."

Pivoting, Margot hurried from the room, gripping the newspaper tightly with one hand. She rushed down the hall. She was only half-conscious of Jake behind her as she entered the den and turned on the lamp. After sitting down in one of the high-backed chairs, she read the first several paragraphs in disbelief. When finished, she looked up at Jake.

"You didn't know, did you?" Jake asked softly.

"I—" She stared at him standing along the edge of the room's shadows. "Johnny, he..." She hesitated, then shook her head. "I feel terrible. I never knew." She reread the date. "It happened a couple of days after Johnny was killed. These people worked with my brother. And here I thought no one showed up at his funeral because they were too damned busy. I didn't know they were all dead!"

She tightened her grip on the newspaper, mangling it between her fingers. "They say it was arson. One of the employees. A janitor. They found evidence at his home."

"That's what they want everyone to believe," Jake muttered to himself, knowing damn well who the real arsonist was.

"What did you say?" Her gaze narrowed. "Are you telling me that they don't have the right person?"

Damn. That was stupid. He needed to learn to keep his opinions to himself. One wrong move from him and Margot would get suspicious. Then sooner more than later, she'd be asking Malcolm and anyone associated with Miltronics questions. If she did that, she wouldn't live long. Not with Malcolm.

And that scared Jake. In far too short a time, he'd come to like this woman. He'd realized that the second he thought Malcolm was going up to the house to confront her. Jake had raced out of the barn, thinking to head him off. Instead, he'd found the bastard leaving the place. God, the relief had almost brought him to his knees.

Jake folded his arms and shrugged. "I never said they had the wrong person. Don't put words in my mouth."

She stared back. It looked like she wasn't completely convinced. But hell, it was damn hard to act convincingly when the idea of someone else taking the fall for Malcolm's criminal activity tasted like crow. Granted, the guy they caught hadn't exactly been a model citizen with two prior arrests and an outstanding warrant for burglary.

"I need a drink."

Jake bit back a retort. If she wanted to drink herself under the table, that was her business. After all, that's what she, herself, pointed out so eloquently the other day. Frustrated, he watched her fling the newspaper on her desk and stride from the room.

Times like now, he questioned her relationship with John. Granted, they could both be obstinate, but he'd always considered her brother mild-mannered—so far off the scale from Margot. At work, John had been the cool, collected, calm one. He'd been dubbed Clark Kent, the alter ego of Superman.

From day one, the name had stuck. The resemblance had been uncanny between the character and John. John had found the idea amusing, and played along, by exchanging his old wire-rimmed eyeglasses for a pair of ugly, thick black framed ones. The joke had gone so far, that on his birthday, Jake and the others had a fake, but very authentic looking driver's license made for John under the name of Clark Kent.

Jake smiled at the memory. John had kept that thing in his wallet and would breeze into their department and flash it around when someone would get stumped in reading X-ray results or a glaring error would show itself in the Miracell model. "Not to worry," he'd say, "I'll get to the bottom of this. I have super-powers."

According to Johnny, there'd been a deep bond between him and his sister, closer than most siblings. He had often confided to Jake about Margot. Nothing in any great detail. More of his hopes and worries. He'd been very proud of her accomplishment with the tough time she'd had with her parents. Jake knew, though, when she'd left her husband and lost her job at her law firm that same year, John had worried. But he'd never explained, and Jake had never learned the reasons why. Maybe now, in hindsight, he should have.

Jake moved over to one wall lined with books, where he was deeper in shadow. He glanced over at the shelves and realized he was in the paranormal section. The *Encyclopedia of Death* caught his attention. Not exactly reading material he wanted to get into. It came too close to home. The book beside it wasn't much better. *The Vampire Book: An Encyclopedia of the Undead*. He slipped it from the shelf and quickly leafed through the pages.

Topics ranged from movies and books to mythology, psychological perspectives and sexuality of vampires. He re-shelved it and pulled out another alongside it. This was far more interesting. *Vampire Myths*. Opening the book, he glanced at the index. Case studies of people claiming to be vampires, historically on up to the present day. These were individuals from across the globe, India, Japan, the United States and Canada. According to the introduction, it was a scientific study conducted by several reputable and renowned doctors. He didn't recognize any of the names. How accurate or authentic was anyone's guess.

"What do you have there?"

He snapped the book closed and shoved it back in the shelf. He cleared his throat. "Nothing. Just looking at what you have here." Glancing over, he saw the half-empty glass of red wine in her hand. Again, he told himself forcibly, it wasn't his business. "It looks like you have an extensive collection."

She smiled, a gentle curve of her full lips. The first smile he'd seen of genuine pleasure. "It's taken me almost two years to get this far. Compared to many, it's pretty modest."

"How did you get into something like this?"

"By accident. I was looking for an out-of-print book I'd loved as a child, because I wanted to give it as a gift to a friend's daughter. I stumbled across it on the Internet. Pretty soon, people were asking me to find this book and that. It just snowballed from there, and now it's starting to take a different turn. The whole book industry is drastically changing, and I'm scrambling into the future of electronic formats."

"Why such a drastic change from being a corporate lawyer?"

Her smile didn't look so genuine now.

"I'd like to know." He trailed a finger along the edge of a shelf. "Johnny said you'd lost your job. I know he'd been really worried about you for a time. It takes guts to dive in and try your hand at something completely different."

~~*~~

He wasn't just being polite, Margot realized. He did want to know. She took a large swallow of wine and sank down in a chair. Why not tell him? She didn't like the memories, but if she talked enough about them, maybe, just maybe, they might fade in time.

"I lost my job right after the divorce. I'd been the one that filed. I think—no, I know—it really hit Malcolm's ego. He fought me all the way—until the end. Then he got really nasty. He even claimed battery. Tried to have me arrested. I guess you might say that I had problems coping with it all."

The truth was she'd had a complete breakdown. Margot glanced down at the glass in her hand. She'd tried not to sound bitter, but, damn, she was. She tipped the glass and emptied it down her throat. Briefly, she closed her eyes, savoring the taste, full-bodied with just a hint of smoke and spice. "I missed too much work. They considered me unreliable. They needed someone they could count on. I can't blame them really. If I'd been them, I'd probably have fired myself long before they ever did."

Henry, her direct boss and a die-hard chauvinist, had actually called her flighty, too emotional for the image they needed to portray. That had stung. She'd never thought of herself as that.

She rubbed the back of her neck to relieve muscles gone tense. The silence was thick and far too awkward. She sat in her chair, feeling like a fool. She'd talked way too much. The wine. God, the wine was dangerous and loosening her tongue. But at the same time, she felt this strange sense of release by telling a near stranger things she'd never been able to tell her best friend Joyce.

"Do you want to go back into law?"

She glanced up, not realizing he'd sat down several yards away in a matching chair of deep green velvet. "No," she answered truthfully. She made an arc with her wine glass. "I've got my books."

"Sounds lonely to me."

"I'm alone, not lonely. There's a difference. I don't need anyone. I've become self-sufficient. And I like it that way." She raised a brow. "Why? Are you lonely? You're not married, with two children, a loving wife and a picket fence, now are you?"

She stiffened. He actually could be. She'd just assumed for some crazy reason that he wasn't married. My God, and she'd been kissing him. No chaste peck, but open mouthed, hot and wet, and so deeply erotic that it still had the power to curl her stomach in remembrance.

"No. I never had the opportunity."

The muscles in her body eased, and she sank back into her chair. "Why?"

"Work always came first."

"Do I detect a note of regret?"

He'd been casually rubbing a gloved palm along the chair's armrest, but his hand stilled and he lifted his head to look at her. "I had my priorities wrong," he admitted. "Family, friends, the little things. I took them for granted. I should have learned from my parents. Hell, they were perfect examples of what not to do. Both workaholics. One a professor at a leading university and another a Dean to a prestigious college. They're both so wrapped up in their positions and titles that I don't think they have any real feeling or passion for anything or anyone beyond their careers.

"One thing I have learned in spite of them and myself, and that is that life's too short and far too precious to bury yourself in a job that can drain the life blood out of you."

Margot shifted and clasped her hands around the stem of her wine glass with rigid fingers. Such conviction, such deep passion beneath his words. She didn't want to think they held any truth. To her, life was long, painful, and filled with disappointment after disappointment. "Is that why you quit?"

He laughed, a harsh, deep sound of bitterness. "Quit? No. You could say I was terminated." He rose quickly to his feet and said gruffly, "I think I'll go on a walk."

She watched him slip from the room. They'd both lost their jobs and been rejected by their employers. She could relate to his bitterness, taste it on her own tongue. Having your job ripped from beneath you could shatter your self-confidence and also your sense of purpose or direction.

When she heard the front door close, she walked over to where he'd been standing by the books. He'd been looking at a certain book, a hardback set in the middle of the shelving unit with a dust jacket the color of blood. She lifted a hand to run a finger across the spines. When she saw the bold, black letters of the title against the red dust jacket, her hand froze in mid-air.

Vampire Myths.

My, God. Vampires.

Stiffening, she glanced over to the doorway but found it empty. Now that she thought of it, Jake reminded her of a shadow, dark, silent and without substance. He had an uncanny ability to move throughout the house and slip into the same room on soundless feet.

She'd never witnessed him eat anything. For that matter, the only time she'd seen him was at night when he was shrouded in darkness.

Ridiculous. She laughed aloud. "Come on, Margot. Get your head together. First ghosts and now vampires. You're losing your mind."

CHAPTER 7

A hushed stillness enfolded the house as Jake stood over Margot's bed and watched her sleep. In an hour, the first rays of the sun would touch the sky, but for now only the stars and moon illuminated her bedroom.

Earlier that evening, he'd had to get away from the house and Margot. He'd been too angry, too frustrated, and too damn close to spilling his guts about Miracell, Miltronics, and every sick detail. Jake had a pretty damn good idea Margot didn't know what was going on, and he wanted to keep it that way. He needed to keep her safe for John. He owed his friend that.

She lay on her side with a cheek pressed to her pillow, exposing the long, smooth column of her throat. Moonlight cast her neck and limbs to cool, silver marble, but he knew her skin would be warm against his hand. The temptation to touch her overwhelmed him. He wanted to stroke his lips and tongue along the sensitive spot below her ear and feel her pulse quicken with desire. Oh, God. How would she react? Would she arch her throat up against his mouth, would her body grow taut beneath him as he buried his hands in her thick, raven hair? He curled his fingers into fists at his sides.

She'd kicked off the top sheet, and her silk gown had twisted up around her thighs and pooled around her hips, leaving a healthy expanse of long, creamy legs.

Jake caved into temptation. Leaning forward, he trailed fingers over the satin skin of her calf, up around to the side of her thigh. She felt beautiful to the touch. He moved his hand up to the curve of her hip, inching the material higher until the fabric bunched up into his palm.

Her scent wrapped around him, womanly and exciting. Breathing deeply, he edged closer and eased down on the side of the bed. As the mattress sighed under his added weight, she shifted and turned onto her back. He stilled. A sigh slipped from her parted lips, but she continued to sleep, oblivious to him and the desire raging through his body.

He glanced over at her night table and saw the empty wine glass. She was dulling her pain, her anger, all her feelings beneath a haze of alcohol. And there was nothing he could do to stop her.

"Margot," he breathed her name. "How can I help you when I can't even help myself?"

~~*~~

It was just past 9:00 in the morning when Margot stepped out of the double doors of the post office. She almost went back inside when she saw Carl leaning a large boned hip against the side of her Cherokee she'd parallel parked along the road. She tightened her grip on the handle of the plastic postal bin she used to mail her book orders.

"Just what I need," she muttered between stiff lips.

"Hey, Margot."

"Hi, Carl."

She hurried past him to the rear of her 4X4. Maybe if she kept moving, he'd take the hint. Nope. No such luck. He was right there beside her when she opened the back hatch and tossed the bin in the back. Carl had a hand on the hatch before she had a chance to close the car or protest.

"Here, let me."

He slammed it shut with enough force to rock the vehicle.

"How about we go to Pinetop for dinner?" he asked, his breath a cloud of warmth against the frigid air. "Hell knows you don't get out enough. I bet you can't remember the last time you went out to a dinner or a movie." He rocked back on his heels and stuffed his bare hands into the pockets of his navy, down jacket. "It's not healthy."

"I'll be the one to worry about my health, Carl. But thank you." She added the last for his sister, Joyce.

"Oh, come off it, Margot. What's a bit of dinner? It's not like I'm asking for sex."

She flinched. For some reason, she hadn't expected something like that coming from Carl. He might hit on her, but he'd never been crude. Even if for some bizarre reason she found him wildly attractive, she still wouldn't be interested in any relationship, especially with a man like Carl. He retained too many antiquated ideas about women. Plus, she'd had more than enough with Malcolm.

"Carl, I'm not interested in dating right now. I'm not ready. It's too—"

"Soon?" His thick lips thinned. "Give me a break, Margot. It's been a good two years since you divorced Malcolm and came back here. You can't live locked up in that house of yours forever. And the drinking sure as hell isn't helping. The way you've been going at it, you're going to kill yourself. You know John would flip out if he saw you hitting the bottle like you've been doing. Joyce's really worried about you. We all are. You've got to cut it out."

Shock left her momentarily speechless. "I can't believe Joyce's been talking to you behind my back! What else have the two of you been talking about? My sex life? Has that also come up? Is that why you mentioned it?"

He raised his hands from his pockets. "Now don't get all emotional on me. Joyce was just thinking of you."

As he shifted, the sun glanced off the shield attached to his dark blue jacket, reminding her that he was a cop. It was enough to smother the nasty retort on her tongue. "I've got to go. I'm starting to freeze out here."

She skirted around Carl to get to the driver's side. Unlocking and opening the 4X4 with a fumbling hand, she jumped inside and slammed the car door right behind her. After starting the Cherokee, she guided it away from the curb with a tight-fisted grip on the cold, leather steering wheel. She turned off the main street, and Carl's pudgy figure disappeared from the rearview mirror.

She couldn't believe Joyce had opened her mouth to Carl of all people. Granted, he was her brother, but he was also a notorious gossip. Anything Carl heard, he repeated within a twenty-four-hour period. Joyce knew that. The whole town probably now knew every miniscule, boring detail of her life.

God, she wondered what everyone in town was saying about her. Was she now the town drunk? The crazy woman up at the house raving on about ghosts and other nonsense? Or the frigid bitch that couldn't get a date if her life depended on it?

Okay, so maybe she was exaggerating, but hell. It hurt to have her best friend talking about God knew what behind her back. Darn it. Days like today, she wished she'd stayed in Boston where a person could lose themselves in anonymity, not some sick Payton place, where a person stepped out the front door and everyone knew the color of their underwear.

As Margot pulled up the drive, she quickly noted the absence of Jake's pickup. Now he was a different story. She didn't know him enough to tell whether or not his words were coated with lies. He was a mystery. And she hated mysteries.

What could he be doing right now? Or for that matter, what in the world had he been doing since he'd arrived at her doorstep? Margot hadn't seen him once during the day or heard anyone mention him in town. She would have thought she'd get one or two comments regarding Jake from someone.

Maybe it was about time she asked where he disappeared to during the day. She frowned. He had her constantly thinking, wondering and questioning him. He was in her thoughts far too much. So much so that he was materializing in her dreams. And they weren't just innocent dreams, she admitted as she slipped from the car. They were vivid, erotic dreams. Even with the snap of winter around her, she felt her face warm with the memory.

In the dead of night, she'd fantasized about him coming to her room. Without a word spoken, she'd sensed not only his desire but also his need. The taste of his finger upon her lips, the scent of his male body had been so real. At times, she could swear they were a reality and not a fantasy.

Just this morning as the first light of dawn touched the windows, she'd woken. Her sheets had been down around her ankles and her nightgown had twisted and hiked up to her waist. She'd lain there, body flushed, hot and damp, her breasts swollen and heavy, and she'd been overwhelmed with such a frightening feeling of intense desire.

Enough. She closed her eyes against the hunger. It had been too long since she'd slept with a man. Since Malcolm. She hadn't had the guts to move past the point of friendship with anyone else.

She hurried across the crackling snow and up the steps to the porch. That's when she saw the front door. She'd thought—no, she knew she'd locked up.

The door now stood ajar, the wood along the jam frayed and splintered. It wouldn't have taken much for someone to force their way in. What with the wood being old and the lock not the latest technical gadget.

That same someone could be inside the house this very minute. Fear crawled up her spine as she stepped back. She should do the logical, sane thing by getting back in her car. But since when had she ever done anything logical recently?

She stepped gingerly inside and glanced around. Nothing looked touched, but as a precaution, she left the front door open. She walked further down the hall and peered into the kitchen. That's when she saw what they'd done. She stood frozen as if coated in ice and as easily shattered.

Whoever had been here was long gone, leaving behind their apathy and malevolence. Cabinets and drawers stood half-opened with pots and pans spilling out from within. Kitchen utensils lay scattered across the counters and floor. The dishes. At least some of the dishes had been left alone. In a daze, she sidestepped a clay pot, shattered and lying on its side, the plant inside uprooted and the dirt splattered across the white linoleum. Glass crackled beneath her feet.

Why? Why would someone do this?

She swallowed. They couldn't have gone through the whole house. Raped every room. Could they? Pivoting, she hurried from the kitchen, the need to know catapulting her down the hall and into her den, her sanctuary, the place she could hide and—

Her worse fears struck her head on.

Shelves lay barren. Books and more books had been tossed onto the floor, their pages creased and mangled from others piled on top of them, their boards bent backward, ruining fragile spines and hinges.

"Margot?"

She opened and closed her hands. Pain closed around her throat and strangled the ability to speak. She stepped over a mound of modern fiction hardbacks and worked her way to the corner of the room and her personal bookcase. These were the books she'd put aside, the rare, expensive volumes she'd kept for sentimental and investment reasons. The window case had been shattered, the lock meaningless. Shards of glass dotted the carpet and volumes.

The person or persons who'd swept through the house had turned vicious, even vindictive here. She lifted a book on top of a pile of ruined volumes. The boards had been ripped from their bindings, the pages torn, the jagged papers flung everywhere.

"Margot!"

The sound of steps rushed across the hall.

"Oh, no!" Joyce cried from somewhere behind her. "What happened? Who did this?"

"I—" Margot cleared her throat and dropped the book to the floor. "I don't know."

"We need to call Carl. Get him over here. Now."

"No."

Joyce's raised her brows. "What do you mean, 'No'?"

"Just that." She rubbed her mouth with a palm. "I don't want everyone knowing about this. I don't want every little detail of what happened here brandished about."

"You don't know what you're talking about. Someone just trashed your house. Are you seriously going to let them get away with it? They could come back. This time you might be in the house when they do." Joyce gasped. "You weren't here when—"

"No." Margot sighed. She gripped the bridge of her nose with a thumb and forefinger and closed her eyes briefly. "You're right. I hate the idea, but I do need to report it. At least for insurance purposes. It's just I don't trust Carl to keep it quiet. Or you for that matter right now. You've been talking about me to your brother behind my back. Things I thought were private— things I thought were just between the two of us."

Joyce flushed. "Yes, well. I'm concerned. We all are. You've been acting stranger than—" She bit her lip.

"Stranger than normal?" Margot finished for her. She should feel hurt, offended, but strangely didn't.

"That came out the wrong way."

"Yes, well, why don't you call your brother?" she asked instead of getting into a confrontation. Now wasn't the time. "While you're doing that I'll go see what upstairs looks like."

Margot went through the second floor, mindful of not touching or moving anything for Carl. She found Marmaduke, safe and unharmed, hidden under a chair in one of the guest bedrooms. Thank goodness the vandals hadn't hit that room or the other guest rooms. But they'd hit her bedroom. Hard. With complete carelessness and disregard for anyone else, they'd shoved her mattress to one side, upended drawers and tossed her clothing aside. Tampons, hair ribbons, sheer, dainty nylons and undergarments littered the floor. Anger, hot and corrosive, eroded away the hollow, numb feeling in her gut.

Why? What had she ever done to this person to make them lash out at her like this?

When she came back down, Joyce was waiting by the base of the stairs. Margot saw the question in her eyes. "There are three bedrooms upstairs. They went to work on my room but didn't mess with the others. I don't know why."

"Maybe they heard your Cherokee and took off before you came in," Joyce suggested

"Is anything missing?" Carl asked from the front entrance. He rubbed the dirt and snow from his boots onto the mat. The front door still stood open, allowing winter air to sweep inside and chill Margot's already cold body.

"Nothing that I can tell." She rubbed her arms. "The TV and radio are still here."

"What about guns?"

"No. I've always hated the things."

Carl disappeared into the den. "Holy shit."

A few minutes later he came out with a grim expression. "It almost looks like they were looking for something. That or they've got it in for you real bad."

Margot grasped the glossy wood top of the stair, newel post.

"You don't have any enemies that would do something like this, do you?" Carl asked.

She rested her chin against the top of her hand, closed her eyes and tried to think. It took all of a second to come up with a name. Tension rolled through her. "There's Malcolm. He's been in town."

"He's got a temper." Frowning, Carl rubbed the back of his neck.

"But it doesn't seem his style," Margot quickly argued.

Carl's gaze narrowed. "What about this guy? This renter of yours Joyce has told me about? Where's he at?"

"He's usually gone during the day."

"Where to?" He shifted and hitched up the side of his pants with his belt loop. "Seems awfully strange. Why hasn't anyone mentioned him in town?"

"I don't know!" She shook her head, getting completely frustrated. She hated how Carl had a very valid point and she couldn't give him a straight answer. "I don't keep tabs on him. He's just renting a room for a couple of weeks. He knew Johnny. And he needed a place to stay."

"He did? What's his name?"

"Jake Preston."

"Well, I've yet to see him here or in town. No one's mentioned him or seen him either."

"Are you calling me a liar?"

"Of course he isn't," Joyce cut in.

"Now, don't get emotional on me, Margot. I'm just trying to get a picture here." Frowning, he rubbed his chin slowly. "Let's see. What else can you tell me about this Jake?"

Margot leaned heavier on the newel post. She didn't know a thing other than what Jake had told her. God, she was beginning to feel and sound stupid. "He worked at Miltronics. The same place as Johnny and Malcolm."

"Is that it?"

Carl didn't say it but it was there in his face. Also Joyce's. Skepticism. "Yes."

That one word tasted like curdled milk. She was coming out looking like a complete flake.

"So you're renting a room to a guy you hardly know. Seems to me like you're not making very good judgment calls these days."

"You might be right, but do you have to point it out?" Margot straightened. "You know, I'm getting sick of this attitude of yours."

He looked almost as frustrated as she felt. "What do you expect, Margot. You're not helping me out here. This Jake—no one's seen. You've talked about him but no one's yet laid an eye on him. It's not like he can lose himself in Greyson. People notice someone new. Maybe that bottle of yours is finally—"

"Carl!" Joyce protested. "That's enough! You're being far too hard on her."

Margot slapped a palm against the newel post. "You don't believe me! Well, let me show you something, Mister!" She pushed off the wood beam and strode down the hall to the room Jake had been using.

At the doorway, she flung her hand out and pointed. "See? Does that look like my imagination?" For just a moment, one split second of time, Margot did wonder, until she glanced inside. The vandals had also struck this room. The mattress sagged half off the box spring and onto the floor, clothing littered the floor, but the dresser drawers looked untouched. Almost as if she'd interrupted them in the middle of their destruction.

"Hmmm." Carl was back to frowning again. "How well does he know Malcolm?"

Again she really couldn't answer him. "I didn't get the impression they were really close."

Joyce grasped her brother's elbow. "Come on, Carl. Let's give it a rest. Margot's had her whole house destroyed. Being grilled is the last thing she needs right now."

"Just do what you have to and please go." Margot followed them back down the hall and to the front door.

"I'll be out of your hair once I dust around this door and a couple of other places." He rubbed his chin. "You're going to have to get a new lock and fix that door jam."

Margot sighed. "I'll give Charlie a call. He's the best, or should I say the only, handyman we have around here."

Joyce wrapped an arm around her. "While you're on the phone, I'll start cleaning up the downstairs guest bedroom."

Less than an hour later, Carl left, but Joyce remained to help. By late afternoon, though, Margot had managed to get Joyce out the front door. She'd wanted to help more, but Margot wouldn't have it. The locksmith had come and gone, while the kitchen and a good part of the downstairs had been cleaned. They hadn't worked on her bedroom or den. Margot wanted to do those on her own. That way if she broke down, she'd do it privately.

From the kitchen window, she watched Joyce's Land Cruiser disappear through the trees as she gripped the counter with two hands. With everyone gone and time to herself, the events of the day were crowding in on her.

She didn't want to go in the den, didn't want to face the destruction...and the pain that would come with it. But she had no choice. She needed to make some sense of all the chaos. Her computer was waiting with orders. Orders that paid the utilities and the food in her kitchen.

She grabbed a full bottle of Beaujolais and a wine glass. She needed something to help her through that room. To hell with what people thought of her drinking. She didn't give a rat's ass. Let them judge. They hadn't walked in her shoes.

Stepping over to the doorway of the den, she faltered. The magnitude of the mess spilling across the room slapped her with vicious hands. To think someone she might know did this. But could it be Malcolm? Was this his way of getting back at her? He'd never forgiven her for being the first to file for the divorce. His damn ego might have spurred him on. After all, he'd always had to have the last word. Maybe this was his way of showing her once and for all.

Still standing in the hall, she glanced over at the guest bedroom. Could Jake be behind the vandalism? His room, although messy, didn't compare to the magnitude of the den's destruction. If he did happen to be the vandal, he would never have left his room untouched, not if he had an ounce of intelligence. Suspicion would have pointed to him otherwise.

She strode into the guest bedroom. She put the wine bottle and glass on the dresser and eyed the room with belligerence.

Did Jake have something against her? If he was the person behind this, what could she have ever done to have him feel like he had to hit back at her? Or was he, in fact, searching for something? But to be so vindictive about it seemed so sick, so personal.

She grabbed the neck of the wine bottle, uncorked it, and filled her glass. She blinked back tears. Whoever did this wasn't going to make her cry.

Glass in hand, she walked over to the door leading into the adjoining bathroom. The small window across the sink and mirror did little for illumination, so she flipped the switch, flooding harsh, fluorescent light into the cubicle. Toothbrush, mint toothpaste, a black comb rested along the lip of the porcelain sink. Nothing unusual and nothing here that someone could hide.

Then she glanced at the opaque ice blue shower curtain drawn completely across the bathing area. Someone might have slipped back into the house after Carl had left. They could have hidden in the bathroom while she'd been cleaning another part of the house with Joyce. Someone could be behind the shower curtain right now.

CHAPTER 8

Her heart rate accelerated and drummed inside her ears. Goosebumps rose across the flesh of her arms and at her neck. She crept closer, grabbed the edge of the curtain, and lunged, shooting the drape aside in one fluid motion. White tile, white tub, silver fixtures, shampoo and conditioner—nothing else.

"This is absolutely crazy!" Her voice echoed against the walls. "Get a grip."

But she couldn't halt the trembling of her hands. She'd been holding her wine glass with her left hand and some of the wine had sloshed onto her wrist. She rinsed it off under the sink and shut off the faucet.

Another sound immediately followed. Almost as hollow to the ear. She took a cautious step into the guest room but found it empty.

"No. I won't have it," she said to the air around her as she walked into the bedroom. "Johnny, if that's you, cut it out. I can't handle any strange other-worldly things happening to me tonight."

Margot rolled her shoulders and eyed the room with suspicion. She hadn't been the one to pick up the mess in here. Joyce had done this room, while she'd focused on the kitchen.

If Jake was behind the vandalism, this was the perfect opportunity to search his room, and she didn't plan on stopping until she came up with something. The man was hiding something.

She placed her glass on the dresser by the bottle and stepped around the bed to the closet. She opened the door and peered inside. Several shirts, a pair of boots, but little else. Sighing, she turned away and thrust her hands on her hips and eyed the floor by her feet.

Absently, she noted the bed skirt brushing against the carpet. The last time she'd been here, Jake had scared the devil out of her. She hadn't seen him come out of the bathroom because she'd been preoccupied with something. Yes. She inhaled sharply as the memory flashed to the forefront. Her foot had hit a dark object protruding from beneath the bed.

She dropped down on her hands and knees and lifted the bed skirt. Two suitcases were shoved beneath the box spring. The vandals must have missed them.

"Yes!" She laughed, ecstatic. "Gotcha!"

She pulled out the one closest, which was a smaller, navy blue case with a carrying handle and wheels at the base. Sitting Indian style, she shifted the traveling bag up against her knees and looked for a lock. There wasn't one.

"Come on luck. Keep it up. Show me what Jake might be hiding."

The zipper slithered open with perfect ease. She pulled open the flap. Inside were several smaller bags and cases, a bottle of makeup—foundation of all things—and something— something she didn't know what to make of. She touched what felt like some type of animal pelt. Frowning she gingerly picked it up. Dark chestnut hair. Human hair.

"My God," she breathed.

It was a wig. She touched a silken strand between two fingers. It was the same color as Jake's hair. Why would he need a wig?

Heart skittering against her ribs, she grasped a square, black box from inside which was similar to that of a makeup case. She snapped it open and looked inside. The upper section had...

She frowned again. What in the world? Gingerly, she slipped what looked like an eyebrow or mustache, the same color as the wig, from one of the compartments. She brushed the small piece with a thumb. *My God.* A tube of glue sat in another compartment while—

A rush of air raced over her, stirring the hair against her cheek. Something hit the bed.

What? Who?

Jerking back in surprise, she glanced sideways, only to have her view blocked by the comforter rushing at her. The material hit her head-on, blanketing and blinding her. She shoved at the comforter, knocking the case from her lap. Someone had slipped into the room with her. They could rush at her any second, could rape, kill—

Panicked, she fumbled for an opening and found none. Growing frantic now, she jerked to her knees and shoved at the suffocating material. Finally, she flung it off her head, throwing her hair on end. She whipped around, gasping for breath.

Dragging air into her lungs in deep, loud gasps, she rushed to her feet and backed away from the bed. She swept her gaze back and forth over the room but found no one. Still, she didn't relax but stood tense, ready to run or fight if she had to.

"Who's there? Why are you hiding?" She swallowed down fear and frustration. "Show yourself."

No one appeared, which didn't relieve the tension clawing at her shoulders and limbs. For a second she thought she was going crazy, but then she glanced down at the comforter caught around her ankle. It didn't attack her all by itself.

Impatiently, she kicked the bedding aside. "Okay. Come on. The joke's over. You can step out now. You've had your fun."

She waited, shifting back and forth on the balls of her feet, ready to bolt if the need arose. Slowly, ever so slowly, as her gaze darted over every conceivable hiding place, she edged toward the doorway.

And that's when she felt it. Someone or something right behind her. She screamed as she whipped around, stumbling in her hurry to see. But nothing or no one was there. She could have sworn...

Her laughter crackled and died against the four walls around her. Maybe she was going crazy. But the blanket. Could she, herself, have pulled it from the bed by accident?

She hated, really hated doubting herself.

She lunged for the bottle and glass from the dresser and backed out of the room. She hugged both against her chest and continued to walk backward down the hall.

"This isn't funny, Johnny!" she called. "I know you were always a jokester, but this has gone far enough.

"If someone's here," she yelled, "show yourself!"

She was crazy. She'd finally gone over the edge. She found herself back in the den as she hit a heel against a damaged book. The chaos of the room smacked her hard, sucking the breath from her lungs and the energy from her body. She stumbled over the ruined books and found an empty spot beside the couch. With the bottle in one hand and the glass in the other, she slid down its side, her back rubbing against the quilted fabric. Her bottom hit the floor.

After sitting there for God knew how long, and when nothing or no one appeared, she uncorked the wine and poured a healthy measure. No one was going to jump out at her, because no one was in the house with her. She didn't want to think she'd made up the incident, because it scared the hell out of her.

She made a conscious effort to pull her thoughts toward something else and focused on the room around her. She swore under her breath. Much of her inventory was ruined. It had taken her two years to get to where she'd been this morning. Now it was all gone. The work involved...

With the back of one hand, she brushed angrily at a tear that had slipped past her lashes. Crying never solved anything. At least not in her life. She'd learned while growing up that tears only brought censure or indifference. A Davenport never cried or showed any sign of deep emotion. That's probably why she'd failed both parents.

She drank the rest of the bottle. The wine coated her fear, deadened her feelings and pulled her into a world of oblivion. Sleep finally dragged her under as she slumped against the couch.

~~*~~

That's where Jake found her. An empty bottle of wine on one side and an overturned glass on her other.

"Damn it, Margot," he whispered, frustrated. "Alcohol isn't going to make your life any better. It'll only push you down deeper."

He took both bottle and glass from her side and shoved the bottle in the trash beneath her desk and left the glass on top by the computer.

It didn't take much to pick her up, carry her over from the side of the couch and gently set her down on the cushions. Her head fell limply to the side and a wave of raven hair slipped across her cheek. He slid the strands aside, exposing her flushed cheek—a cheek where deep hollows clung below the bone. From the photos he'd seen around the house, she'd lost weight—a lot of weight. If she lost any more, her health would be in danger, if it wasn't already.

Jake didn't look around the room. He'd already seen enough. The guilt of it buried itself into his gut. He might not have torn the place apart, but he was equally to blame. Malcolm knew he was here. It was also obvious Malcolm suspected another copy of the formula was secreted away in the house.

Reluctantly, Jake left her on the couch. He had to right some of the wrong done to her. Less than an hour later, when he came back and found Margot still sleeping, he sank down on the edge of the couch and caressed her forearm with a gloved hand.

"I'm sorry," he murmured, knowing she couldn't hear. "For having Malcolm follow me. For all the destruction and all the pain it's caused. And for frightening you with the blanket. I never meant for you to doubt yourself, but I didn't see any other way to stop you. You were going to discover everything. I can't let that happen. I can't put you in any more danger, or myself."

Her lips parted, giving him a glimpse of even white teeth. He touched her bottom lip with an index finger and then trailed it down across the line of her jaw and smooth column of her throat to her delicate breastbone and the scooped neckline of her dark brown sweater. Her low-slung, faded jeans clung to her hips and thighs in all the right places.

He groaned. He shouldn't be thinking of sex. She had enough problems without him adding to it. But he *couldn't* help but think of a sexual relationship with her, however short. He couldn't ignore his body's reaction—a reaction that both amazed and alarmed him. He'd never been that sexual. Work, more importantly, science, had been his life, something that had always taken precedence over anything else.

He'd had women, of course. There'd never been a problem getting sex. As to his looks or his sexual prowess, he'd never had complaints. But any relationship he'd encountered had lacked any great feeling.

Damn. What a cold ass he'd been. He'd made the mistake of letting everything important fall unheeded behind him. Until now. Now with his mortality threatened, he hungered for life and everything it involved.

He slid his index finger back up over the column of her throat. Dissatisfied, he pulled away. The gloves masked the feel and texture of her skin.

Margot stirred. Her lids snapped open and she stared at him with large, thick-lashed eyes. An indefinable emotion flickered in their depths before they widened. She scrambled along the couch and away from him.

"You've done this before. Sat there, watched me, touched me while I've been sleeping, haven't you?"

The question threw him. How could he explain without sounding like a pervert?

"It's not what you think," he insisted. But wasn't it? Hadn't he crept into her room in the middle of the night and watched her sleep? Hadn't he touched her? Hadn't he wanted to take her in his arms, have her naked and crying out his name?

"You've been in my room. Late at night while I've been asleep." She shoved her knees up to her chin and wrapped both arms around her jean-clad shins. She regarded him with huge brown, liquid eyes. "I had such dreams... I thought they were my imagination. I'd wake up in the morning feeling so—I thought—"

Sudden awareness flared between them. He felt it, saw it in

her eyes and heard it in the quick intake of her breath as his own breathing escalated and his groin throbbed and hardened.

"I wanted you." The admission seemed dragged from her lips. "In my dreams I wanted you to go further than a simple touch."

~~*~~

It was the truth, Margot realized in dismay, acutely conscious of Jake sitting on the same sofa with her and aware of being in a dark and isolated house together. The idea both horrified and aroused her. He was darkly dangerous, darkly male and darkly mysterious.

His sudden stillness told her he'd been affected by her words. She sensed his desire across the short distance and her body responded, hunger wrapping, then squeezing itself around her belly.

"You don't know how tempted I was to do more than touch you," he admitted.

His words, deep, rough and thick with desire washed over her, weakening what little resolve she had. "Don't." She lifted her chin. "You don't have any right to steal into my room. I sure as hell didn't invite you."

"But you wanted me. Late at night, alone in bed. At least your body did. You'd arch up, urging me to touch your breasts, curl my fingers between your legs and—"

"Stop it!" She stumbled off the sofa and stepped on a book. The pages ripped beneath her foot. She stared at the crushed volume and remembered everything. Her body once hot and flushed turned icy. Oh my God—to think for a few moments she'd forgotten the vandalism. She glanced over at Jake still seated on the sofa. "I want you out of here."

She dodged a mound of books and snapped on the lamp on top of her desk. She blinked at the brightness, while the sudden throb of a headache pressed against her temples. She could thank the wine. Rubbing at her brow, she looked at the books thrown at her feet.

Jake saw her glance at the floor and then look at him. The

accusation on her face was unmistakable. His heart rate faltered, then galloped full tilt. "You think I did this?"

"Of course. Who else? Can you tell me that? It seems damned strange that you show up at my door and this happens! It took Joyce and I hours just to clean a portion of the place—your room included." She tossed several raven strands over one shoulder. "I don't want you here. I'll give you enough time to pack before I call the police. It won't take Carl long to get here."

"That doesn't make sense! Why would I trash my own stuff? Can you answer me that?"

"I don't know!" She balled her hands at her sides. "I don't know you! Or what motivates you! For all I know you could be some sick lunatic."

Jake rose to his feet, but he wasn't ready to leave yet. "I'm not some lunatic. How can I convince you I didn't do this?"

"Can you give me proof?"

"Proof? You want proof?" He turned, intending to walk the length of the room, but stumbled over a book. He picked it up and leafed through the pages. Did he dare tell her? No. Once she knew, matters would escalate. More questions would be raised, more people would become involved. Someone else would get hurt or even die. He couldn't handle that. Margot might not value her life, but he did.

"I have no alibi," he said, his voice weary and tired as he placed the volume on an empty bookshelf beside him. "I was alone." Palms upward, he raised his hands. "Damn it, Margot. You've got to believe me. I had nothing to do with this. If I'd known it was happening, I would have done something to stop it."

"Even if you had nothing to do with what happened today—something's going on. Why else would you make an effort to disguise yourself? The wig. The glasses. You're hiding from someone or something. I want to know what it is. I want the truth. And I want it now. Are you running from the police?"

He ignored the panic. How could he have ever thought she'd forget her little discovery in his bedroom? What did he say? What could he say? Did he tell her the truth? He rubbed the back of his neck where the label of his turtleneck chaffed at his skin.

"Well?" She folded her arms across her middle. "I want answers. Do I have to call Carl? Because I will. Maybe he'll get to the bottom of this. Maybe he'll be able to find out what you're hiding."

When he still didn't answer, she strode over to the desk, reached over and put her hand on the phone. Damn it! He bounded over a pile of books to get to her side and covered his gloved hand over her own. The light was shining on him, damn it, but he couldn't let her make that call.

She tried to pull away while retaining a grip on the receiver, but he held on. "Don't," he breathed into her ear, unable to mask the desperation in his voice. "Don't call the police."

She turned as if in slow motion—her waist twisting, her neck arching sideways as she lifted her head to look at him. The light on the table hit every pore of his body. She'd know. In a second she'd see the light illuminate his features, his mouth, his teeth—

He continued to hold her hand down against the telephone, as he slammed his other hand against the lamp's candelabra. The light skirted across the table, tipped over and crashed against the floor.

Utter blackness enveloped the den, then slowly, very slowly moonlight whispered into the room, painting a myriad of different shades of gray against the furniture and fixtures. Blessed shadows shielded him from her eyes. Only then did he let go of her hand.

She stumbled back. "Why did you do that?"

"It was an accident." He backed away from her, tripping over another damn book with his clumsy feet. He grabbed an empty shelf along the wall to steady himself. "I can't have you call Carl—or anyone else for that matter."

"Then tell me," she insisted.

He bowed his head. For too long he'd kept everything to himself. Years now. There'd been his co-workers of course, but he had yet to confide with anyone outside of Miltronics. No one else knew the details of his research, not even his sister.

He lifted his head and glanced across the distance of the room. Jaw ridged, tension radiating from her slim figure, Margot stood waiting.

"Fine," he finally said. "I'll tell you."

CHAPTER 9

MARGOT STARED AT him across the shadowed, office room. "I need some light in here. You might be able to live in the dark, but I can't."

She wove through the debris and lit the fireplace. Flames bloomed from the ceramic logs, and a yellow glow illuminated the room and flickered across the wall and the window. Because of the fire's reflection, Jake couldn't see past the glass to the world outside, but anyone on the other side could easily observe Margot and himself.

He strode over and pulled the drapes from the wall anchors and brought both sides of the thick velvet material together.

"So are you going to give me some answers?"

Jake turned from the drape and saw that Margot had sunk down in a high-backed chair. Faded jeans hugged her slim hips and shapely legs, while the dark brown sweater accented her pallor. Even with the dim lighting, she looked exhausted. If he hadn't shown up at her house, maybe she wouldn't be going through what she was right now. No. That wasn't necessarily true. He shouldn't feel guilty. There were other players.

He cleared his throat. What the hell was he doing? If he spilled his guts, he'd put her in jeopardy. But at the same time, he couldn't let her start asking questions. Then she'd be in deeper trouble. What had Malcolm said? She wouldn't be worth one of her 'dime store books'. Damn. How he hated that phrase and the careless, apathetic way it had been said. When it came down to it, Jake guessed supplying her with some answers was the better of two evils.

"Where do I start?"

"How about at the beginning."

The feminine huskiness of her voice floated across the room, reminding him all too clearly of his attraction to her. He'd been battling it since that night she'd run into him—even before really. She'd felt so good in his arms. Curves in all the right places. Well, if he were any type of man, he'd fight this thing he had for her.

"I guess I'll start with Miltronics."

"Why am I not surprised?" Leaning forward, she rested both elbows on her knees. "Go on."

He shifted. Getting the words out was proving more difficult than he'd anticipated. "I asked John to safeguard a disk for me. It was a duplicate of a scientific discovery we had been diligently working on for several years. We'd just completed it last month. Granted, there were a few minor glitches, but it was a relatively pure formula. I had a copy made. It was the only smart thing I did. At the time, I hadn't been using my brain or paying attention to the people around me. I didn't see it coming—not really. I was so damn euphoric. Our department was humming with excitement. We'd actually hit pay dirt with the hypothesis we'd reconstructed!"

His hands were damp beneath the leather gloves and the temptation to rip them off was overwhelming, but of course he didn't. He dragged in a deep breath and saw he'd captured her rapt attention. But did he dare tell her what part he'd played? The entire scenario? Shame and self-loathing decided him against the idea. What he'd done was unforgivable.

He exhaled. "To make a long story short—a critical portion of the formula was destroyed. I've been trying to reconstruct it without success. The only other complete copy is the one I gave John."

"And that disk is here, isn't it?"

"Here or in the lab."

She jerked to her feet and swept an arm around her. "So you decided to do a little hunting and to hell with my house!"

"No! I told you I didn't do this!"

"Then who?" She glared at him. "Can you tell me that? Can you?" Hands on her hips, she waited. She opened her mouth to say something, and then closed it. Suddenly the anger in her eyes dissolved. Surprise and understanding washed over her pale features.

"Malcolm. It's Malcolm, isn't it?" she asked. "It all makes so much sense now. A while back, I thought it might be him, but only for a short time, because I couldn't come up with his motivation. He'd stopped being vindictive over a year ago. But he's the one looking for the formula."

"Yes."

"And you? What about you? You want this formula too. That's why you're here, isn't it? For the copy? You've been going through my house searching for it." An expression of what looked like disgust flashed across her face. "Did you get what you came for?"

Even though she tried to mask it, Jake heard the hurt beneath the bitterness. It made him feel that much more of a creep. "No. It's still missing. At least, I think it is. I don't think Malcolm's found it."

"But he might have—the way he went through each room. Then again, there's a lot of anger and frustration behind the destruction, which might mean he didn't find it." She hugged herself. "It has to be pretty important for Malcolm to break in and rampage through here like some crazed person. Then there's you, secretly sneaking around, digging into places you have no business. What's on this disk? This scientific formula?"

Jake stiffened in surprise even though he knew she'd eventually ask that question. "I can't tell you." The firelight illuminated the objection in her face. "Please. Believe me. It's for your own safety."

"My safety?" She rubbed her arms. "Come on, Jake. You don't expect me to believe that—"

"It's the truth! Too many people have died because of this.

The whole wing of Miltronics was completely destroyed. Twelve people were murdered. These were people I worked with on a day-to-day basis. Many of them I considered friends, not just co-workers." And he was to blame. Because of him, they were dead. "I was the only one that got out of the building alive. Every day I'm so damned thankful I'm still breathing, and I want to keep it that way. That's the reason for the disguise."

"But the newspaper said the police caught the person." Frowning, she walked around the back of her chair.

He could tell she didn't believe him. "The real killers found the perfect scapegoat for the police. They hired a janitor who'd spent some time behind bars. They had to know his record. They do background checks on every employee. He wouldn't be any different. What better person, than someone with a prior record for burglary and not too swift in the intelligence department? At least not enough intelligence to work with those type of explosives."

Bitterness roughened and deepened his voice. "He was a patsy, and the police on the case, either lazy or incompetent, decided to zero in on him. Hell, who could really blame them? He'd been spotted on several occasions loitering around Miltronics after his shift. And of course, there was the evidence he'd conveniently left around his apartment."

She placed both hands across the top the chair. "You sound like you know who did it."

He heard the question in her voice and decided enough was enough. Margot needed to know how dangerous her ex-husband really was. After all, didn't she have a right to protect herself? "I can't prove anything, but I know Malcolm was involved. He might not have lit the fuse, but he was right there planning everything."

"Malcolm? Malcolm had something to do with those deaths at Miltronics?" Her voice rose in amazement. "My, God! It explains so much! The way he came barging into the house the other day. And he has it in him. There's a dark, almost black side to his personality. But to actually cross that line—act on it. It's all so hard to imagine."

"Yes, well, you better believe it. He's more than motivated. There's a lot of money at stake. His, and a number of other investors." Jake stepped over several books. "I'm surprised Malcolm hasn't talked much to you about Miltronics. I can see John keeping quiet, but I would think Malcolm would have confided in someone."

"Oh, now I understand. You suspected me of knowing what Malcolm was doing. What with Malcolm being my ex-husband?" Hurt and reproach thickened her voice. "But now, you don't still think I'd—"

"Of course not," he returned quietly. "Granted, in the beginning I had my doubts. But it didn't take long to figure out that you're not in any way involved with Malcolm's schemes. Plus, you are, after all, John's sister. That says something in itself. I trusted him. He was one of few I could count on."

"Thank you, I think." She pulled a wisp of hair back around her ear and laughed without humor. "As to Malcolm—he's never gone into any great detail as to the goings on at Miltronics. That doesn't mean it wasn't important to him. Quite the opposite in fact."

She rubbed a palm across the back of her chair. "He was so fixated with that company. He didn't need any children, not when Miltronics was his baby. I used to ask him about his work, but he guarded every little thing that went on there. After a while, I gave up. Then I didn't care. Our marriage had never been a good one. It took all of one year to figure that out."

Jake tried to tell himself he wasn't jealous of her time with Malcolm. He tried to tell himself he wasn't bothered that she'd had a relationship with the bastard. Maybe he'd also be able to convince himself it didn't hurt to know Malcolm had had his hands on her or that he'd held her, done things to her that Jake had only been able to imagine.

Margot shook her head. "Johnny really hated him near the end. He never told me why, but I'd just mention Malcolm's name, and he'd act like a scalded cat, ready to leap the walls at the least little provocation. I had no idea."

"Yes, well. It's just as well you didn't. That might be why you're still alive."

She frowned and shook her head. "My brother—" Then she stared at him. Even with the room's distance, he felt the sudden intensity of her gaze. "Is that why Johnny's dead? Because he knew too much?"

"Margot—" An explanation lay blocked deep in his throat. What could he tell her? The truth? And shatter her world or what little belief she had in it now? He'd never wanted her to find out.

"I'm beginning to see."

The look of horror on her face wrenched at Jake's gut. He attempted to close the distance between them, but she warded him off with a raised hand.

"My brother's car accident—wasn't an accident. He was murdered, wasn't he?" It was more a statement than a question. The conviction, the realization was there in her face. "He was murdered all because of this formula."

"It's more than that. It's not just the formula."

"Then what?" she demanded, her voice rising in anger and disbelief. "I want to know why! I deserve to know why my brother was killed!"

She pushed at the chair with such force that it rocked forward and dropped back on all four legs.

"Margot, I can't prove anything. Remember that. This is all conjecture."

She frowned. "But you believe it."

He sighed. Some things he just couldn't lie about. "Yes."

"But the car accident. There's no explanation. He hadn't been drinking. They couldn't find anything wrong with the vehicle. He never mentioned having any enemies. Why would someone want him dead?"

"He threatened to start talking about what was going on at Miltronics if—Well, the reasons are unimportant now. The fact is—Malcolm couldn't let John talk."

"Malcolm? No. I don't want to hear this." As she stepped back, her heel caught the glossy cover of a book, and she slid sideways. Quickly, she righted herself, and turned, stumbling over the debris to the doorway.

She was running. He didn't want her doing that, hiding, wounded and alone. He rushed after her. Before she reached the door he caught her by the arm and swung her around. She lunged at him. He dodged before her knuckles connected with his cheek. With both hands, he caught her wrists and hauled her into his arms.

"Don't—" Her face a mask of anguish, Margot pushed against him, using her hips, stomach and chest, but Jake didn't let go. Instead, he drew her closer, cradling her against his body, leaving her no leverage to break free. After a moment of struggling, she slumped against him and clutched his shoulders.

"Why?" she cried. "I don't understand."

Margot buried her head against the hollow between his neck and shoulder. The wild beat of her heart against his chest pounded in time with her deep sobs of despair which wracked her body. With a trembling hand, he smoothed the silken tendrils of her raven hair from her brow and just stood there, holding her. For how long? He didn't know, and he didn't care.

She was in shock. And who wouldn't be if they'd just learned their brother had been murdered? His throat tightened with helplessness and shame. He was indirectly to blame for her despair. How he wanted to take away her pain. Somehow find a way to make her life easier. But he didn't know how. Then he realized he was grasping at some fantasy.

He didn't have the ability to help Margot. How could he? A man doomed to die can't help the living. He can't seek revenge and...he can't do a damn thing.

Her breath whispered against Jake's neck and jaw as she lifted her head. The reflection of the fire shimmered off a lone tear doggedly clinging to one cheek. With a gloved thumb, Jake brushed the drop from her skin. Even though she'd stopped crying, he didn't want to let her go. As she eased gently from him, he reluctantly dropped his hands to his sides. She stepped away, letting cool air touch the fabric of his shirt and his heated skin.

"I need to think," she muttered. "This is all so crazy."

Margot walked over to the fireplace. He watched her stare at the flames as she regained her breath and her composure. The glow of the fire touched her skin to gold. Other than the soft hiss of the fire, the only other sound was her breathing which had slowed somewhat. Even so, he sensed the tension coiled within her.

She bowed her head, and a thick wave of hair fell forward, obscuring her expression, but he knew she must be feeling raw and exposed. From what he'd learned, Margot valued her privacy and probably hated having him catch her at such a weak moment.

"You know," she said, her voice hoarse and low, "Johnny never told me a thing. He was in trouble—probably way over his head—with no family member other than myself to turn to. But he didn't come to me. He didn't trust me enough for that."

"No," he argued, compelled to ease her pain. "You're wrong. He wanted to protect you. He knew if he told you anything about the goings on at Miltronics, he'd be putting your life in jeopardy. Especially since you were so close to Malcolm."

"Close?" She laughed, an ugly, harsh sound. "For all of six months!"

With her gaze still on the fire, Margot straightened and pulled her hair back around an ear, exposing her profile and the determined lift of her chin. "Malcolm isn't going to get away with this. I'm not going to allow it."

As she turned to face him, Jake tensed. "I don't like that look. Whatever you're thinking—don't."

She lifted her chin even higher. "Oh, I'm thinking. For the first time in a long while—I'm thinking. Maybe it's about time I really faced Malcolm—held my own. Show Malcolm that—"

"Shit, Margot." He advanced on her, but still had the forethought to keep far enough into the shadows. "Don't even think of messing with Malcolm."

"Why? He's only a man—"

"—with powerful friends. You tangle with him and you'll get someone upset." He sighed, growing more aggravated. "It goes further up than Malcolm. To people even I don't know. But one thing I do know, these people have money and power. Lots of it. What is that saying—*power corrupts and absolute power corrupts absolutely*? Well, Malcolm's on his way. He's always had money, but now he has a glimpse of the power he can have with Miracell, and it's gone to his head. So don't mess with him, not when it comes to Miracell or Miltronics."

He wanted to shake that stubborn look off her face or, better yet, kiss some sense into her. "What do you think he's going to do if you threaten him and Miltronics? He's not going to calmly take it. Didn't you just tell me Miltronics is his little baby? Well, he'll be just as fierce and protective as any father. He'll retaliate harder and deadlier then you can even imagine."

The determination in her face didn't ease, much to Jake's dismay. Damn, but she could be pig-headed.

~~*~~

Turning away from Jake, Margot walked back to her desk and once again stared into the fire. She didn't want to argue. On Malcolm, they'd never agree. Plus, Jake would only get upset if he knew she had every intention of exposing Malcolm for the killer he was.

She'd start by looking into Johnny's car crash. The answer was there. Some small piece of evidence had to have been missed. Someone had to be hiding something. And she was going to be the person to find it. She might have failed her brother while he was alive, but she'd be damned if she failed him in death.

Margot inhaled a deep, shaky breath and found her gaze captured by the fire's hypnotic orange and yellow flames. Their heat was deadly, yet soothing. She was exhausted yet tense, numb yet focused. Johnny. She would make sure he hadn't died in vain.

"Are you all right?"

She stiffened, all thoughts of Miltronics, her brother and Malcolm disintegrating as she became aware of Jake right behind her. She felt his warmth, smelled his cologne.

"Yes," she whispered.

He slipped a hand onto her shoulder, his fingers curving

over to her collarbone. The leather cold, yet oddly hot, felt erotic against her skin. Margot didn't dare move. She sensed him directly behind. Inches away. If she backed up, her bottom would push up against his hips and his sex. The thought whirled through her body, tightening her breasts, heating her blood. Her breathing changed, grew deep and shallow. Desire. It squeezed below her belly, weakening her legs so much so that she latched onto the edge of the desk with both hands.

"I—" She cleared her throat. "I'll be all right."

The thick, hoarseness of her voice gave her away. Jake had to know now. He had to know she wanted him, wanted something to happen between them. God help her—she wanted it bad.

It had been so long. Gritting her teeth, she fought against the hunger. Self-control. She needed self-control. Oh, but how her body screamed for Jake's touch, a brush of his lips against her skin, the feel of his palm against her naked flesh, the caress of his breath against her hair as he moved inside her.

Then she felt Jake's hand on her hip, branding her through the thick material of her jeans, sliding up over the fabric to her waist. For a brief second, she fought against the pressure of his palm, but only for a second. She turned and looked up into his face. Shadows clung to his rugged features. Then there were his glasses. Those stupid glasses. They shielded his thoughts, his emotions. Yet...

She sensed his desire, the hunger in the pressure of his fingers at the small of her back as he nudged her closer. She parted her lips in anticipation. Then she was completely blinded by shadows as his head dipped and he claimed her mouth.

His lips, firm, supple, warm, against her own, weakened her legs yet further. The touch of his tongue, experienced, hot, knowing, wrenched open the last of her restraint. Wanting more, so much more, she inched closer, clutching his arms and pressing her hips against his own. His biceps bunched beneath her grasp as he slid his hands down to cup her butt.

The heat of his arousal against her belly ripped the breath from her lungs and played with an already wildly beating heart. He wanted her, really wanted her. The tremble in his hand, the roughness of his touch did more to her than any practiced lover's. He felt exactly what a man should feel like. Hard. Rugged yet gentle. So very gentle, she realized, as his lips slid over the line of her jaw to trail inch by silken inch down the slope of her neck.

Closing her eyes, Margot arched her neck to give him freer access. She slipped her hands up around his waist, and up under his sweater to his back where she ran her fingers across tight skin over hard, taunt sinew and muscle. He felt so right.

"Perfect," she sighed, awash in sensation as she slipped her fingers from beneath his sweater and reached up to play with the silky strands of his hair at the nape of his neck. Margot stilled. The hair entwined between her fingers wasn't natural.

"Your hair," she said in a thick, husky whisper. "Is it brown or something else? And your glasses. Your eyes. I don't know their color."

"It's blond," he replied, his voice uneven and just as thick with desire. "And my eyes—my eyes are blue."

Abruptly, Jake broke away from her embrace, grasped her wrists and pulled them from around his neck. Before she had time to react, he'd drawn away completely and pivoted on his heel. With shaky fingers, she touched her lips where the imprint of his mouth still lingered and stared at his back in shock. She leaned against the desk for support. Her legs were far too weak to hold her weight right now.

She lowered her fingers and asked between short, ragged breaths, "Why?"

Jake stuffed his hands in his pockets and continued to face the empty shelves. He might have his back to her, but the way he was inhaling and exhaling large chunks of air told her he was having just as hard a time recovering.

"I shouldn't have done that."

She blinked and could actually feel the skin around her face tighten at his lack of explanation. "You shouldn't have? Then why did you? Can you tell me that?"

He'd wanted her. She knew that even if he decided to lie. She wasn't so inexperienced to confuse an act and something genuine. Yet he'd turned away from her and the sexual chemistry burning between them.

"Is there someone else?"

"No. Nothing like that."

"Then what?"

His silence was answer enough.

"Then if you can't—no—if you won't tell me why, then stay away from me. I can't take this—being turned on and off." She took a deep breath, hating the raw emotion in her voice, but unable to keep the truth to herself. "It's been a long time since a man made me feel the way you have. But I'm not going to subject myself to one rejection after another. So don't come near me again if you have every intention of stopping things."

Pride in shreds, not about to wait around for yet another rejection, Margot rushed from the room. When she didn't hear Jake behind her, she didn't know whether to be relieved or disheartened. Some sliver of hope had her imagining him following her, sweeping her up into his arms and—

It didn't matter. She'd stopped believing in Prince Charming years ago. Or fairy tales for that matter. They were all wild imaginings of a lonely little girl.

She climbed the stairs, leaving Jake and his silence behind. She was walking away from one disaster and into another. Her bedroom along with the den had been the only rooms she hadn't had the stomach to clean. But now she couldn't wait any longer. Margot had to face her room and put some order into it so she could sleep. Stepping past the threshold, she hit the light switch. As the room flooded with light, she inhaled sharply.

She'd expected clothing on the floor, her items flung this way and that, the mattress upended. But that wasn't what she found.

CHAPTER 10

THE HARDWOOD FLOOR lay empty of clothing, while the mattress again rested on top of the box spring. Her sheets and comforter, once pulled from the bed and tossed aside, were replaced with light pink and cream printed bedding. The dresser drawers, having been upended with their contents scattered about the room, now sat back in their slots. The room was warm and inviting, just as it had been before the vandalism.

Someone or something had gone through and systematically cleaned and straightened her room.

Jake. It had to be. Who else but him? Johnny? No. Impossible. No, it was Jake. Jake was the one who'd slipped into her room. Not her brother's ghost. Jake was the one who'd carefully restored her room to its original condition.

Surprisingly, she wasn't upset. Not really. She did feel a little vulnerable and exposed, having him see such a personal side of her. Yet at the same time, she felt oddly touched that he'd come up here to restore her room while she'd slept downstairs. He must have known how much it would bother her to do it herself.

That is, unless—it was his excuse to look for the disk.

No. Slowly, she backed from the room. She didn't want to think that of him, but the thought wouldn't go away. She didn't trust him. God knows, she wanted to. It would take more than words to sway her. It would take actions—and time. She'd learned her lesson with Malcolm. Glib words wouldn't blind her to everything else around her.

With every intention of confronting Jake, she turned to go into the hall and downstairs. At the bedroom's threshold, she faltered, grasping the doorjamb. No. She couldn't go down there now. Not after the things she'd said, the demands she'd made of him. Her face burned at the memory. She'd actually told him not to touch her again unless he planned on sleeping with her. Maybe not in so many words, but the implication had been there. They'd both known it.

Margot closed the door. She didn't have the stomach to face him right now. Not when she still hurt from his rejection. Maybe tomorrow, when her feelings weren't so raw and the memory of his touch no longer lingered in her thoughts.

With an index finger, she followed the contour of her bottom lip. She could still feel his mouth there, could still remember the taste of him and the smell of his cologne. She changed into her nightgown, slipped beneath the covers, and closed her eyes, all the while trying not to think of being all alone in her big bed while Jake slept one floor below, or of the way he'd made her hunger for him.

The gown slithered across her skin as she twisted to get a more comfortable position. After a moment, she kicked off the sheets and buried her face into the feather pillow. The air cooled her skin but not her thoughts. God, she burned. She burned for the heat of his skin against her palms, for his touch on every inch of her body, for him to make her experience every blessed sensual sensation her imagination could envision.

She didn't know she'd fallen asleep until she woke. With her knees tucked close to her chest and her hands cushioning her head beneath her pillow, she lay on her side. Breathing slowly, she listened and watched the red glow of her clock on the night-stand turn to 3:14.

She lay under the cover of night, cloaked in a thick, deep blanket of blackness. Nothing stirred from outside. At least nothing that she could readily hear, while inside, the house was just as deathly silent. But she continued to listen. And wait.

She gripped the pillow beneath her. As she strained to hear, her breathing quickened. Nothing. Yet...she knew. Somehow she knew. Jake. The man she couldn't get out of her mind. The man that made her blood hum with desire and longing. He was coming to her on silent feet, through the darkness, climbing the stairs to her room and bed.

And God help her, she wanted him to.

~~*~~

The metal doorknob, probably as old as the house itself, was cool against Jake's palm as he turned it beneath his grasp and eased the door open. He shouldn't be here, creeping through the house like some sick pervert with no self-control. He should be in his room, in his bed downstairs, attempting to sleep. Lust, need and loneliness all mingled and shredded together, compelling him up the stairs and across the threshold to her bedroom.

Margot. Her name was a soft sigh on his lips. He didn't want just any woman. He wanted—her—with an inexplicable, driving need. He had since she'd first tumbled into his arms that moonless night. And like the selfish bastard he was, he was going to see if he could take her and damn the consequences. He licked dry lips. It was the perfect night for it. Totally black. Thick, impenetrable clouds obliterated any light from the moon and stars.

Dragging in a lungful of air, he paused. Even though he couldn't see her bed, he knew its exact location. He'd been in here many a night as she slept. Those first couple of times, frustrated, angry at Miracell, Malcolm, Miltronics——the whole situation—— he'd come up here to brood, but somehow, every single time her sleeping form, so serene, so ethereal would calm him.

As he crossed the room with sure, bare feet, the hardwood floor creaked beneath his weight.

The sound cracked loudly in the room—at least to Margot's ears.

She shivered. Any second, and Jake would be alongside her bed. She didn't know what to do—turn and acknowledge him or pretend to sleep. She couldn't remember having a man, single and oh so very male come to her bed in the dead of night. Other than Malcolm, there'd been only one other in college, and that experience didn't even compare to the emotions churning inside her.

Was he naked?

Lying frozen, her back to him and the door, she forced the air in and out of her lungs in as natural a rhythm as she could manage. The thought of him touching, stroking her with sure, experienced hands left her heart rate at a distinct disadvantage and her limbs all weak and tingly. And her breasts. They ached already for his hands.

She was wet, throbbing, ready for him when she heard the soft sigh of sheets. The mattress dipped as he slipped in behind her. It had been so long since she'd had a man touch her, caress her. She turned at the waist, but he cupped her shoulder with a hand.

"Don't," he whispered, gently but firmly holding her so her back faced him as he slid up against her and wrapped his heat along the length of her body. "I tried but I couldn't stay away."

Oh, God. He *was* naked. Absolutely every hard and sleek part of him. He brushed a muscled thigh over her hip while curling her closer to his body. His arousal, hot, hard, burned through the sheer fabric of her nightgown and into her butt.

This time, she lost control of her breathing. She drew in air with short, sharp pants as his hands roamed over her body and he nibbled at the sensitive skin below her ear, his breath mingling with the downy wisps of her hair. Goose flesh rose along her arms and the nape of her neck.

"Jake—" She twisted beneath his hold, desperate to touch and taste him.

"Shhh," he whispered into her ear while holding her firm. "Relax."

How could she relax when he had a hand cupping her breast and was brushing a thumb over her nipple? How could she be calm when he was using his other hand to brush her hair from her nape so he could play his tongue and mouth along the curve of her spine?

"Jake," she breathed, turning her neck so she could see him, but the night blinded her. With the loss of that one sense, all her others heightened to an almost painful clarity. She reached behind to touch his hair-roughened thigh and up over the silken skin of his pelvic bone. The movement pressed her breast deeper into his palm. She clutched his hand, a hand minus gloves, a long-fingered, seemingly flawless hand that was doing beautiful things to her nipple. "Jake. Your hands. They feel perfect. Your gloves. Why—"

Cupping her chin in a gentle hand, he shifted over her and quieted her this time by molding his lips over her own, delving inside, pantomiming what he would do later with another part of his body. She forgot everything but the kiss. It was hungry, filled with passion and longing.

He broke the kiss with apparent reluctance. The heat of his mouth then trailed over the line of her jaw and down the side of her neck to nip lightly at the curve between her neck and shoulder. His breath whispered just below her hairline behind her ear, sending delicious shivers down Margot's spine. Oh, God. He knew exactly what to do with that mouth of his.

Nudging her legs apart with his knee, he wrapped an arm around her waist to splay his fingers briefly against her stomach before lowering his palm, then caressing her thigh with feather-light fingertips, circling ever higher, teasing, tormenting until he touched her...there. Exquisite longing shattered what little thought she had left. She caved into the sensation, letting it wrap itself around every pore of her body. She throbbed for him, ached for him. She'd do anything to him, with him...

Margot let him help her out of her nightgown and pull her up on her hands and knees. His hands whisper over the small of her back, over her flanks, down one last time to slip a finger into her before he replaced it with something harder, larger and hotter. Ever so slowly, he entered her from behind, his shaft, satin over hard muscle, filled her, burned her right to her womb. She whimpered as he held her hips and slid out, then back in with one sure, controlled stroke. She tried to buck beneath him, to move, to take control, but he had her impaled, positioned in such a way that she couldn't do anything but take the sensations he created.

With gentle fingers, he caressed her back and butt, running random lines across her muscles, which sent a delicious quiver across her flesh.

"Oh, baby," he whispered by her ear as he slipped both hands around to cup her breasts. "Such beautiful breasts. So perfect." He flicked his thumbs over their tips. "Such tight little nipples."

Groaning, all four shaking limbs anchored to the bed, Margot closed her eyes. She dug her fingers into the mattress, twisting the bedding beneath her hands as he teased, touched and played with her breasts, all the while rocking her, thrusting, then withdrawing, teasing, tempting, driving her nearer to the edge. He caressed the underside of her breasts one last time before sliding his hands over her abdomen and stomach to massage her inner thighs with both palms and tease the slick, wet nub between her legs with his raised thumbs.

She moaned.

"You like that, don't you?"

He did something with his fingers that shot desire throughout her entire body.

"Oh, God."

"Tell me," he demanded, his voice, dark and husky as his fingers played her.

"Yes—yes," she cried. "I like it—I—"

"Are you sure? Are you sure you want all of me? I can stop." His fingers stilled and he withdrew until only the tip of him remained, teasing, taunting her with what he could do with it and with her. "Do you want me to stop?"

"No, please," she cried, beyond caring what she said or did, beyond anything but this second, this moment. "I want it. I need it. I need you!"

"You got me. All of me." He thrust into her again and again, relentless, driven. "No one but me."

She took all of him, wanted all of him. She was on fire, yet cold, shaking with a different type of fever as tension curled around her with each lunge of Jake's hips. Blindly, she clutched the headboard and arched her neck as the tempo increased and the tension, delicious, so delicious, tightened and tightened. She was almost there. So close. So very close. He scraped his teeth along the side of her neck as his large hand covered her own on the headboard, entwining his fingers between hers, while he continued to stroke, tease, and torment her.

He surrounded her, filled her so completely. She cried out as her body contracted one last time before exploding. Oh, God. It was heaven, she was in heaven. Her climax went on and on, squeezing her, pulling her under. Pinpricks of pure, inundated pleasure pulsed through her. Sensation. Such a beautiful sensation.

He came quickly after, clutching her hips with shaking hands, growling his pleasure as he pumped into her while his ragged breathing fanned over her damp neck and danced with her own, sharp, shallow pants.

The shaking. She couldn't control it. It swept through her body and wouldn't let go. If it wasn't for Jake's arm hooked snuggly around her waist, she would have collapsed. But his grasp held her steady and eased them both down onto the bed. She'd never, never responded so completely, or with such shattering intensity

She lay cradled in Jake's arms, the beat of his heart against her back a soothing and hypnotic comfort. Words. She couldn't think of a one that wouldn't ruin what had just happened. She'd had enough experience to know what went on moments ago didn't happen to everyone. The whole sexual experience with Jake had been like a beautiful, moving dance.

The caress of his fingers, slowly, even tenderly, combed the strands of her hair away from her brow and temples. Exhausted, sated, she smiled and said, "Thank you," before sleep pulled her under.

~~*~~

Jake knew the second she fell asleep in his arms. Her body tucked up against his had grown limp and heavy while her breathing had evened out. She slept like an angel, while he remained awake with his demons. He was more tense now than ever before. A heavy weight lay deep in his chest. Sex for him before had been mainly an itch, something that needed to be done, and nothing like what had just happened. He was no romantic, never had been. He'd always been a man of science, but tonight, he couldn't explain the feelings Margot had dragged out of him. He held a lock of her hair and rubbed the strands between his fingers.

In her sleep, she snuggled deeper into his arms and sighed something. He stilled, his fingers frozen in her hair. For a moment there, he'd thought she'd told him she loved him. No. That was impossible. It was just his imagination, his tired brain deciphering words that just weren't there.

Sex. What was between them was great, mind-numbing sex, nothing more. At least, that's what he told himself. But hell, he didn't believe it. He might have learned these last couple of months to be a damn good liar to everyone around him, but he hadn't yet learned to lie to himself.

He was getting involved. Jake had no business in her bed or in her life. He had no future and nothing to offer a woman. He let her hair slip from his grasp and sighed. Tonight, he'd used her, purposely driven her to a point where she couldn't think about anything but the sex. He'd applied every trick he'd learned over the years to have her quivering, receptive to him and his touch. If her mind had strayed, if she'd had a chance to think of the man in her arms, to see him for what he was, she would have—

Jake flinched.

"—you're dead." Malcolm's words came back to haunt him. "A freak of science. You don't exist."

Jake would have to let her go before anything could come of it. He had to. Before she saw him for the monster he was. But damn it, his whole mind and body rebelled at the idea.

Closing his eyes, he leaned over and pressed a kiss against her temple. He lingered for a moment, then slipped from her bed.

~~*~~

Sunlight woke Margot. Its rays pierced through the lace and

cream linen curtains and streamed across her bed and into her eyes. She rolled over and buried her head beneath the pillow while sliding a hand across the flannel sheets. They were cold to the touch. She popped her head from beneath her pillow to find the other side of the bed empty. Jake had left with the rising sun. Or had he? Had last night been a delicious figment of her imagination? Some erotic dream of her own making?

She was beginning to doubt what had happened last night until she rushed across the cold floor and into the bathroom. That's when she caught sight of her reflection. She paused before the full-length mirror and stared back at the woman in front of her. She disliked the image. Her raven hair was tangled about her shoulders, mussed no doubt by Jake's wayward hands. But it was her eyes that bothered her the most. A new vulnerability shone from their brown depths. She hated the look. She didn't want to be vulnerable to anyone or anything again.

She lifted her chin. As much as she wanted to deny last night, explain it away as some figment of her imagination or as a very hot and erotic dream—what she found proved otherwise. Arching her neck, she brushed her hair back over her shoulder and touched the evidence with an index finger. Jake had marked her with his mouth above her collarbone.

CHAPTER 11

HE SPIT ON the snow, inches from her booted foot. Margot didn't move, didn't flinch, didn't look away. She waited. She wanted answers.

Max Sawyer cleared his throat again, but thank God, didn't spit a second time.

"You know," he said, rubbing his gray, military shaved hair with a nicotine and grease-stained hand, while a lit cigarette dangled between the fingers of his other hand. "There's nothing I can tell you that you haven't already heard. John hit the railing and went down."

He opened the door into the front office of Max's Auto Shop and slipped inside. Not about to walk away with that type of answer, Margot followed.

It was late afternoon, yet deep shadows hung over the waiting area. No one was about, which wasn't surprising. People came here only as a last resort, and she had a good idea Max knew it. Even so, he probably didn't worry much. He had enough business being the only shop in town. The next place was over sixty miles of mountainous road to Pinetop.

She stepped over to the window and twisted the wand attached to the side of the closed blinds. Watery, winter light slanted in and a layer of dust wafted to her nose. Impatiently, she brushed the particles from her face with the wave of a hand

and turned back to Max. At least now with the blinds open, she might be able to read his expression. It was difficult enough with that week's growth of beard.

"But what about records?" she asked.

"There's nothing." Jamming an elbow on top of the front counter, Max rested a hip against its side and crossed a leg at the ankles. "At least nothing I have. Carl didn't want me doing anything. He had someone in Pinetop take care of the wreck. From what I gather, it wasn't a nice sight. The car was totaled on one side. There was a lot of blood—"

"Please, we're talking about my brother—"

"Sorry." Max winced. "Didn't mean to get all detailed on you. Your brother was a nice guy. Seemed so, anyway. Didn't know him real well—him being years younger and going off to college. Sorry I didn't make the funeral."

"Yes, well. That's all right." She swallowed. She was not going to get emotional. "Do you know the name of the garage in Pinetop?"

He rubbed his unshaven chin, then took a deep drag from his cigarette and exhaled loudly. "No. Can't say I do. You'd have to ask Carl."

That wasn't what Margot wanted to hear. Carl already thought she was the town drunk. If she started asking him strange questions about the accident, God knew what he'd say behind her back.

"Thanks, Max."

She managed—but barely—to keep the frustration out of her voice. As she turned to the front door, she caught sight of a paperback copy of Hemmingway's *A Moveable Feast*. Who would have thought? Max had always given the impression he liked working with only his hands.

Stepping outside and hunching deeper into her down jacket, she inhaled a large breath of clean air. The cigarette smoke, grease and oil had burned her eyes and nose.

She shivered against the cold. The temperature had dropped dramatically. The top layer of snow had melted earlier in the afternoon, but now a thin sheet of ice had formed, coating the tree limbs. She quickly found it also covered much of the ground as she slipped on the cement slab leading to Greyson's small but well-stocked grocery store, which Joyce owned since her parents passed away. Inside, she didn't find her friend but the short, stocky clerk Joyce hired to fill in for her. Margot quickly grabbed a half-gallon of milk, a frozen dinner, a bottle of wine, and a can of cat food for Marmaduke. Enough staples to get her by until tomorrow when she'd go into Pinetop for her weekly trip.

Fifteen minutes later with bagged purchases in one hand, she stepped out of the store and gingerly crossed the parking lot to her car.

"What the hell do you think you're doing?"

Glancing over her shoulder, Margot didn't pause as she continued cautiously over the icy blacktop. Carl didn't seem concerned about the slippery ground, though. The way he rushed across the street toward her, it was a wonder he didn't land on his butt.

Carl reached her car door first. She stopped and eyed him warily. Right now wasn't the time to ask him about Johnny and the accident. Not when he looked like he was in a fine snit. The fading light didn't completely shield the flush to his face or the anger in his narrowed gaze. He was also breathing heavily, but that could be caused by the short jaunt across the street. From what she knew or remembered, he'd never been particularly fit.

When it looked like Carl wasn't planning on budging from in front of her car door any time soon, Margot coolly returned, "I'm getting in my car and going home. That's what I'm doing."

Carl snorted and of course didn't take the hint and move out of her way. "I'm not talking about what you're doing *now.*" He jabbed a thumb in the direction of the building across the street. "What were you doing over at Max's shop?"

Her lips thinned. She'd been there less than an hour and already the whole damn town knew about it. She'd thought Max was one of the more closemouthed types in town. Obviously, she'd been wrong. She knew Carl would find out eventually, but she hadn't expected it this soon.

"I was asking questions," she said.

"Exactly. That's why he called me."

Margot frowned. Carl was breathing down her neck like she'd committed some grievous crime. Well, she hadn't, and he wasn't about to make her question her right to ask about her brother's accident. She didn't care whether he was a cop, Joyce's brother or the President of the United States. She'd had enough.

"You know, Carl, why do you have to have your nose into everything? Can't you mind your own business? If I want to ask about my brother, I have every right. It's my business. And mine alone. Not yours. And even if it were your business, I wouldn't trust you. You can't keep your mouth shut for two seconds without repeating it to someone else."

Carl laughed, but he sounded far from amused. "I'll have you know that I can keep a secret just as good as the next person. Even more so. When it counts—when it really counts—I can keep my mouth shut. More than you know."

"Fine," she didn't bother acting like she believed him. "I don't know why you're so upset anyway. I just asked Max if he had any records on the car Johnny was driving. It's not like I was getting classified information from the FBI!"

He sighed, expelling a large cloud of air. "You need to stop."

"Why?"

"Why?" He stared back at her in disbelief. "Well, because— he's dead—of course. What's the point of asking about that type of stuff? It's not going to bring him back. It's pure craziness if you ask me. You've got to let it go. He's dead, Margot."

"I know that. There isn't a day that goes by without me realizing it!" Straightening, she raised her chin, not about to back off now. "But I'm beginning to think he died pretty strangely. Johnny took that corner by Bloody Basin too many times in his life. He knew how dangerous it was. Why all of a sudden does he decide to go racing around that turn? It doesn't make much sense, now does it?"

Grunting, Carl lifted his down jacket, then hefted his pants up with both hands. "I don't care if it makes sense or nothing. Just stop asking questions. It's not going to get you anywhere other than a whole heap of trouble. And keep the hell away from Malcolm."

She narrowed her eyes suspiciously. "Why? Is there something I don't know?"

"Of course not," he was quick to argue.

She searched his face, absently noting his flushed cheeks, wide brow and full lips now thinned into a disgruntled line. He wouldn't look directly at her, which told her everything. In some aspects, he was just like Joyce... a terrible liar.

"Carl, please." She touched his forearm, unable to mask the urgency and anxiety in her voice. "I want—no—I need to know what you're hiding."

A brief yet charged pause came from Carl. Then he said in a deep, gruff voice, "Nothin'. I'm not hiding nothin'."

He turned and walked back the way he'd come, across the street and down to his car parked in front of Max's Auto Shop. She stood and watched him and wondered. That was the very first time Carl had been the one to walk away from any conversation between them. It said much.

Carl was hiding something. But what? Could he have been involved with Johnny's death? God, she didn't want to think it. She'd always taken Carl for granted. He'd always been just there, her best friend's brother. She'd never really paid attention to him.

She got in her car and drove off, somewhat ashamed at how she'd always treated Carl over the years. He'd never done anything to warrant it. No. She wasn't going to start thinking that way, Margot told herself, as she guided her car up the drive to her house. All she had to do was remember the way he'd treated her after the vandals had struck her house.

She parked and got out with her bag of groceries. Jake's pickup wasn't around. Only the mournful sigh of the wind was there to greet her. The last whisper of light hovered in the sky before it would sink onto the other side of the world. She didn't want to go inside. She didn't want her own company. Yet, she didn't want Jake's either. She wasn't ready to see him.

Memories of last night were still far too vivid. She slammed the car door and trod through the snow. The feel of him. The heat, the hardness, the satin touch of him on her and in her. Margot hugged the bag of groceries to her chest. She'd never wanted, never hungered, never shattered like that before. Control. She'd lost every ounce of it. He'd had her begging, crying for him. He'd had her so mindless, so sensitive to his every caress. No one, not even Malcolm—especially not Malcolm—had pulled her under such a sensual spell.

The wind picked up and swept through her hair and brushed across her cheeks as she climbed the steps to the veranda. As she shivered and pulled her thoughts back to the present, the heel of her boot caught on a patch of ice. She slid sideways. The bag in her hands went flying and crashed against the wood porch.

"Damn it!"

Margot didn't have to look to know the bottle of wine had broken. She picked up the bag. Wine leaked onto her hands. The cold air immediately hit her damp skin, stiffening already chilled fingers. She didn't dare rub them on her clothes. The stains would be impossible to get out.

Muttering to herself, Margot walked around the wrap around veranda to the garbage by the side door. After rescuing the can of cat food, pint of milk and carton of frozen macaroni and cheese dinner, she stuffed the bag and most of the broken bottle into the trash. A thin layer of wine had already crystallized into ice, gluing fragments of glass to her other purchases. She banged the side of the canned cat food to get the pieces off. Finally, giving up after several vain attempts, she secured the top of the trashcan with several bungee cords to keep the raccoons and other small animals out and walked back along the veranda.

By the time Margot turned the corner and looked over the railing to the driveway, it was too late. A car was parked alongside her own. Tensing, she glanced across the porch. Ten feet away, Malcolm stood by the front door.

Her heart skipped a beat than galloped hard against her ribs. As she stepped back, the bottom of her boot pressed down on a board. The wood beneath creaked. Malcolm turned, and for several long, silent moments they both stood watching each other.

Malcolm had his collar turned up, protecting his neck from the cold as a frigid breeze played with the sandy locks of his hair. Black leather gloves covered his hands and a thick jacket in matching leather sheltered him from the winter air. He looked casually elegant, the exact impression she knew he always strove to portray. Image meant everything to Malcolm. She'd found that out while sharing a bathroom with him. After the first week, she'd given up the battle and she'd used the guest bathroom.

Attractive, wealthy, sophisticated. He was all of those. An impressive package for any unsuspecting female. But not this female. Not anymore.

"Hello, Margot. I'm glad I caught you at home."

The smile, the congenial tone of voice didn't fool her. Not when she saw the cold, calculating sheen in Malcolm's eyes.

"What do you want?" She kept the fear from her voice. The best—no—the only option she had was to play dumb. She knew nothing, suspected nothing, didn't know a damn thing about the fire or her brother.

He stepped casually toward her. "I think you know."

"No, I don't." Thank God. Her words had just the right tone of disbelief, just the right amount of acid. "I'm not a mind reader."

"The disk." He took another step. This time it was measured, not the least casual. "I want it."

"What disk?"

Swallowing, Margot tried to tell herself she wasn't afraid. But it wasn't working. She was deathly afraid. She didn't have a weapon—didn't have anything to protect herself. Her brother's murderer stood only a few feet away. And she didn't particularly like the way he kept on opening and closing his hands like that. It looked like they were itching to get around her neck...and squeeze the life out of her.

To think she'd lived with this man, slept with him, sat at the same kitchen table—

"The disk John gave you. You know, your brother? The one that took a nose dive over the cliff?"

She stiffened. God, she hated him. She didn't know how

someone who looked so beautiful could be so ugly. "Johnny didn't give me a disk. I don't know what you're talking about."

Abruptly, Malcolm pivoted and looked out over the darkening landscape. He sighed. "I wish I could believe you."

She watched his profile uneasily. Maybe she'd be able to get out of this with her hide intact. "Well, it's the truth."

"Damn it! There's got to be a copy." Frustration thickened his voice as he leaned over and placed both gloved hands along the railing. "It's got to be somewhere in your house. I can't think of anywhere else it could be at."

Her grip on the milk, frozen dinner and cat food tightened. The sting of glass fragments cut into her palms. "You did it? You broke into my house? You deliberately destroyed my things? All because of a stupid disk?"

"It's not just a 'stupid disk'. It's my damned future! Without it, I don't have one! All my money's riding on that 'stupid disk'." He turned to face her, and she saw the desperation, the fear in his eyes before he masked it. "If you know anything, I suggest you tell me."

"You didn't answer my question. Did you break into my house?"

He pushed back a lock of sandy hair from his brow. "What if I did? What are you going to do about it?" He raised one brow. "Sue me?"

To see the answer in his eyes and have it verbally confirmed, hit hard. Frustration, anger and fear burned the back of her throat. She felt helpless. Then again, Malcolm might have the brute strength, but she had her mind. She could outsmart him.

She shouldn't have doubted Jake, shouldn't have believed even for a moment that he was capable of all that anger and violence. He wasn't like Malcolm. Now she knew, at least on this, Jake had told her the truth. But was he right about Malcolm's involvement? Was her ex-husband capable of killing her own brother? One moment she believed it and the next she just didn't know.

She looked into Malcolm's sky blue eyes and wondered. What if she just outright asked him? No. That was far too dangerous.

Ignoring the stiffness, the slow numbing of her hands against the packages, Margot straightened. "It's obvious you didn't find the disk from the way you went through my house." Bitterness sharpened her voice. "You could have at least been more careful. You didn't have to destroy everything you touched."

Malcolm's casual shrug made her forget caution, forget anything but the anger. She waved her frozen dinner at him. "I want you off my property. Now."

He caught her wrist. "Or what?" He pulled her toward him until he peered down at her and his breath, moist and hot, brushed her temple. He arched a brow. "You'll beat me? Or better yet—spank me? Sounds kind of kinky, but I'd like that. You still have a tight little body—at least from what I've seen of it. I could go for a little T. and A. right now."

She jerked her wrist from his grasp. "You make me sick!"

"I never used to." He reached out to touch her cheek, but she stepped aside. "There was a time when you liked it." His voice turned husky. "Seriously, Margot. It was good there for a while between us. You have to admit that."

He was being serious. She saw it in his eyes and was stunned, so stunned that she couldn't form a coherent response.

"Remember when we'd go to Jackson's after dinner." His face softened. "Damn, but you knew how to dance. The way you moved that body of yours."

She finally found her voice. "Sex. You're talking about sex. For a brief second, I thought you might have changed, might have actually had some feelings for what we once had."

He looked insulted. "Of course I did! Why do you think I married you!" Anger darkened his face. "And we'd still be together if it wasn't for you. You and your damned divorce!"

"My divorce? You're the reason for the divorce. Any sane person couldn't live with someone like you. Your temper is frightening. You lose control all the time and—"

"Are you calling yourself sane now?" His lip curled at the corner. "My. I don't think that would be the correct term to use... not with your past record——"

"Don't!" He'd hit way below the belt on that one. Her voice turned sharp with anger. "I've had enough of you and your snide innuendoes. You always have to push me, back me into a corner every single time until I can't do anything but hit back. I think in some sick way you enjoy doing it. I don't know why, and I don't want to know why. But I do want you to leave. I don't want you here—now or anytime in the future. Got that?"

A red flush stained his cheeks. "Oh, I hear you. Loud and clear. You can yell all you want, and I'll be the only one able to hear you. It's just you and me up here. All alone. All by ourselves. *Got that?*" He stepped toward her.

She didn't move back. They were only threats. She wasn't about to show him they bothered her as she walked past him, brushing a shoulder against his arm on the way to the front door. And anyway, she could threaten just as well as Malcolm. "I'm leaving, and if you're not gone by the time I get to the phone, I'll call Carl."

"Carl? You can't be serious. The guy's a joke. I've had the bad luck to meet him twice, but hell, that'll do me for a lifetime. He's got the brain the size of a pea. The only thing *not* funny about him is the way he blabs and snoops into everyone's business. If he doesn't watch it, someone's going to make sure he shuts his trap for good."

"You might not take him seriously, but what about another restraining order? Will you take that seriously?" Stopping at the front door, she looked over her shoulder and watched his expression change, the slight tensing of his jaw, the angry glitter in the back of his eyes. She'd hit home. "I'll do it again if I have to."

"Don't push me, Margot."

Fear shot into her veins. That low, deadly tone of voice was far too familiar. If she let herself remember... No. She wouldn't let herself think back. She hitched her chin up a notch and stared back, hoping like hell she looked self-assured. "Then don't push me, Malcolm. I won't be pushed. Not anymore. You'd be smart to remember that."

She hugged the groceries against her chest and fumbled with the key to unlock the front door. Her hands were stiff, dangerously close to being frostbitten, which right now was almost a blessing. The cold masked the pain from the slivers of wine bottle embedded in her palms. She didn't want to think how they would feel when warmed.

Sighing with resignation, she gripped the brass doorknob. Suddenly, Malcolm lunged, shoving her away from the door and barring her path into the house.

"Is that a threat?" he asked harshly by her ear, his palm pressed flat against the doorframe.

Margot froze. He was so close that she smelled peppermint on his breath. "It's more than a threat, Malcolm." She stood her ground, not about to back away with fear. She wouldn't give him that satisfaction. Clenching her jaw hard, she glared at his chest and said through gritted teeth, "It's a promise. I swear if you step into my house one more time without being invited, I'll call the police and happily press charges. If Carl doesn't charge you with breaking and entering, I'll be damned sure I find something else he can arrest you for. Assault and battery is a good one for starters. I bet you'd like that. And what about stalking? I think Arizona has a law against—"

Malcolm grabbed her upper arm. His hand on her made her react without thinking, and she swung the carton of milk. It landed against his cheek. The thin cardboard cracked open, spraying milk everywhere. Chips of broken glass frozen to the carton caught on his cheek, scraping his smoothly tanned flesh and drawing blood.

Margot broke free and dragged frigid air into her lungs as icy milk trickled from her face, down her neck to seep into her sweater and jacket. For several, long heartbeats they stood without moving, breathing heavily, staring. A muscle ticked along the edge of his jaw while milk coated one side of his face and dripped from his ear lobe. Then Malcolm growled and lurched for her with both hands.

She stumbled back onto slick ice. This time, she couldn't regain her footing, couldn't do anything but helplessly clutch at air.

Her skull hit the side of the railing as she went down. White pinpricks flashed across her vision as the world blurred around her. Then she was falling into blackness.

CHAPTER 12

HE WASN'T A violent man. At least, he'd always thought that until now, Jake realized as he sank back and rested his neck against the chair's backrest and stared up at the ceiling of John's lab.

In high school, he'd been the stereotypical geek, the awkward, gangly boy with his head buried in a book, the type girls avoided and disliked as much as an outbreak of acne. He'd been into science, math, everything that wasn't considered 'in'. Then out of high school, he'd grown into his large-boned body and acquired a new self-confidence, and suddenly women were finding him attractive. But he hadn't changed. Not really. He still had his head buried, but now it was in front of a computer.

Fat lot of good that had done him.

Why hadn't he learned to have fun? Or gone out drinking and chasing girls like the rest of his male counterparts? Maybe if he'd been able to relax, let his hair down, so to speak, he wouldn't be in such a dire situation right now.

If only he could go back and start from the very beginning. He would never have accepted the position at Miltronics, never have let himself get caught up in Malcolm's enthusiasm and his own inflated ego. A chance to change the world. The possibilities of a Nobel Peace Prize, and...disaster. Why hadn't he seen the dark side of the formula? Had he been so damn self-centered that he hadn't understood its two-edged sword? Of course, he'd understood the ramifications. He'd ignored everything, because he'd wanted it all—money, fame, colleague recognition.

Jake gripped the vinyl armrests and pushed out of the chair. Right now, he couldn't work. He was too wired to concentrate. Anger and self-loathing rolled through him. Oh, yes. He'd never been a violent man, never been put into a situation which forced him to see the darker side of his personality. But now— well, now he wanted to lash out, pound something with his bare hands. The rage inside him at times completely consumed him. Then there was the hopelessness. They were both dark, insidious companions that dogged his every step. He had no business dwelling on such unproductive emotions; he couldn't afford to. If he caved to either one, he wouldn't have a future.

Sighing, he turned away from the desk and computer and with two thumbs rubbed at the pressure points by his temples. He needed to be rational and formulate some backup plan. Jake snorted. He couldn't think of one he hadn't already attempted.

Maybe he should go back through Margot's house and search again. The disk had to be there somewhere. Granted, John hadn't said it was at Margot's place in so many words, but the implication had been there all the same. What else could Jake make out of, "I've got you covered. It's tucked away where only my sister can find it."

Maybe if he had Margot's help, this time, they'd be able to find it. Though he hated the idea of involving her further. Damn it. He'd told her far too much already, endangering her life when he had no right. He'd caved in and spilled his guts, instead of fielding Margot's questions like he should have. But he'd needed to talk to someone other than himself.

Walking over to the window that faced Margot's house, Jake stretched, twisting his waist and arching his back. The joints between his vertebras popped, easing a back cramped with tension. He saw an unfamiliar car parked alongside Margot's 4X4. Jake's own pickup was hidden away on a back road alongside Margot's property. Most days he parked there and backtracked to John's lab—his way of ensuring Margot didn't start asking more questions.

Frowning, he drew nearer to the glass. She was up there on the veranda with someone, but he couldn't get a good view because of the branches from an aspen tree. Shifting, he pressed closer only to have his warm breath fog the icy glass panel. Impatiently, he rubbed the condensation away with a fisted hand.

Then suddenly he saw up the hill to the house.

Malcolm. Even with the fading sunlight, he'd recognize Margot's ex-husband anywhere.

Jake stiffened. What the hell was Malcolm doing there with Margot? Something wasn't right, but Jake was too far away to gauge either's expression.

He watched Margot turn her back on Malcolm and reach for the front door. Then Malcolm sprang. No. They were struggling. Malcolm was touching her, hurting her. Suddenly, she crumbled to the porch.

Jake sucked in air. No.

She didn't get up.

Fear moved him. Fear that Malcolm wasn't done. Fear that he wouldn't get there in time.

Margot. She couldn't be hurt. He wouldn't let it happen. He couldn't let it happen.

Rage catapulted Jake across the linoleum floor to the front door. He dodged a table and a trashcan. Blood pounded against his ears. His heart crashed against his ribs. He'd kill Malcolm. He'd use his bare hands and strangle the life from him.

Two feet from the front door, it hit him, slamming him to a halt. The pain. It ripped through his limbs, ate through his veins and ligaments to sear his skin. Crying out against the pain, Jake pushed himself forward. One step. Two. He stumbled. He fell to his knees, the flats of his hands landing on the tile as he gasped for breath.

Jake didn't blackout. But almost. He held on, curling into a fetal position on the floor. Fighting the crushing pain only seemed to make it worse, so he gave into it and rode each wave that pounded against him.

How long he lay there, he didn't know. When he became aware of everything around him, the cold tile against his jaw and hip, the soft purr of the computer across the room, Jake realized pain no longer crippled him.

He uncurled his fists and pushed himself up into a sitting position. Every joint protested. He shook his head to clear it. He'd thought his attacks couldn't get much worse, but he'd been wrong. Dead wrong. With this one, his mind had ceased to function. Any coherent thought had been beyond his grasp. It scared the hell out of him.

Grasping the corner of a table, Jake rose to his feet. His legs shook from his weight. He had to get to Margot. If he was too late—

No. He wouldn't think it. Drawing in a fortifying breath, he fumbled his way to the lab's door. He grasped the knob and flung the door wide. Strength was returning to his limbs, but not half as fast as he wanted. He trudged through the snow-covered yard. The going was too slow. Slick snow and patches of ice impeded his way up the slope to the house. Plus his damn legs. They weren't working!

Jake fell once and had to grab a brittle branch from an aspen tree, which cracked and nearly snapped beneath his weight as he heaved himself up. His arms and legs wouldn't respond to his brain's signals. They were too damned sluggish and uncoordinated. Everything about his recovery seemed slower, so much slower than all the other attacks. Jake knew it was a bad sign, but he didn't dare think about that now. He needed to focus on Margot.

He glanced up. The sun had almost dipped over the horizon. But still enough light illuminated the way to the house and the empty space beside Margot's 4X4. Malcolm was gone.

Jake pushed himself harder, racing up the remaining snow-covered hill, then pounding up the stairs to the veranda. She lay on her back, twisted at the waist, her arms flung to her sides. Choking back a cry, he dropped down beside her, his knees skidding across the icy wood deck.

"Margot..."

She was still unconscious. But for how long? A few minutes, an hour, or longer? He didn't think it was too long, but he hadn't been paying attention to the time when he'd first seen her from the lab. Quickly, he checked her pulse and found it strong beneath his fingers. With gentle hands, he explored her scalp and found a large lump on the side of her head. The skin was unbroken, but that didn't discount the severity of the blow to her head.

He brushed a gloved knuckle across her cheekbone.

"Margot."

A soft groan parted her lips as she stirred, shifting and moving both legs. That was all he needed. He hauled her up into his arms and carried her into the house. He closed the door with a heel. Still weak from the attack in the lab, he strained beneath her weight as he carried her down the hall. She was much heavier than he'd expected. Grunting, he hefted her higher against his chest.

Margot's head fell back, limply cradled against the crook of his arm, exposing the smooth, long column of her throat. Her hair fell away from her face, affording him a clear glimpse of her clean, delicate features. She was beautiful. The blue-black hair, milky complexion, red, pouty lips were so like his childhood visions of what Snow White would look like if she'd appeared in his make-believe world of dragons and wicked wizards.

He found the sofa in her den and carefully placed her across the cushions. After flipping on her desk lamp, he hurried back and sank down on the floor beside her. Taking both of her frigid hands in his he began rubbing them to get some warmth into them but froze at the feel of them against his fingers.

"Damn it!"

Even with the muted lighting from the room's lamp, Jake saw it all. Blood. Glass. Tiny slivers cut the insides of Margot's hands, while streaks of blood clung to the creases of her palms, her cuticles and beneath her nails. Her hands were a mess. Jake didn't know how, and he was almost afraid to find out. He hadn't seen any evidence of broken glass, but then again he hadn't been looking for it.

He needed a flashlight, tweezers, hot water, antiseptic and a cloth. It took him a while to find everything, but he needn't have worried. She hadn't yet stirred.

Jake wedged the flashlight into the crease between the cushions of the couch and worked it till the beam shown down on her hands, but faced away from him. The last thing she needed was to get a real good look at him. Then she'd have a bigger scare than any Malcolm could ever give her.

She shifted several times as Jake wiped the blood gently away with a damp cloth, careful not to pull at the pieces of glass. When he used the tweezers to pull out a fragment, she finally woke up.

"Ouch!" She jerked her hand from his grasp. "What are you doing? Trying to kill me?"

~~*~~

Margot squinted at Jake but couldn't see clearly because some stupid light shone right in her face. But she did glance down and got a good look at her hands. She winced. "Did I do that?"

"Did you?" Jake reached over, grabbed the flashlight and quickly shut it off. "Or was it Malcolm?"

"Malcolm?" she asked. Margot was having a devil of a time remembering. "I—I—"

"I swear he'll regret the day he touched you."

"Touched?" she croaked. God. Stupid questions, but she couldn't seem to get her brain working right. Jake oozing such fury didn't help things either. Those sunglasses of his didn't hide his clenched jaw or rigid posture. He looked ready to jump up, go after her ex-husband and use his flashlight on Malcolm.

"No... It didn't happen like that." Her encounter with Malcolm came back to her with far too much clarity.

Using her elbows, Margot twisted around and tried to sit up, and then wished she hadn't. Her head felt about ready to explode from the rest of her body.

"Here, let me."

Before she had a chance to protest, Jake set down the flashlight, gently grasped her beneath her arms and eased her gently up against the armrest. He sat back on his heels and frowned. "How's your head?"

Margot lifted a hand to touch the back of her skull and stopped in mid-air when she saw and remembered the condition of her hands. The last thing she wanted to do was get her hair tangled in them. "It feels like someone took a baseball bat to it. That or a battle ax."

"You probably have a concussion."

She laughed somewhat self-consciously. "I guess I'm more of a klutz than I thought."

"I saw you struggle with Malcolm."

"Yes, well. He was provoked. I hit him with a milk carton. He didn't take too kindly to that."

"Hmmm."

Jake didn't sound convinced...if she could go by that growl of his. In fact, he sounded angrier than before.

"Here, let me see your hands." He snapped on the flashlight and shoved it back between the sofa's cushions to shine on her hands. "I need to get this glass out."

Margot offered both her palms. "Yes, well. He didn't hurt me. He might have wanted to, but then again maybe he didn't. I'll never know now. Anyway, before he had a chance to touch me, I slipped and fell." God, she was rambling. But she couldn't stop even if she wanted to. "I might have grabbed him for balance. Maybe that's the struggle you saw. So, I'm the one that banged up my head, not Malcolm."

She hadn't a clue why she was protecting Malcolm. He didn't deserve it. Then it dawned on Margot—she wasn't protecting Malcolm. She was protecting Jake. She didn't want him going after Malcolm and getting hurt.

"Hmmm."

That sounded a little less angry, Margot decided in some relief as she watched Jake's bent head in silence. He might be upset, but his hands, encased in black leather, were gentle. How he worked so easily with those gloves was beyond her.

Only last night he'd used those same hands on her. Then they'd been naked, supple and so very knowledgeable as to how to please her. But it was so much more than just his touch that had left her shattered. It was the *way* he'd touched her, the emotions behind his caresses and just as importantly—how they'd made her feel.

She'd touched him back, entwined her hands with his and felt their strength and their power. His hands had been nothing like she'd imagined—somehow flawed or disfigured. "Why do you wear gloves?"

Jake's touch on her stilled, but he didn't look up. "Why do you ask? Is it important to you—that they're scarred?"

The questions were casually asked, but Margot sensed a motive behind them. "No," she returned softly and in all honesty.

He cleared his throat. "Good."

And then he returned to administrating her hands in silence. It was a new, awkward silence, one filled with tension. And it all had to do with that one question. Were his hands that badly disfigured that he didn't even want to talk about it? His ten digits were all intact and in working order. She knew that. All she had to do was remember last night.

"Are you self-conscious about them? Is that it?"

Jake shifted. "It's not that."

"You needn't be self-conscious."

"Well, I am! They're ugly. Can you drop the subject?"

"Sure."

Jake sighed and paused long enough to say, "I didn't mean to snap, but it's a sore subject. Maybe in time—"

"It doesn't matter." She shrugged to show she wasn't bothered. "It's none of my business."

After opening a tube of anti-bacterial ointment, he dabbed a dot onto her palm and spread a light coating over each cut.

"I'm almost done," he said.

Jake glanced up at Margot again and looked at her through those stupid black glasses of his. She couldn't see anything behind either lens. That was something else she wanted to ask him about. Other than the flashlight hooked up to shine on her hands, the room was in deep shadow, which didn't explain why he wore his glasses now. But she didn't think asking him about it was a good idea right this minute. He hadn't wanted to talk about his hands, so she had a good idea getting into this new territory would only end up in more silence.

Plus, hadn't she just said that it was none of her business anyway? And she most assuredly didn't want to wonder why it bothered her so much that it was none of her business. She'd made a point of keeping out of other people's lives when she'd moved back. That way, they'd stay out of hers. Margot should be happy about that. After all, that's what she'd always wanted, wasn't it?

No—Yes. Of course it was.

"Did I hurt you?"

"No. Not at all." She hadn't realized she was muttering aloud. "You're very gentle. Now I know what they mean by 'doctor's hands.'"

"I'm not that kind of doctor."

His words were clipped and impersonal. He'd turned cold on her.

"You really should have seen Malcolm's face," she said, interjecting a lightness to her voice. Anything to erase the strain between them. "He didn't look too attractive with a pint of milk dripping from him."

"I can imagine it wasn't pretty."

Margot might not be able to see behind those glasses of his, but she saw a definite twitch of his lips.

She nodded. "And the shock on his face. He looked like an albino fish, his mouth opening and closing, spouting all that milk."

"Now *that* would be something I'd have liked to see."

Ah. Now she definitely heard some humor there. "I think it was the first time I've ever seen him so shocked."

Margot laughed at the memory of Malcolm's reaction, then immediately winced.

"Your head?" Jake's voice deepened and warmed with sympathy.

At the pain, she blinked back tears, afraid to nod and worsen the sudden throbbing in her head. "I forgot for a moment."

"Well, let me have a look. You might have broken the skin after all." He recapped the tube of ointment and set it down with the towel and tweezers. He rolled the glass fragments in another thick towel and placed it alongside the other items. Quietly, he rose from his place on the floor and moved around the sofa.

Margot felt him right behind her. The soft sigh of his breath, warm and scented with cinnamon, touched the curve of her shoulder and whispered by her cheek. His fingers, the merest of touches, probed the back of her skull, parted her hair, then slid deftly through the strands and sent little shivers across her neck. But even so, when he touched the spot right behind her left ear, she flinched.

"Sorry."

"That's okay." Her voice sounded a little too breathless, a little too unsure. "How bad does it look?"

"I don't think it looks too bad, but it's hard to say with all this hair." A small pause. "You have beautiful hair. So thick. And silky. I love how the light turns it to silver in places."

She closed her eyes. He glided his fingers through her hair once again, but this time she knew he did it because he found pleasure in touching her. She sat rooted to the cushion and struggled not to remember last night.

"Can you give me that flashlight?" he asked.

"Ah. Sure."

She handed it to him over her shoulder and waited impatiently. He was far too close. Margot could actually feel the heat radiating from him as he stood behind her.

"The skin's not broken, but you'll definitely have a contusion."

"I'm not surprised with the way it hurts."

"He hasn't hit you before, has he?"

Margot didn't have to ask who 'he' was. Not with the way Jake's voice had lowered to that dark, dangerous, almost savage pitch. She shivered. Jake might appear the mild-mannered man at times, but there were other times like now, where she wondered just how dangerous he was. God knew he was dangerous to her peace of mind. He had her completely confused, even dumbfounded as to what she wanted from life.

"Has he?" Jake asked again, obviously not about to drop the subject, as he placed the flashlight on the floor by her side.

"No."

It was the truth, she told herself as Jake clasped her shoulders with his hands. He pressed his thumbs into the muscles below her neck and made strong circular movements. After a few minutes, the throbbing in her head eased and she closed her eyes and sighed in pleasure. Beneath the steady massage of his hands, she found herself relaxing and melting into the cushions. But that all changed with his next question.

"He did something to you, though. Didn't he?"

She bit her lip, opened her eyes. "Don't ask me questions when you yourself aren't willing to answer any."

His fingers stilled on her shoulder. "Touché."

They were back to where they were just five minutes ago. "Yes, well, if the shoe fits..."

He slipped his hands from her shoulders and walked around to her side. "I saw what happened on the porch. He went after you."

He wouldn't leave Malcolm alone. She shrugged. "He was a little upset."

"Come off it, Margot. Malcolm doesn't get a 'little' upset. His temper can get pretty scary—even for me."

"Okay," she admitted in a disgruntled tone. "He was a lot upset."

Jake hunched down beside her. "Why?"

She laughed a hollow, somewhat bitter laugh. She couldn't look at him. "The disk, of course. He wants it. And I just happened to tell him something he didn't want to hear. This disk sure is becoming quite popular. I'm beginning to wonder just how much it's worth. Probably enough to retire. Right?"

"And then some."

"Well, so far Malcolm's not getting any closer to retiring. He's starting to sound pretty desperate."

"Which makes him a hell of a lot more dangerous. Today, he came too damn close to seriously hurting you. I'm not going to give him another chance to hurt you or anyone else. I should have done something long ago. My mistake. But not anymore."

Margot grunted. "That's easier said than done. There's no proof tying him to Johnny's death. I can't think of anything to put him behind bars. At least anything legal."

"Why does it have to be legal?" In one fluid motion, Jake grabbed the flashlight on the floor and rose to his full height. He tapped the light against his thigh.

Jake's words sent her nerves jangling. "What do you plan on doing?"

He laughed harshly. "Don't look so horrified. I'm not going to kill the guy."

She didn't relax. "Then what are you going to do?"

Bending down, he picked up the tweezers and other items from the floor. "I better clean this up before someone steps on it."

"Fine. Ignore my question." She lifted her hands to rub at her face in frustration, then saw the cuts and dropped them back down into her lap. "But you're not doing anything without me."

"I need you to stay out of this."

"That's not going to happen. It's payback time. I'm not going to sit back and watch you squash Malcolm without having my hand in on it. He's ruined everything I've held dear. My self-respect, too many lost years—more importantly—my brother!"

Swinging off the sofa, she stood up too fast. Pain pounded against her skull.

"I need a drink."

"You don't need a drink," he growled. "You need to sit back down and rest."

She glared at him. "I want a drink."

"No. You're not going to get one."

Headache momentarily forgotten, Margot dodged around him, slipped under his outstretched hand, but didn't get far—not by any means. He caught her belt loop from behind and yanked her back. At the unexpectedness of his move, she lost her footing and stumbled against him.

Her bottom pressed up against his hips right where it counted. Jake let her go immediately, but not before sexual awareness smacked her all over. Margot turned around and knew immediately that he felt the same tension. It scared her. This hunger, this clawing need.

"Fine." She backed down, taking a blind step away from him. "I'll have one later."

"We'll see about that."

"God, you can be so stubborn!" Margot swallowed and clamped a tight fist down on her anger, frustration and hunger. "I'm going to—" *bed.* She'd caught herself just in time. "We can talk about this tomorrow. I'm tired. Goodnight."

Not waiting around for an answer, Margot slipped from the room. She walked casually down the hall, the soles of her shoes clattering against the polished wood floor, but she wasn't calm as she climbed the stairs. All she wanted to do was run, fly up the steps and dash into her room. Run from Jake and her feelings.

CHAPTER 13

MALCOLM REACHED INSIDE his jacket and touched cold metal. He wrapped his fingers around the gun's handle but didn't pull it out.

He watched Margot step out of the post office. She hadn't seen Carl, but Carl had seen her. The cop stepped out from the squad car, yanked up his pants and walked along the shoulder of the road in her direction. When she caught sight of Carl, even from this distance, Malcolm recognized Margot wasn't thrilled at his appearance. Not that he blamed her. He'd never liked the guy. Granted, he'd only met Carl twice, but that had been enough to know the cop wasn't worth a minute of his time. But by thinking of Carl as just stupid, Malcolm made the mistake of underestimating him. Something he hated to admit. Malcolm didn't make mistakes. Not important ones.

A wall of thick, gray clouds marched across the sky. It brought with it a cold, dry wind that bit into his skin, pulled at his hair, and tossed the flag hooked above the entrance to the post office. The cloth flapped loudly against the otherwise quiet downtown street. No one was about. It was still too early in the morning for the tourists or even the locals. The only place open other than the post office was the donut shop on the edge of town and Flap-Jacks, some dive that offered breakfast Malcolm hadn't dared touch. The diner probably hadn't seen the likes of a health inspector for years. He'd always known Greyson wasn't exactly a Mecca for haute cuisine or five-star lodgings, but it wasn't until these last couple of weeks that he'd found out firsthand the lack of amenities in this stinking town.

"Hey, Margot!" Carl called.

Malcolm pressed against the corner of a brick building and nervously fingered the gun. He watched Carl stop in front of his ex-wife. Damn it! If Malcolm took a shot now, he'd hit both. He needed Margot off to the side to get a clear aim at Carl.

Malcolm didn't particularly want to kill anyone. Not because it went against any code of ethics. Shit, no. He'd had enough of self-righteous bastards in his life. He'd learned all too early that they were a bunch of hypocrites. Even Jake had turned on him. But he didn't want to think of Jake. He'd only get angry, which he didn't need right now.

No. Killing someone was just messy. It would add more complications and questions. Unlike the explosion at Miltronics, Malcolm didn't have a ready alibi to extricate himself if the cops started sniffing his way. Then there were a couple of prissy-assed investors who hated any type of headlines. But what the hell else was he supposed to do? It all came down to self-preservation.

He couldn't afford to wait another day. Not with Carl walking around with too much information rattling around inside his head.

~~*~~

Margot watched Carl come toward her. He was the last person she wanted to see this early in the morning, particularly when he didn't look any happier than when they'd last talked. She rocked the plastic handle of the mail bin between her fingers and paused long enough for him to reach her side. Then Margot slowly walked toward her car as Carl fell into step beside her.

"We need to talk, Margot."

Carl also didn't sound any happier than last time. She sighed. "What about?"

An explosive bang ripped through the quiet of the morning. Margot jumped and dropped the plastic carrier. The bin clattered against the pavement. Pivoting, she searched the street. The door to the post office swung closed. Someone must have just stepped inside. At Max's, the blinds on the front window and door were shut tight. A car's engine rumbled down the next street, while the flag above the post office door slapped at the wind.

Margot turned back to Carl and met his stunned expression. He opened his mouth several times but said nothing. At the same time, they both glanced down and saw the hole in his jacket to the left of his chest. Before either had time to react, another loud explosion ripped through the chill morning. A hole appeared inches below the other. Carl staggered back, clutching at his chest.

"Carl!"

He crumpled. Margot grabbed his arm but the jacket's nylon sleeve slipped from her grasp. He fell hard, awkwardly, without the buffer of outstretched hands. His shoulder took the worst of the hit as he landed on his side.

She dropped down beside him, scraping her thinly clad knees across hard concrete and dagger-like pebbles. Nudging him over on his back, she unzipped his jacket, pulled it apart and wished she hadn't. Blood, vivid, scarlet, terrifying, stained his white shirt and ate up the snowy fabric with alarming speed.

"Oh, God." She sucked in a lungful of air. "I—no."

Margot leaned over. Carl didn't turn, didn't do anything but stare at the sky. Pain twisted his face into a pale mask of harsh lines. His breathing was ragged, watery, frightening.

From across the way, Max sprinted toward her.

"Don't worry, Carl," Margot assured. "Help's coming. You're going to be all right."

"What happened?" Max slid to a stop beside her, winded and flushed. "I heard a noise and then saw Carl on the ground here."

"He's been shot. He needs an ambulance. Please—"

She didn't have to say more. Max sprinted toward his shop.

Margot needed to remain calm. For once in her life, she had to be strong, to hold true. She couldn't run away or cave in. Not this time. She had to get Carl through this. She just had to for Joyce.

What would Joyce do if something happened to Carl? He was her baby brother, her only brother.

"Max's calling for an ambulance. It'll be here any second." The closest hospital was in Pinetop, a good hour away by car. Margot suspected he'd never make it that long. The only other way was to helivac him out. "Just you hold on."

"Margot."

The word came out like a sigh more than anything else.

"Ssh. Don't talk. Don't say anything. You need to save your strength." Margot choked back hysteria that threatened to bubble up her throat. Shrugging out of her jacket, she reached over and lifted his head in gentle hands and bundled her jacket beneath his head.

As she pulled back, Carl clutched at her arm. It was a weak attempt at best. His lips moved, but all he managed was "I—"

"Don't talk—" She bit her lip to smother the sob.

"I—I can keep a secret—" Carl grabbed her hand, his palm cold against her fingers. So very cold.

"Carl. Listen—"

But he wasn't listening. He was struggling for words.

There was an urgency in his grasp, in the way he tried to speak. "I'm not... I'm not as stupid as everyone thinks—" Carl's voice turned more forceful as he clutched at her hand. "No one knows. The car accident. There's more. I did something. Not even Malcolm or J—" Suddenly, Carl inhaled. Liquid gurgled in the back of his throat as he struggled to speak. " John—"

His hand bit into her flesh then slackened and completely went limp. Carl stared at her, but then he didn't.

He was dead.

Margot sat on the dirt and concrete, oblivious to everything but the wind bitterly caressing against her face. She became aware of cries in the distance, people rushing forward.

Someone led her away. She didn't know who, and she didn't care. Just like that. Carl was dead. He'd been standing right beside her one second, then the next he'd been laying in his own blood.

She was the one to tell Joyce later that morning. She was the one to hear her friend's cries of anguish. She was the one to hold and comfort her until Joyce's aunt and uncle drove in from Pinetop. And throughout it all, guilt, raw and painful, dominated every thought. From as far back as she could remember, she'd never treated Carl with any respect, never had anything nice to say to him. It all seemed so crazy, so very pointless. No one had a clue as to why Carl had been shot. It wasn't gang related. The town wasn't big enough.

Why?

Because of this secret he was hiding? Had he been about to reveal it? Had someone wanted him silenced because of it? And why mention Malcolm to her? Had Carl known all along that Johnny's car crash wasn't an accident? Could he have been tied in with Malcolm? Could they have both been involved? Could her ex-husband have shot Carl dead? God knew Malcolm was already a murderer. One more body wouldn't matter. But killing Carl seemed so bizarre. She didn't understand the reason behind it.

So many questions and suspicions, but no answers or clues.

Before driving home, Margot dropped by the mini-mart and bought herself a bottle of Merlot. With her nerves completely shot, she struggled through the checkout and the drive home. She was on the edge of an abyss and so close to falling that it terrified the hell out of her. At least the wine would get her through the night, because she intended to get thoroughly drunk. She didn't have anyone around to tell her otherwise.

Jake was gone. His pickup missing. Margot hadn't seen him all day, which was fine by her. She'd have her wine without anyone nagging at her. God, who was she kidding?

She needed Jake. She wanted to deny it, hated to admit it, but, oh, how she craved his strength, his support and comfort. He'd crept into her life. If Margot wasn't careful, she'd start relying on him. The way he'd cleaned the cuts on her hands with such tenderness. The way he listened—really listened—to what she said. The way he cared...

No. Margot wasn't going down that road.

She stepped into a house absent of light and color. The sun hadn't broken through the dense cloud cover yet and didn't look like it was going to anytime soon, as if the weather somehow reflected the day's terrible events. For a moment, Margot just stood in the hall and listened. Nothing. No strange sense of being watched or odd moving objects. Margot hadn't experienced any of that for the last week. Maybe all that had been her imagination—an unconscious part of her hoping for a sign that Johnny still lingered somewhere, some sliver of comfort that he was on another side.

Margot walked into the kitchen and opened the bottle of wine. She shouldn't be wallowing in self-pity. Not when Joyce was dealing with her brother's death. Sadly, Margot knew exactly how her friend felt, and she wouldn't wish that on her worst enemy.

The first glass went down really smooth. It tasted wonderful against her throat. Just a touch of spice.

Bottle in one hand, glass in the other, she retreated upstairs. After setting both down on the floor by the tub and turning on the bath water, she stripped, tossing her clothing on top of the closed hamper. Then Margot stepped into the tub and gasped. Hot, steaming water slipped over her calves and higher, closing over her hips, waist and breasts and on up to her neck as she slid deep into the tub. She rested her head on the inflated pillow she'd attached earlier and let the bite of the water lap against her reddening skin. The intense heat drained the energy from every pore of her body, while three-quarters of a bottle of Merlot helped drain every searing thought from her brain.

~~*~~

Jake flipped the light on in the bathroom, saw Margot and panicked.

In a glance, he took in her limp arm and outstretched hand over the side of the tub, the overturned wine glass on the floor just beneath her fingers, and the cool marble of her skin against the black porcelain tub. They were all vivid and horrifying images against the fluorescent light.

"Margot!"

When he'd first stepped into the house, he hadn't yet worried. But when his calls went unanswered, uneasiness had turned quickly to dread. He'd seen her car out front and knew she had to be inside, so he'd searched every room downstairs. Then he'd hurried up here only to find this...

Jake fell to his knees. Margot's long, black lashes and full, red lips, parted as if on a sigh, were stark contrasts against her translucent skin. Bath water pooled just beneath her chin. A few bubbles hugged the sides of the tub and did nothing to conceal the full thrust of her breasts, the narrow waist, the flare of hips and her long, pale legs. She lay unmoving, vulnerable and exposed.

Heart pounding in fear, Jake checked her limp wrist for a pulse. He found one, steady and unmistakable, against his shaking fingers.

Margot was going to be okay.

She'd scared him. Scared the hell out of him. Angry now, Jake gripped Margot's shoulder. Her damp, raven hair, snaked around his gloved fingers as he shook her—hard.

"You little fool. Wake up!"

Margot winced, shrinking away from him. "Don't yell—my head—"

"Damn it! You're drunk!"

Margot squinted up at him. She didn't look the least bit guilty.

Jake grabbed the edge of the tub. Better that than a part of her body. "Are you out of your mind? You could have drowned! Do you know that?"

She folded her legs up against her chest, and wrapped both arms around her knees, shielding her nakedness from him. With the heel of her hand, she rubbed at her brow. "Leave me alone."

"The hell I will!"

He reached into the tepid water and hauled her wet and naked body against him, drenching his jeans and long-sleeved sweater. He hooked an arm beneath her knees and heaved her into his arms. Damn, she was heavy. Until Margot, he'd never made a habit of picking up women, but now it seemed commonplace.

And Jake didn't like it one bit. Both times he'd had her in his arms he'd thought he'd lost her moments before.

Straining beneath her weight, Jake shifted to get a better balance. His blasted heel caught on a puddle and nearly landed them both on the floor. Granted, he might have saved them from a tumble, but in the process, he whacked his elbow against the wall and knocked his funny bone to hell and back.

"Damn it, woman!" He wanted to shake her. "What were you thinking?"

She slapped at him. A sad attempt at best. "Leave me alone."

The light from the bathroom shone into her bedroom and gave him enough visibility to get to her bed without breaking a leg. He set her down on the foot of the bed none too gently, rushed to get a towel in the bathroom and started to rub down her skin.

"Stop it!"

Ignoring her well-placed smacks to his face and arms, Jake dried most of her off and pulled the bedding back for her to slip underneath. After she had the sheets up to her chin, he asked, "Where's your nightgown?"

"Under my pillow."

Jake immediately stuck a hand beneath her pillow and pulled a ball of silk from underneath and shook it out.

She jack-knifed into a sitting position while still managing to hold onto the covers. "What do you think you're doing?"

He ignored her outraged cry and stuck the hole of her gown over her head. "I'm getting you dressed. It's obvious you're in no condition to do it!"

Margot's head popped through the material. Sputtering, she rammed the silk material down to her waist and squirmed around to get the gown situated. It looked like she was having a devil of a time untwisting it from around her waist. If at all possible, her face looked paler than before.

"I think I'm going to be sick."

"Well, you're not going to get any sympathy from me. You deserve an upset stomach. What were you thinking? Any fool knows you don't fall asleep in a tub full of water. And the added craziness of drinking on top of that! You could have drowned yourself!"

"So?"

"So?"

That one little word made him want to yell that much louder. Jake managed—just barely—to bite back an angry retort. His emotions were high, near breaking from the shock of finding her lying like that in her bathtub.

He'd thought the worst. And who the hell wouldn't? Anyone walking in and seeing her so deathly pale against that black tub of hers would have thought the same.

Margot eased back against the pillow, dragging the bedcovers up to her chin again and closing her eyes. A deep sigh shook her slender frame. At least she'd stopped shivering from the cold, but she still looked too fragile. What would have happened if he hadn't walked in and found her? She might have slipped beneath the water. She might have drowned.

The possibilities drove him nuts. "That's it! I've had enough. You're not having another glass! I'm going to make damn sure of it! It's killing you."

He stopped. Revelation hit him. "But that's what you want, isn't it?"

She put both palms over her ears. "I don't want to hear this." Margot glared at him, but the beam from the bathroom light caught the glitter of tears at the corners of her eyes and the tremor of her chin. "I can't handle any more confrontations. Not tonight."

"Why?"

She dropped her hands to her sides. "Because Carl's dead. Someone killed him! Right in front of me. I was there, two feet away. One minute I was talking to him—and the next—the next he—"

Margot broke into sobs, deep, pain-filled cries that slashed at his heart.

"Oh, Jesus..."

Her words knocked his legs from under him. He sank down hard on the end of the bed.

"I'm sorry," he whispered, clutching her knee over the comforter. "I didn't know. I swear. I had no idea. Believe me. I would never have acted like that..."

With hesitant fingers, he touched her hand, which rested against her lap, then slid his other hand up over her arm to cup her shoulder. She didn't reject him as he feared but sat up and eased into his arms. He tucked her head against the crook of his shoulder and rocked her.

Jake cleared his throat. Calm. He had to get a grip on things. The last thing Margot needed right now was for him to jump all over her again. But damn, the situation was driving him nuts.

"Can you talk about it?" he asked. "I mean—about what happened?"

She clutched the sleeves of his sweater and twisted the fabric between her fingers. "I was just talking to him... I forget about what. I guess it wasn't important," she said between rapid, shallow breaths. "He was hit in the chest by two bullets. Before I knew what was going on, he was on the ground. There was blood. So much blood."

Ice rushed over his flesh.

"It was on my jacket. I couldn't get it off. It was everywhere. I—I had to throw it out. The jacket."

"Do the police know who did it?"

"No. The other two deputies don't have a motive. At least none they know of or are willing to tell me. But I think I know who killed him." She gripped his arms tighter, pressing her nails through his sweater and into his skin. "I just don't know why."

"Malcolm," he breathed the name, answering for her. He clamped down hard on his jaw to contain the words about to spill from his lips. Margot didn't need his anger and bitterness.

She inhaled sharply. "Yes. I'm pretty sure."

Jake looked over her shoulder to the headboard with a narrowed-eyed gaze. "Well, you don't have to worry. Malcolm isn't going to hurt anyone again."

Margot stilled in his arms. "Why do you say that?"

Jake closed his eyes and rubbed his chin over the soft wisps of her hair. He heard the uncertainty and dread in her voice and didn't have to ask to know what she thought. "Don't worry. I won't kill anyone. Nothing as crazy as that. But something needs to be done. Too long I've waited around while Malcolm does whatever the hell he wants. I can't do that any longer. Not if I'm ever going to have any respect for myself."

To his surprise, Margot didn't say anything.

For the life of him, Jake didn't know how to take her silence. After all, she'd once been married to Malcolm. There could still be some lingering fondness for her ex-husband. Tension wrapped around his muscles, while fear kept him from pulling away to see her expression. He couldn't handle her disillusionment. Granted, he'd never told her he was a shining example of humanity. But Jake wanted her respect. It scared him how much he wanted it.

"Thank you."

Those two little words knocked the tension from his limbs. "Anything to keep him away from you." Jake pulled her even deeper into his embrace. "He'll never touch you again. That's a promise."

Her sigh whispered across his throat. "I still can't get over Carl's death. It happened so fast, yet it seemed every second lasted forever. I was there, but then again, I was so far away, looking in from somewhere else."

Jake couldn't find the words to ease her horror and didn't even attempt to try—he knew they were useless. Instead, he held her, just held her. After a while, he slid his fingers over the slick satin across her back and rubbed slowly over the taut muscles along the length of her spine, and over her shoulders and nape. Only when her body melted deeper against his own did he attempt to draw away.

But she would have none of it and latched onto his arms.

"Please stay with me. I can't seem to get warm." She whispered against his throat, her limbs shaking against his. "And I don't want to be alone."

"I wouldn't think of leaving. I'm just going to drain the tub and turn off the bathroom light."

Jake told her the truth. He couldn't leave her if he wanted.

She wasn't just John's sister. She'd grown to mean more than that. It was already too late for him. He'd become involved.

After turning the bathroom light off and closing the drapes, he kicked off his shoes. Shrouded within a black cloak of darkness, Jake yanked off his gloves and stripped down to his briefs, leaving a pile of damp clothes beside the bed. Then he dropped his sunglasses somewhere beside them and slipped under the blankets with her. Sighing, she slid up against him and tucked her head against the indentation between his shoulder and chest. As he watched the red numbers of Margot's clock change with each minute, her body relaxed against his. Her ankle crept upward and slipped over his calf, and her arm curled around his waist.

Jake should never have gotten into bed with just his briefs. He should've at least left his damn pants on, no matter how damp and uncomfortable they were. The warm silk of her skin against his was killing him. Anything would have been better than this hunger, this gnawing away at his insides.

Minutes ago, thinking of Margot in any sexual light had been the farthest thing from his mind. But now, he couldn't think of anything else but her body against his own. It was pure pleasure and pure torment having her lips, so soft and silken against his neck, and her breath, warm and moist, feathering the sensitive spot below his ear.

His hold on her tightened, and he glanced up at the ceiling. Jake wasn't going to take advantage of her now. Not tonight. If he could help it, not ever again. So he held her, gave her what support he could while he drank in her warmth. With his arms still around her, he slid his free hand over her hair, tangling his fingers through silken strands still damp from her bath.

Soon, Margot would be safe. Jake would take the necessary steps to make sure Malcolm never touched her again. He wouldn't kill the bastard. As much as he hated to admit it, Malcolm had been right. Jake didn't have the guts to step over that line and commit murder. He smiled grimly. He might not be able to kill Malcolm, but he knew of a way to ruin him.

CHAPTER 14

MARGOT WOKE UP to silence. She opened her eyes and wished she hadn't. Even with the closed drapes and the room drenched in soft shadow, the headache deep in her skull still crashed against her brain.

Groaning, she turned away and glanced at the other side of the double bed. Empty. Just like inside her heart. Margot slipped her hand over the rumpled sheets and found them cool to the touch. Jake must have left long ago. But what had she expected? That he would stay? Keep holding her forever?

She'd loved having his arms wrapped around her middle, his chin resting against the crown of her head. He'd been there for her, lending his gentle, yet silent support, his strength. If Margot wasn't careful, she'd find herself falling in love.

No. She wasn't ready for that. She wasn't ready to be vulnerable. She wasn't ready to be hurt again. But, oh, it would be so easy to let her heart lead her down that path.

Pressing a palm against her brow, Margot struggled from the tangled sheets and stumbled to her feet. The shower's warm water drumming over her chilled body did nothing to soothe her head. Turning the water too hot didn't do any better, and it especially didn't do anything to lessen her tumultuous thoughts. Carl. His murder. His life gone forever. Malcolm. Why? She couldn't understand. She was afraid to understand, and she didn't want to.

After donning a pair of jeans and a wool sweater, Margot went downstairs and into the kitchen. She froze by the counter. Three wine bottles lined the top. All empty. She hurried over to the cabinet where she kept a spare, white wine she didn't particularly like. Gone. Someone had tossed it in the garbage with a bottle of scotch. Both empty.

Anger surged and burned through her veins. Jake had no right. None whatsoever. If he thought he was going to get away with pulling this stunt then he had another thing coming. She'd tell him so the minute she saw him.

Then she saw the note taped to the refrigerator.

"I had to run an errand. Will be back in a couple of days. Yours, Jake."

At Jake's salutation, her heartbeat accelerated into a jumble of hope and excitement. Then just as quickly, she smashed those emotions. No. She wasn't going to read anything into that one little word. She didn't believe in hope. Plus, why should she even feel like that when only a second before she'd been angry with him?

~~*~~

For the next two days, if Margot wasn't working at home doing e-book conversions for her clients or at least trying to make sense of the mess left of her business, she went into town, visiting and helping Joyce, and searching for hard to find books.

No matter how busy she kept, Margot couldn't stifle her loneliness, a constant companion these last couple of days. Margot didn't know how to fix it, even though she knew the cause. Jake. Far too quickly, she'd come to rely on him. Something Margot didn't like one little bit, because when it came down to it, she didn't trust him. Not completely. Maybe if she knew he wasn't hiding something, she might not be so leery.

During the day, Jake disappeared, doing God only knew what. At first, she'd kept silent and avoided a confrontation because it was none of her business. Then later, she'd been afraid of Jake's answers, afraid of the oddness of the whole situation—the gloves, the glasses, and the way he moved around the house so silently. But this evening as Margot sat in front of the computer uploading a number of e-book conversions to one of the online distributors she used, suspicions were getting in the way, growing stronger than any fear she might have of Jake's answers. She needed to face him, discover what he was hiding. Otherwise, it would drive her crazy.

The sound of the front door opening and closing echoed down the hall and into the den. On the off chance Jake came back tonight, she'd left it unlocked. She'd also kept the lights off in the hall and front porch, knowing how much he hated the light.

Margot scrambled from her chair, hurried into the hall, and caught him going toward his room.

"Jake!"

He stopped but didn't turn around.

"We need to talk."

"About what?" Finally, when Jake turned around, she wanted to rip those stupid glasses from his face. How could she read a lie when she couldn't gauge an expression?

"Where have you been?"

"Boston."

"Boston?" She frowned. "But that's where Malcolm lives."

"I know where he lives."

Something about his voice, about the way he held his body, sent dread burrowing into her stomach. "What did you do? You didn't confront him, did you?"

"No. I didn't talk to him, but I made sure he'll never bother you again. I didn't even have to touch him. All it took was an anonymous call to the police, a few witnesses, and something planted in his car and then in his house. It doesn't take much if you have the right resources. So you don't have to worry about—"

Jake gasped, cutting off the rest of his words, and he stumbled, striking a hand out behind him, grappling for the wall but meeting air.

"Jake!"

"I—" He dragged in air, a loud hiss of pain. "Go. Now. Please—"

She took a hesitant step forward. "What's wrong?"

"Go!"

Powerless with shock, Margot watched as he staggered and slammed back against the wall. Then his legs buckled, and he crashed to the wooden floor on hands and knees, his head bowed between his shoulders.

"Jake!"

Rushing over, Margot skidded down onto her knees beside him. He collapsed on his side, doubled over with his back facing her, and panted between high, heart-rending whimpers. She clutched Jake's shoulder in panic. His muscles quivered beneath her fingers. Oh, God. He was shaking all over.

"What's wrong?" She gripped his shoulder harder. "You've got to tell me!" Margot thought of the empty vials she'd found in his room. "Do you need medicine?"

Jake couldn't seem to speak, only draw in harsh, rapid gulps of air, which the wooden floor and walls amplified to a terrifying degree. Rising to his knees, he curled into a ball, wrapped his arms around his middle and bent his head into his chest.

"I'll call for an ambulance."

She rose, hand on her knee, but Jake caught her wrist, digging into bone and flesh, forcing her back to the floor.

"No!"

"But what's wrong?" Her voice turned hoarse with fear. "You've got to tell me."

"I told you to go."

"I can't leave you like this—"

Jake turned his face to her, only for a second, but long enough for the faint light from the den to touch his features. There was something about his face. Something odd...

"Get the hell away from me!"

Margot jerked back as if slapped.

Jake shoved her away. The force pitched her sideways. She caught the floor with one hand just as he lurched to his feet. She scrambled after him, grabbing at the sleeve of his shirt, digging and twisting her fingers into the fabric, but Jake tore loose, and the material slipped through her fingers. He escaped into the bedroom, slamming the door shut.

The sound of wood against wood thundered through the hall. Margot stood panting, shaking, and staring at the closed door. What in God's name was going on?

Something crashed on the other side. Margot flinched. Opening and closing her hands, she faced the bedroom door as an unearthly silence descended throughout the house.

Margot was scared. Scared for herself, and scared for Jake. Scared of what or who was on the other side. Inhaling quick, ragged breaths, she wrapped her fingers over the cool metal of the doorknob.

An unholy cry, animal-like in its intensity, carried from the bedroom. Gooseflesh raced up her spine. She recognized it as the same sound she'd heard those other times during the night. She jerked her hand back from the knob. What should she do? What could she do?

She turned the knob back and forth and found it locked. With shaking fingers, she inched up on her toes and searched the top of the doorframe for the safety key and didn't find one.

"Jake?" She pressed a cheek against the door and listened. Silence. What if he'd passed out? "Jake? Can you hear me? Are you okay?"

"Damn it! Margot, if you love your brother you'll leave me alone."

The mention of Johnny in a voice thick with pain and anxiety urged her away from the door on unsteady legs. She backed further down the hall until she reached the entry into the kitchen. Once there, she slipped into the other room. Margot couldn't stop shaking. She also couldn't stop thinking of Jake's pain, his intense rejection, and her inability to help.

God. She needed a drink. Now. But Jake had dumped everything she had down the sink. She glanced up at the clock. Too late to go to the local grocery store. She grabbed onto the edge of the counter and took in several long, deep breaths as she struggled against the need that clawed at her insides.

Two minutes. Just another two minutes and the craving would dissipate. Isn't that what she'd read somewhere when it came to addictions?

~~*~~

Jake rushed into the bathroom, hitting a hip against his laptop and throwing it to the floor. At the threshold, he tumbled, colliding with the bathroom door, which slammed against the wall. His legs gave way, but he managed to break his fall with the flat of his hands. The tile was ice even through his gloved palms. He was damn hot.

He whipped his glasses off then pulled off the wig which suffocated and burned into his scalp. It didn't relieve a thing. Nothing could. Jake had to ride this through to the end if he didn't die before that.

Knives licked at his insides, searing into every cell of his body. Jake closed his eyes against it, struggling not to black out. His room. It had a flimsy lock. Margot could come in if she had a safety key. See him like this. Without his disguise—

Jake gasped as a tide of fire rolled through his body. His arms and legs gave way, and he fell to the floor. Then as suddenly as it came, the pain subsided. He opened his eyes and focused. Crimson drops stained the white linoleum. Blood. His blood. He wiped his nose with the back of his hand. His glove came away wet.

"Shit."

This was bad. Real bad.

Death came for him, and he couldn't do a damn thing to stop it.

Jake wanted to scream, lash out at the injustice. He didn't want to die. Not now. Everything was slipping from his grasp. He'd taken his mortality for granted. So damn stupid. He'd always thought there'd be a tomorrow. Well, he was living tomorrow with no children, no wife, no one to call his own.

Margot.

If only...

The sudden loneliness bearing down on him seemed almost as debilitating as his attack, and thoughts of Margot didn't ease the ache. It just made him feel worse. He was coming to love her. Well, it didn't matter now. He'd caused irreparable damage between them tonight by scaring the hell out of her.

Jake grabbed the edge of the sink and pulled himself up, then snatched a towel from the rack on the wall. He rubbed the sweat from his jaw and back of his neck with one side of the towel, and used the other side to wipe the drying blood from his nose. After tossing the towel down by his feet, he stripped and dropped his clothes and gloves on the floor beside it. Shivering, he showered and dried himself quickly.

Stepping into the bedroom, he found the room empty and the door closed and still locked. Relieved, he crawled into bed and wrapped himself in a warm cocoon of flannel sheets.

Even though mentally and physically drained, Jake couldn't sleep. His mind raced with thoughts of the formula, Malcolm, Miltronics, but particularly Margot. He couldn't get her out of his mind.

He heard Margot outside his room. The creak of the stair gave her away as she made her way up to the second floor. Jake lay on his back with his head pillowed by his hands and stared at the ceiling. Her bedroom was directly above his. A few minutes later he heard the shift of the bed through the floorboards.

Despite his weakness, Jake wondered what she was wearing. Damn it. He didn't care what the hell she wore. He wanted her naked again. Naked and writhing beneath him. He wanted to feel the smoothness of her skin beneath his fingers, smell the scent of her hair against his cheek, and hear her moan against his throat. He wanted her arching beneath him in surrender as he came into her. He wanted all of her.

Jesus! She haunted him.

Jake pounded his pillow and turned on his side. Nothing was working. Nothing but a miracle would get him to sleep tonight.

~~*~~

Margot woke from a fitful sleep, glanced at the bedside clock and groaned. A little after three in the morning, and she was wide-awake and dead sober. She hated both.

The programmed thermostat had shut off during the night, throwing a chill into the room. Turning over on her side, she pulled the down comforter over her ear and snuggled deeper beneath the covers.

She stilled.

Jake was in her bedroom.

Margot hadn't heard him come in, couldn't see him, but she knew he was there. The scent of him, woodsy and all male, drifted to her through the night. She sensed his stillness, his hunger in the darkness. Her breathing quickened and her stomach knotted in anticipation.

Oh, God. No. She didn't want him here. Not now. She was too raw, too frightened, too everything. And too sober. Without the haze of alcohol, her senses and emotions were far too heightened. She was terrified of who he was, what he was hiding, but most importantly, the power he had over her. She still hadn't recovered from witnessing his break down.

The rustle of sheets, the sigh of Jake's breath whispered from behind. At the touch of his palm, warm against her bare shoulder, she stiffened.

"Jake..." Margot didn't think she had the willpower to say no.

"I tried, but I couldn't stay away. You smell so good..." His breath touched the nape of her neck, warming her exposed skin and ruffling the fine hairs at the nape of her neck. He nipped at the lobe of her ear, then used his mouth to burn a hot and seductive path along the slope of her neck.

Margot shuddered and closed her eyes against the hunger. Her veins burned with it, her stomach ached with it. Desire raged through her body. The way Jake's body cupped her from behind, the way his skin seared through the thin silk of her gown chipped away at her resolve.

"Jake—I—"

"Don't, Margot." He urged her on her back with gentle hands and pressed a finger against her lips. "Don't tell me to go. I need you tonight. I need you like I've never needed anyone in my life."

She looked up. The night, thick, black and total hid his profile from view, but she heard the desperation in his voice. How could she turn him away when she would be denying not just him but herself?

"Why?" Her throat tightened, making speech difficult at best. "Why are you doing this to me, Jake?"

Jake cupped her cheek and caressed the line of her jaw with the pad of his thumb. "When it comes to you, I have no control." His deep voice sounded emotionally charged. "I can't stay away. I know I should—for both of us. I—" He inhaled sharply. "I'm sorry Margot. I just can't leave you alone."

His words and their honesty touched her like nothing else could. "Then don't."

Jake caught her parted lips with his mouth and slid over her, covering her body with the hot, hard length of him. Then raking his fingers through her hair, he anchored her head against the pillow and opened her lips wider with his mouth and tongue. Margot clutched at his shoulders, digging her fingers into the naked flesh of his muscles. His kiss deepened, took and devoured until she was a mindless mass of sensations, unable to deny him or herself.

Sweet heaven. He tasted wonderful. Pure sin and pure pleasure. The desperation, wildness in his touch excited her that much more. Margot couldn't get enough of his mouth, his tongue, his hands. Oh, Lord, those hands of his touched her in places that made her hunger for him that much more. She wanted him, all of him, around her and in her.

~~*~~

Jake dragged in a breath of air. Lust. But far more than that. His feelings were involved, deep feelings of love and devotion. For Margot, he'd do anything, be anyone. He'd protect her, even from herself or die trying.

Easing her legs apart with his knees, Jake sank back on his heels and tugged roughly at her gown with shaking hands, drawing it up over her hips. She arched, freeing the fabric and helping him pull the garment from her body. Jake tossed it aside. He needed to touch every naked, satin inch of her, to feel her legs wrapped around his hips, to hear her cry out as he moved inside of her.

He couldn't see her. Though, he could hear her shallow little pants, the rustle of sheets as she moved restlessly against the bed. He wanted to see her in the light, see her dilated eyes and her ivory skin flush with desire.

Clasping her knees, Jake drew them further apart. They quivered beneath his fingers as she tried to close them, but he wouldn't have it. He wanted Margot vulnerable, open to him. He wanted her complete surrender.

"Jake. I don't think—"

"Sssh... For once don't think," he whispered. "Just feel. Let me make you feel."

When her muscles relaxed beneath his hands, Jake slid his fingers over the silken flesh of her inner thighs, inching his thumbs up higher and higher, inch by slow inch, until he reached the apex of her legs. Then he stroked her with his thumbs. She was wet, ready for him.

Damn it. Sweat formed on his brow as he fought the urge to take her right then and there. Control. He needed control. Not a quick tumble. Granted, his body screamed for it, but he wanted the moment to go on and on. He wanted tonight branded into Margot's thoughts. He wanted her to think of no other man but him. Only him.

Mindful of his rough jaw against her skin, he followed the same path across her inner thighs with his lips. When he reached the juncture of her legs, he touched her clitoris with the tip of his tongue, a light, fleeting caress, but he soon grew bolder and took her with his mouth.

She gasped and shifted against the bed. Encouraged by her excitement, Jake didn't stop the pressure of his tongue or mouth as he slid his hands over her hips and belly until they covered her breasts. He molded them beneath his palms, grazing his fingers again and again over her hardened nipples.

She clasped his head between both hands and drew him deeper against her as she arched against his mouth and cried out. Jake's own excitement turned hot with hunger as she came against his mouth.

He didn't give her any time to recover, but rose up and slid deep into her, clutching her butt with both hands and pulling her to him. Groaning, she wrapped her legs and arms around his body.

One thrust and Jake thought he'd come right then and there. She was hot and tight and...perfect. She squirmed beneath him, trying to set the pace, but he grasped her hips and slowly drew out, then back in, using short, deliberate thrusts to tease, to tempt again and again. Then he drove deep, once, twice. When he sensed her nearing the edge, he paused deep inside.

"Jake, please—"

Her nails bit into his shoulders and her legs tightened around his hips.

"It's okay, baby. I've got you."

"But I—want—I want—"

Margot used her body to try to throw him to the side and take over, but he dug his knees and elbows into the mattress, holding her tight against his body. He caught her mouth, delving deep. She matched him with equal passion, twining her fingers into his hair to hold his head steady as she mated with his tongue.

Jake broke the kiss, nipped at her bottom lip, and ran his tongue gently, ever so softly over the same spot. With some primitive urge goading him, Jake found the pulse above her collarbone and suckled, marking her as his.

Margot was no one else's. She had to see that. She had to see that he loved her. Yes. He loved her, loved her more than any other woman in his life.

Drawing her legs from around his waist, he slid them up over his shoulders. He grabbed the extra pillow and nudged it under her bottom while rising to his knees, impaling himself deeper inside of her.

"Oh—" She gasped.

"Am I deep enough now?"

"Yes—" She said between hard, ragged breaths. "Oh, yes."

Grasping her hips, he withdrew and plunged into the warm, tightness of her. "You feel so damn good."

He closed his eyes and grappled for self-control. She was so feminine. He loved the curves beneath his hands, the long, length of her legs, and the way she responded to his every touch.

Jaw clenched, Jake quickened his pace—each thrust deliberate as he moved faster and harder. He stroked her hips and waist, urging her on. "Come for me, baby. That's it. Feel the rush."

Beneath his hands her body tensed, grinding against his hips as she arched off the mattress. Her cry of release broke the night. Jesus. Jake lost it then. Heart pounding, he clutched at her hips, his own bucking and straining above her as he came inside her. He shuddered. His climax went on and on, draining the life out of him. Careful of Margot's legs, he eased gently down beside her and curved an arm around her, drawing her snuggly against his chest.

"I didn't hurt you, did I?" Jake stroked her damp hair from her brow.

"Hurt? Never that." She laughed, a deep husky, even sultry sound. "But I'm weak, all wobbly. If I got up right now, I'd embarrass myself and land flat on my face."

Smiling, Jake glided a thumb tenderly along her jawline. He tightened his free arm and drew her soft curves even closer to his length.

"You're not the only one. With you, I've never... I mean it was more than hot sex." He cleared his throat. He'd never been good at explaining his feelings. "It was beautiful. You're beautiful."

"Beautiful?" she asked, a smile in her voice. "I like the sound of that. Keep the compliments going, and I just might let you stay the night."

With Margot cuddled in the circle of his arms, her cheek against his shoulder and his mouth by her brow, Jake closed his eyes. Her scent drifted to him in the darkness. She smelled of him. He smiled once again and drifted into an exhausted sleep.

~~*~~

Margot woke to something soft stroking her cheek. She wrinkled her nose and pushed it aside. Another gentle swipe brushed at her mouth. She opened her eyes and found Marmaduke hunched inches from her face. As she opened her mouth, he decided then and there to rub up against her face and present her with a mouthful of cat hair.

"Yuck." She rubbed her mouth with the back of her hand and pulled him up against her stomach. "I don't exactly like eating cat hair. And what are you doing up? It's too early yet, stupid. You're going to have to wait for breakfast."

The sun hadn't yet risen over the horizon, but moonlight now seeped into the room and thrust the furniture into varying shades of gray. Lifting her head from her pillow, Margot looked to the empty space beside her and slipped her free hand over the cool sheets.

No. Not again. Jake had left before sunrise.

Margot let go of the cat, who scrambled off the bed and disappeared into the hall.

She knew he'd been with her most of the night, having woken up a few times with Jake's leg over her own and an arm curved around her waist. But now he was gone to God knew where.

So he'd left. Margot told herself she shouldn't be hurt by it. Otherwise, that would mean she was vulnerable—a weakness she'd promised never to allow herself after Malcolm.

Margot laughed harshly. Who was she fooling? Last night had been pure heaven. Everything about Jake left her wanting more—his hot, naked skin against her own, the urgent need of his lips and hands, the warmth of his breath against her brow.

Sighing, she threw off the covers. Sleep was impossible. There was no point even trying. Margot slipped from the bed, crossed the cold floor on bare feet and snatched her thick housecoat draped over the bedroom chair. Shrugging into its sleeves, she tied the belt snuggly around her middle and walked over to the window to pull the curtain aside.

The lab, a thick, dark shadow, sat stooped in front of an outcropping of aspen and Ponderosa pine. A light appeared in the window, throwing a shallow glow over the once gray snow.

Margot stiffened, clutching the curtain between her fingers. So that's where he'd gone.

"Who are you, Jake? You've got so many secrets," she whispered, her breath misting the glass's frigid pane. "What are you hiding?"

The barn and the light from within beckoned. Her answers were down there. Answers she planned on learning today.

~~*~~

Malcolm sat in the back of the squad car and burned. Behind his back, the metal handcuffs bit into his wrists. He stared out the window over the manicured lawn of the Georgian styled brick house. His house.

Movement at the corner of his vision made him turn. The neighbor, Harry or Henry—some stupid name that started with an H—walked across the opposite side of the street with his prized golden retriever. His gray, fake hair flopped with each stride. It couldn't be anything else but a sick attempt at a hair transplant, because the guy had been bald as a bat months before.

Back ramrod straight, Malcolm glared through the closed window. He couldn't miss—no one could—the way Harry or Henry rubbernecked to get a look at who sat inside the cop car. After all, it wasn't every day someone saw the police parked in front of a house in the neighborhood. This was probably the most excitement anyone had seen in a while.

Humiliation crept up Malcolm's neck and burned into his face.

He knew exactly who'd done this to him. A stupid kid could even figure this one out.

Jake.

Rage surged and mixed with humiliation. Malcolm didn't want to think of how he'd driven up his driveway to find several cops sniffing through his house. The crack cocaine on the dining room table, the semi-automatic rifles, all unlicensed, tasted like bile against his throat. He'd underestimated Jake. For some reason, he hadn't thought Jake had it in him to lower himself beyond his sick ethics and frame him. He'd made it so easy and so simple for Jake to do it.

He never intended to underestimate Jake again. He'd made two huge mistakes—Carl and now Jake. Well, he'd taken care of Carl, and as far as Jake, he'd fix him just as good. If Jake wanted to play with the big boys, then he was in for a surprise.

Jake might have won this scrimmage, but it was far from over between them.

Malcolm twisted his wrists against the handcuffs, which tightened and dug deeper into his flesh. What other things had he missed?

Or who?

Margot. Hell. Could Jake somehow have involved her? Malcolm mashed his teeth together. She could very well be another threat. What if she had a hand in this whole stinking mess? Maybe she'd been the one to put Jake up to it. It was possible. Hell knew, she could get down and fling dirt like the worst of them.

Well, they were both in for a surprise if they thought this was over.

CHAPTER 15

AFTER SCRAMBLING INTO pair of jeans, a thick woolen sweater and socks, Margot raced downstairs, rammed her feet into a pair of boots and grabbed her jacket. Outside, she turned up her collar and stuffed her hands into the big pockets of her down jacket—anything to ward off the icy air snapping at her exposed skin. Snowdrifts and patches of ice hampered her way to the lab. By the time she reached the building, her breath came out in rapid, cloud-like puffs.

Margot opened the door, stepped quickly inside and shut it tight against the cold. The lab's sterile light glared off the lab equipment and furniture.

No sign of Jake.

Or anyone.

But the computer was on. Frowning, she walked over to the desk and sat down. The chair's warmth penetrated through the fabric of her jeans. Jake must have been here just recently, though, in this chair, working on the computer.

Margot jiggled the mouse. Formulas. They all looked so innocent, but she knew they were deadly. She scrolled down the screen. Nothing made sense. But she didn't know anything when it came to science. The subject in college had never been something she'd aspired to. She'd never had the logic or the patience to understand. But right this second, she desperately wanted to make sense of everything in front of her.

The information displayed on the monitor held the key to Johnny's murder, maybe even Carl's. Could all three, Jake, Malcolm, and Carl, be linked together? Carl might not have been the smartest person, but some way, somehow he could have become unknowingly involved. It was just too much of a coincidence otherwise. But she didn't understand the link with Carl. He'd mentioned a secret Whatever it was, it had to be of grave importance, something serious enough to be murdered for.

A footstep, soft but unmistakable, sounded from behind. Margot pivoted, swinging the chair around 180 degrees.

"Jake?"

The place remained deathly still. The hum of the refrigerator in the back and the computer's hard drive were the only sounds that permeated the room. She clutched the chair's armrests with rigid fingers.

"Johnny?"

Nothing.

The door to the lab remained closed. But she could feel something or someone in the room with her.

She waited, while her heart crashed against her ribs. Her breathing became quick and shallow. Frozen in the chair, she waited longer. Seconds passed. Then minutes. Still nothing.

"Johnny? Is that you?"

Clamping down on her fear, Margot searched the room, not only with her eyes but all her senses. She felt something or some type of presence.

"Fine," she told the empty room with bravado. "Have it your way."

Margot forced herself to turn around and face the monitor. The hairs on the back of her nape rose. She gripped the armrests even harder. Something was behind her.

She was afraid to look. Afraid to see what or who. But the need to know was too powerful.

A crash resounded through the barn. Frigid air rushed into the room. She swung wildly round in her chair. The lab door gaped open, having banged against the wall. Someone must have rushed outside.

"What the—"

Margot stumbled to her feet, raced toward the threshold, and hit a foot against a metal trashcan. Paper tumbled from the basket and kicked up into the air.

She stepped outside and squinted against the sun as its rays crested over the horizon and bounced off the snow. Nothing. No one. Just a bunch of barren trees.

God. Was she going crazy? Was she finally hallucinating? Closing her eyes, she rubbed the bridge of her nose with a thumb and forefinger, mentally shaking her head.

She opened her eyes and began to lower her arm, but stilled. She'd almost missed it. An imprint in the snow. A footprint. And it wasn't hers. The print was much larger. After closing the lab door, she followed cautiously up the embankment toward the house.

She plodded through snow as thick as the silence around her. Every now and then she looked over her shoulder to check if someone followed her. She was still spooked, fearful of what or who might be out here with her. When she reached the steps to the porch, the footprints abruptly disappeared. She'd shoveled off the steps and veranda after the last storm, too impatient to wait for the local teenager she'd hired to come and shovel after each snowfall.

The front door stood closed, just as she'd left it. But whoever had been in the lab was now in the house. Call it gut, call it intuition, or just call it common sense.

If Jake was the one inside, then why had he run from her and escaped out of the barn like that? It made no sense.

But who else could it be? There wasn't any other car in the driveway, no other sign of someone else other than Jake.

Malcolm.

She faltered on the stairs to the porch. No. It couldn't be Malcolm. Jake had said something about jail and him not bothering her again. God only knew what that meant. She was afraid to even think about what Jake had been talking about.

The front entrance showed no forced entry, no sign of

someone breaking the lock. She groaned at her own stupidity. Of course not! She'd left the door unlocked. Stupid. Stupid. She should have known better after the last break-in.

Margot grabbed the shovel resting up against the wall and hefted it in both hands to get a good feel of its weight. She wouldn't hesitate to use it. Granted, she didn't consider it the best of weapons, but it sure was better than having nothing.

With the shovel in one hand, Margot opened the door on silent hinges. She stepped inside and closed the door with the heel of her boot. A quick glance found the place as she'd left it.

Then she saw the water—little puddles of melted snow on the wood floor by her feet. She gripped the metal handle of the shovel tighter beneath her palms.

Margot wasn't alone.

Her breathing, ragged and rapid, sounded far too loud in the empty foyer. She opened her mouth to call out but the words caught against her throat.

The melted snow not only sprinkled the floor by her feet but further down the hall. She followed, all the while holding the shovel in a vice-like grip and high in the air. The puddles led right to Jake's room. She stopped and stared at the closed door.

She lowered the shovel.

Jake. She'd slept with this man, done things with him in her bed that she'd never even done with Malcolm. She'd let herself become completely vulnerable, desperate with want and need, with a man filled with secrets. Mysteries that were dark, dangerous and far too frightening.

What did she really know about him? Only the things he'd told her. Only what she'd really wanted to hear. And what was beyond the door? She knew he was in there right this minute. But what would she find?

The last time she'd stood in front of this very door, Jake had been shut inside and filled with such heart-wrenching pain. Like a wounded animal, he'd turned his back on her to deal with it alone.

Very carefully, fearful of making any sound, Margot turned the knob. It moved easily beneath her fingers. She eased the door open silently into the room, exposing the interior inside.

Margot dropped the shovel. It clanged against the floor. The sound reverberated through the hall and into the bedroom.

Whatever was inside froze.

Shock glued her boots to the floor, froze her limbs, widened her eyes and locked the scream from getting past her throat.

A pair of jeans, an opened shirt, and nothing in it. The clothing hung in mid-air. They both moved as if propelled by an invisible force.

Pivoting, stumbling over feet that wouldn't do what she wanted quickly enough, she raced down the hall. She slipped on the melted snow, almost fell, but grabbed the wall with the flat of her hand.

"Margot!"

Jake.

But not Jake.

What she'd seen wasn't human.

His cry didn't stop her but only made her more determined to get away. She almost slammed against the wall in her hurry to get out of the house. She fumbled with the knob, and bolted out, scrambling down the porch steps and away from the house.

The car.

No. The keys were in the house. In the kitchen. She didn't dare go back.

The lab. It had a lock, even a phone.

Margot veered in that direction, sliding on a slab of ice. It knocked her feet from under her. She landed hard on her hands and knees. The fall stole the air from her lungs. Small, jagged rocks embedded in the ice, cut into her jeans and the palms of her hands. The pain didn't matter. Nothing mattered but getting away.

He was following. She heard him from behind—his feet against the ground, his breathing, heavy, labored.

"Margot! Stop!"

She scrambled to her feet and leaped forward. Margot ran faster, ducked under a tree branch and dove through the snowdrifts, kicking up powdered snow into her face and hair. It hurt to breathe. She struggled for air as she wove through the pines and down the bank toward the lab.

Another fifty yards and she'd make it.

"Damn it!"

Something grabbed her shoulder, something invisible, something not human. Margot yanked her shoulder from its grasp, but it latched on and wouldn't let go. Forced to a stop, she turned around.

"It's me—Jake. Don't be afraid—"

But Margot was. How could she not? This thing in front of her didn't exist, didn't have shape or form. She lashed out, kicking into the pants, slamming her fist into the empty space below the shirt's collar. Her hand connected with skin and bone, human flesh.

She heard a grunt.

It let go. She stumbled backward, almost falling at the unexpectedness of being free. Her hair slapped against her face and into her eyes, obscuring her vision. She scraped back the cold strands, pivoted on the slippery snow and raced toward the lab. Frigid air cut into her lungs as she struggled to catch her breath and push herself forward, but her body was weakening, her strength ebbing. Margot dodged past an aspen, a snow-topped boulder, a fallen log. She slipped once, twice, but regained her balance both times. The lab door came into view. Twenty feet now. If she could just move faster, just—

But she didn't think she'd make it.

It—he followed right behind, his breath at her neck. Knowing she couldn't get into the lab and lock the door in time, she turned suddenly and rounded the building.

She saw the garbage pail too late.

Margot hit the metal can. She grunted. Her feet left the ground. The force propelled her sideways. The lab's window raced toward her. Unable to slow the momentum of her fall, she covered her face with an arm. Then something collided from behind, pushing her backward. Glass shattered. Metal crashed.

Then silence.

CHAPTER 16

F REEDOM. FOR A while there, Malcolm had thought he'd never be able to smell it.

He squinted into the sun. He'd made bail. Thanks to a damn good lawyer. But more importantly, he'd been released because of money. Money talked, money bought and sold people. Money was everything. Whoever said it couldn't buy happiness fed themselves a line of bullshit because they didn't have it.

At an early age, he'd learned quickly that money opened doors, bought allegiance, power and fame. And the only way to get there was by rubbing shoulders with the upper echelon. So he'd lied and cheated his way into a prestigious college, made the right connections and worked like a damn dog. No way would he have it all taken away now.

Malcolm brushed at the sleeves of his jacket. He couldn't get the damn creases out. The minute he'd get home, he'd throw it in the trash. It stank of the hell-hole he'd just been in.

Well, he needed to make a little visit to Arizona. Getting out of state might be a problem, but he'd figure a way. He might have hit a wall, but he'd either climb over it or blast his way through. Nothing would stand in his way of taking care of a couple of things, or more like a couple of people.

Malcolm sneered. Oh, yeah. He hadn't come this far to lose

the game. While behind bars, he'd come up with the perfect solution and, at the same time, a way to get the formula. He'd use the weaker sex against Jake and his stupid principles. Of course, not any woman would do. Oh, no. But then again, Malcolm knew exactly which woman to use.

~~*~~

Flat on her back, Margot opened her eyes. The barn rested to her left, thrusting her in shadow, while to her right, pines knifed upward, stabbing into a vivid blue sky. She grew conscious of the frigid air against her exposed skin and the snow, wet and raw, seeping into her already damp jeans and hair.

Digging into the snow with stiff fingers, Margot pushed herself into a sitting position. Turning, she saw the trash can she'd hit earlier on its side. The lid had snapped off, revealing an empty interior. Harmless looking now.

Carefully, she brushed off glass intermingled with snow from her thigh, then scrambled awkwardly to her feet. Her head pounded at the sudden movement, but other than that and a few bruised muscles, she was uninjured.

A low groan sounded from behind. Stiffening, she pivoted. Glass crackled beneath her booted feet.

"Oh, God."

Tension snapped around her limbs. Jake, whoever or whatever, lay five feet away. Pants, shoes, and an opened shirt lay before her, but where flesh and muscle would normally be exposed to the eye, there was only a void.

Cautiously, Margot walked over. Then she saw the crimson drops against the snow. Blood had seeped from what looked like a gash to Jake's head and then had trailed down to mesh and color a small patch of hair. The short strands were a stark contrast to the lack of substance around it.

Sucking in a lungful of air, Margot sank down beside him. She glanced down at the ground by her knees and blinked. Before her eyes, an unmarked section of snow transformed, almost imperceptible at first, then accelerated with each rapid beat of her heart. The snow, once blinding white changed to faded pink, then dilated and darkened into a circle of vivid red. Blood. It had appeared from nowhere.

Unsettled, Margot turned back to Jake. She now realized he'd thrown himself at her to stop her from crashing into the window. With a trembling hand, she touched where his face would normally be. Her fingers connected with skin, a jaw, then a cheek and temple as she ran them gently across where she knew a face would be. Even with the winter air all around them, what met her fingers felt warm and very much human.

By his temple, Margot touched something hot and wet, but she couldn't see anything against her fingers.

Horrified, she suddenly knew...

Jake's blood. Blood that must be oozing from an unseen gash to his head. For some reason after leaving his body, Jake's blood altered back to normal, or at least what appeared normal.

Jake hadn't flinched, hadn't even moved from the touch of her hand. But she felt the warmth of his breath against her palm.

Memories flashed through her mind—Jake appearing only after sunset, the cries in the night, the pictures in the hall dropping, the keys...which meant Johnny's ghost had only been some silly aspiration on her part. Margot's throat tightened. Not even a small part of her brother's body or soul lingered on this world. Somehow, knowing that, made Johnny's death cut that much deeper.

Jake groaned.

She snatched her hand back.

"Margot..."

Jake's pain-filled whisper lingered in the air. It made her realize just how fragile and vulnerable Jake really was. Inside, he was still the same man as yesterday, with the same doubts, hopes and thoughts as before. Slowly, fear of him subsided, but with it, a new fear formed. A fear for Jake's well-being. From what Margot could tell, the gash to his head looked bad.

At the unexpected touch of Jake's palm around her wrist, Margo jerked in surprise but didn't pull away. Warm pressure from his fingers met her skin, yet it was all so strange when that same hand was invisible to the naked eye. She took a stumbling breath. "We need to get you to the hospital."

"Can't—"

"Maybe if you lean on my shoulder, I can manage to get you to the car."

"No hospital."

She frowned. "What are you talking about? You're hurt, Jake. You need stitches."

"A hospital's out of the question. If I show up there, what the hell do you think's going to happen? Absolute chaos. Not just with the doctors but with the patients." He paused and inhaled sharply. "Within minutes word will get out. Reporters, the government, everyone will swarm down on us. I can't let that happen."

With his hand still clasped around her wrist, Jake rose to a sitting position and swore in a low, gruff voice. Obviously, he was in a lot of pain. Something needed to be done. But Jake had a point. The minute they both showed up at the hospital doors, people would react in ways neither one of them could predict.

"I don't know what to do then, Jake. There's no doctor in town. All we have is a retired vet. Joni's on the other side of town and—"

"No."

She opened her mouth to argue but he cut her off.

"I can't have anyone know about me, the formula, or Miltronics. Too much is at stake."

"Then what, Jake? You're cut bad. You're losing a lot of blood. You need medical attention."

"You're going to have to do it."

She recoiled. "What?"

"Stitch it up. You're the only one I can trust. It's either that or just hope to hell it heals on its own."

Margot looked at what blood she could see. Even for a head wound, there seemed to be just too much of it. No doubt, more blood seeped from his cut that hadn't yet materialized.

When it came down to it what other option did they have?

She swallowed. But even knowing that it all came down to

her, Margot didn't know if she could do it. She'd always hated blood. For God's sake, she couldn't even handle donating to the blood bank.

"You don't know what you're asking. I can't see what I'm doing. It's like asking a blind person to sew a quilt."

"You'll have to go by touch."

After a long pause, Margot gave a jerky nod and stood. She brushed her cold hands against her jacket and held up a hand for him to clasp. She felt his fingers close over her own and the pull as he rose to his feet. He stumbled in the snow and knocked up against her. Then the unexpected weight of his body as Jake draped an arm around her shoulder almost buckled her legs from under her. Balancing his additional weight, she wrapped one arm around his waist and held onto his forearm with the other.

The snow and patches of ice sure didn't help as they both stumbled their way up the hill. Margot clenched her jaw. She was going to get him up to the house or die trying.

Then there was Jake. She knew he tried to keep most of his weight off her, but she could tell he was losing what little energy he had from the way his body sank deeper against her own with each additional step. By the time they reached the porch, she was winded and shaking from exhaustion, while her shoulders and leg muscles burned from supporting Jake's weight.

She had a good idea Jake felt worse than herself. Granted, Margot couldn't see his expression as they staggered up the stairs to the house, but she could feel the tremble of his body against her own and hear the rapid, strained breathing beside her.

After they entered his bedroom, Jake sank hard onto the mattress. The bed springs groaned in protest as he stretched out across the mattress, while Margot rubbed her neck and shoulders. At the following silence and stillness from the bed, she tensed.

"Jake. Please don't pass out on me. Not now. You probably have a concussion. Sleep's the last thing you should be doing."

"Tell that to my body."

Jake's weak attempt at humor was at least a good sign.

"Are you hurt anywhere else? I didn't see anything." Margot realized how ridicules that sounded. Of course, she couldn't see anything. There wasn't anything to see.

"No broken bones I think. Probably just a couple of bruises. At least nothing serious, other than my head."

After hurrying into the kitchen and bathroom, Margot put a bowl of hot water, several towels, antiseptic, and a small first aid kit on the bed stand beside Jake. She'd also found some thread and a package of needles. Florence Nightingale, she was not. Right now, she wished she'd seen a couple of reruns from the ER series. Actually, any television show with a hospital would have helped right now. She hadn't a clue what she was doing.

After Margot sterilized the needle and thread with rubbing alcohol, she squared her shoulders. She needed to calm down. If only the tremor in her hand would go away! She really needed a drink right now.

No. A drink wouldn't solve anything. In reality, it would only make it that much more dangerous by dulling her senses and clouding her judgment. Margot didn't even want to think of what would've happened if she'd been drinking before all this, because it terrified the hell out of her.

She sat down on the edge of the bed. The muscles of her shoulders and back bunched with tension as she peered at the wound or what little she could see of it. At least a thin veneer of blood from before offered some visibility.

Jake must have sensed her doubts.

"Don't worry, Margot. You'll do fine."

For both their sakes, she hoped he was right. She forced a smile. Jake didn't need to know that she shook right down to her toes.

"You know, I trust you. I wouldn't be here if I didn't."

Margot stilled and her smile wavered. "Don't say that. How can you? I don't even trust myself."

"It's simple really. I believe in you."

She felt the sudden sting of tears at the back of her eyes. Jake's words moved her like none other had. No one, absolutely no one in her life had believed in her other than Johnny. Quickly,

Margot looked down at the thread in her hand, wanting to, but unable to, express how much it meant to her to have Jake think highly of her.

Abruptly, Margot stood and muttered, "You give me too much power. No one's ever put that much faith in me—including myself."

She grabbed a towel from the nightstand and sat back down by Jake's shoulder. Margot didn't talk as she worked. She needed to pour all her concentration on seaming both sides of Jake's skin together. Oh, but it was hard. She felt his silence, his pain as his breath fanned against her throat. A soft hiss slipped through his lips every time the needle punctured his skin. Margot knew she was hurting him, but she didn't have any other choice.

A film of cold sweat covered her brow. She rubbed it off with the back of her hand.

"I'm almost done," she whispered, gliding a thumb against the edge of his skin. Margot didn't want to think of the blood slick and warm against her fingers. She couldn't afford to. Otherwise, she just might lose it. "I just have a couple more stitches."

Margot didn't get an answer. Not that she expected one. She was probably stabbing him to death. She felt so inept.

Finally, she finished. Sitting back, Margot looked at the track of black thread. It sat there as if suspended in air. She looked away, finding the image too eerie, too hard to fathom.

"You can't stand the sight of me, can you?"

She tensed. "Jake. I'm still in shock. It's not like I've come across an invisible man before. Give me some time to take it all in."

Margot grabbed another towel from the nightstand and wiped at her hands. Her stomach rolled with sudden nausea. No matter how hard she rubbed at skin Jake's blood continued to stain her hands.

"Why can I see your blood, but not the rest of you? I don't get it."

"It changes its composition when it leaves my body. I haven't been able to identify the reason yet."

She nodded, unable to comprehend the pain and anxiety he'd

gone through these last couple of weeks. It was all too much. It would have broken a lesser man.

"You need your rest." Margot stood, still having a hard time looking at him directly. "I'll also get you some water. You've lost a lot of fluids."

She didn't give Jake a chance to respond but slipped from the room.

When Margot came back with a glass of iced water, silence greeted her. On the bed, Jake's prone figure remained in the same position. She didn't know what to think. This was terrible. She couldn't tell if he was sleeping or not.

She walked closer to the bed. When she noticed the gentle rise and fall of his shirt, she sighed in relief. For one crazy second, Margot thought she'd killed him with a germ-incrusted needle. Until now, she hadn't given herself the luxury of reacting, and she particularly didn't want to delve into her feelings. If she did—

A drink. God, she needed a glass of wine. She hungered for the way it took the edge off of everything. Not one bottle remained in the house. But the store was open. She could run to the car and—

No.

Enough. She'd completely lost control of her life. She'd let alcohol permeate her every waking thought and action. Not something Margot was proud of. But it was something she could change. That is if she found enough strength.

Margot put the glass of water down by the nightstand harder than she intended. Drops sloshed over the rim and onto her hand. She shook with need. Maybe just one glass. She could slip over to the store. No one would know. It would be so easy.

No!

Keep busy. Yes. She needed to keep busy. That should help. Any little thing might take her mind from wanting a drink.

Margot reached over to clean up the first-aid kit and other items from the nightstand when she saw Jake's wallet resting up against the brass lamp's stand. She paused. Knowing she shouldn't, knowing that it was absolutely none of her business, didn't stop her from reaching over and picking up the billfold. Really. When was the last time she'd kept her nose out of anyone's business?

She opened the wallet and saw a Massachusetts driver's license on top of several other cards. With nervous, fumbling fingers, she pulled the plastic from its slot.

Margot's grip tightened on the leather. The picture didn't look familiar. She glanced at the name. Jake Preston. Age, 38. Height, six-feet, two-inches. Weight, 193 pounds. Blond hair, blue eyes. This man looked the complete opposite of the Jake she'd come to know.

Gold hair, thick and cut close to the scalp, capped a strong, square face—a face warmed from the sun's rays and not at all like the pale complexion she'd become accustomed to. Thick brows, several shades darker than his hair, topped light blue, intelligent eyes. His nose and the strong thrust of his jaw were the only characteristics she recognized, but only after studying the picture for a full minute.

She was shocked at how well Jake had disguised himself. The image in the photo didn't compare to the man on the bed. While Jake was dark, this man was light.

Also, there was no denying the man in the photo was gorgeous. The female in her couldn't help but respond to the rugged strength and masculinity of his features. Though the other Jake, the one she'd come to know, was someone she'd responded to on a completely different level. A level far deeper than any physical attraction. It was something more instinctual, more primitive and far more powerful than anything she'd ever encountered in the opposite sex.

Hearing Jake stir, Margot almost dropped the wallet. She glanced over and saw he'd risen up on an elbow.

"You're very attractive," she said without thinking and flushed.

"Why, thank you."

At his amusement, Margot's face warmed yet further. She'd never been good at flirting. She'd never had the time. Getting her degree, working up the corporate ladder had consumed her days. Then she'd met Malcolm, a client, at the firm she worked for. From there, her life had gone downhill. While now—now she couldn't exactly describe where her life was going. But if she'd ever craved excitement, she had it now. More than she could have ever bargained for.

"If it wasn't for the name on your license, I never would have recognized you. You look—well, you look different." She snapped the wallet closed and placed it back on the nightstand.

"Good. That was the whole point. I didn't want anyone from Miltronics suspecting that I'd survived. If word got out, I'd be dead by now."

"But Malcolm knows or at least suspects."

"Yeah, he knows. But he isn't about to talk. He has his own motives. Plus, right now, he needs me."

"Because of the formula?"

"That, but more importantly the antidote." His voice had grown sluggish, making her realize how much talking had drained the little energy he had.

"I'll let you get some rest, but first, I wanted to thank you. I would have been seriously hurt if it hadn't been for you. Instead, you were the one injured."

"Forget it. I would have done it again no matter what."

Something in his voice—a fierceness, an urgency—made her glance over at his figure. She saw the stitches in mid-air, the empty holes below his shirtsleeves and pant legs and looked quickly at the floor. She still found his appearance unsettling.

"You really hate looking at me, don't you? Tell me the truth this time."

She stiffened. "Why do you think that?"

"Oh, come off it, Margot! Who wouldn't have a problem? I'm a damn freak—some sick apparition who'd turn anyone's stomach. Why do you think I tried keeping this from you? It wasn't just the danger. Okay, that had a hell of a lot to do with it. I knew I couldn't handle you looking at me like you are now— with revulsion."

She gazed at Jake in horror. "Is that what you think?"

"Why wouldn't I? Just hours ago you were running and screaming at the sight of me."

He was right. Denying it would be a lie. So instead, Margot changed the subject.

"We need to talk. Not right now, of course. But when you're better. I deserve some answers, and not what you think I need to hear. I want all the truth."

"Yeah. I think it's time."

Nodding, Margot slipped from the room. In the hall, the tears came. She wiped at them, but they continued spilling down her cheeks.

She tried to tell herself that Jake hadn't changed, that he was the same man from yesterday. She thought of those nights in his arms, of how his touch had made her feel cherished, beautiful, needed. He'd made her feel like a woman again.

That had all changed within a matter of seconds.

~~*~~

Several hours later, Jake found Margot sitting at her desk and bent over the computer keyboard. Unable to stand another minute with himself and his racing thoughts, he'd pulled himself from the bed and made his way down the hall. Plus, he couldn't afford to lie around when each minute passed and the future and his mortality loomed closer and closer.

He felt like crap. The ibuprofen helped somewhat, but it still seemed as if his head was on overload and about to crash.

Jake paused in the doorway. The mid-afternoon sun shone into the room from the large bay window. He squinted against the too bright light and winced as his stitches pulled against his skin. He'd become accustomed to the dark, either by using his glasses or keeping to shadowed rooms.

Margot must have sensed his presence, because she stopped typing at the computer and looked up. She swiveled in her chair and glanced around the room.

After a moment, she asked, "Jake?"

"I'm right here. By the door."

Frowning, she turned, then gasped. "I don't see any clothes. My, God. You're naked!"

"Yeah."

Margot stood up so quickly that the chair jerked backward and hit the bookshelves with a thump. She looked about ready to bolt. Probably at the idea of him running around naked and invisible.

Jake sighed. Obviously, he'd shocked the hell out of her. Again. It looked like it was becoming a common occurrence.

"Why!" she demanded. "Why no clothes?"

"I thought it would be easier this way than watching me walk around like some headless horseman. I know how upsetting you find it."

"Oh."

"I just don't want—" Jake hated explaining his fallibilities. "Damn it. I just don't want you seeing me like some sick freak."

"What? Don't even think it!" Her features softened with what looked like sympathy. "Right now, you're just different. If it wasn't for your condition, you'd look like the man pictured in your license, right?"

"Right."

"Plus, it's a temporary condition." At his silence, she frowned. "It is, isn't it?"

"I don't know. I'm beginning to believe it's permanent."

"Permanent? I never thought—I just believed you'd come up with the antidote and everything would be back to normal for you." She closed her eyes as if in pain and then reopened them. "Pretty naive, eh?"

"No, just optimistic."

With Margot and only Margot, he'd let himself become vulnerable. Right now, she was having enough problems dealing with his abnormality. What would she think of him if she learned the complete truth? Any feelings she still retained for him would vanish like dead ash against a bitter wind.

Jake balled his hands into fists. She wouldn't hear it from him. Shame kept him silent. So much of it that he couldn't face his own actions without flinching in self-loathing.

The only one who knew everything was Malcolm.

His tread silent on the thick carpet, Jake walked into the room. Margot's scent drifted to him. Sunshine and flowers.

Damn, but she was beautiful. That thick mane of raven hair begged for him to bury his fingers in their silken strands. With just one look, those oh-so-large brown eyes of hers could bring him to his knees. He wanted to cradle her in his arms and take away the confusion and hurt from her eyes.

He stopped a foot in front of her and brushed a knuckle against her cheek. "I'm sorry," he whispered. "I'm so damn sorry."

Margot flinched and turned away.

Then suddenly, she glanced up, and Jake caught her unmasked expression. It was far from revulsion. Hot brown, liquid eyes stared back at him. Hunger. His groin tightened and his chest expanded. He wanted her, wanted her body locked against his own, wanted her moaning and writhing for him and only him. He lifted a shaking hand, the urge to slide his fingers in those satin strands too overwhelming to ignore. She must have sensed what he planned to do, because she slipped quickly from between him and her desk.

"Don't. Not now. I can't seem to think straight when you touch me." Margot shook her head and backed further away. "I don't want to be more confused than I already am."

She crossed her arms against her middle and pleaded, "Talk to me, Jake. I want to know. I need to know. Where you're concerned, I feel like I've been walking along a precipice. You've got me so confused."

"What do you want to know?"

"Everything. The beginning. The end. Not just the short version you gave me the last time."

"The beginning." Suddenly Jake was bone weary, exhausted beyond his years. He sank down into the nearest chair.

"Yes, the beginning."

"Well, you know a good part of it already." He started to rake his hand through his hair, then remembered his stitches. "Miltronics. Everything begins and ends there. About a week before the blast, John caught wind of a conversation Malcolm had with one of the suits. He heard 'kill' and 'take care of it'. Then there was Malcolm, acting distant, colder than usual. Something was up, and we sure the hell knew it wasn't good. So we acted. Johnny copied the formula and took off. I stayed behind and smuggled several vials of Miracell from the building. The plan was to delete everything from the system. At the time, I hadn't a clue that Malcolm planned to blow Miltronics to hell and back."

"I still don't get that. Why? What's the motivation? Malcolm loved that company."

"John was bailing from the company and threatening to talk. I also wanted out. I hadn't said anything, but I know Malcolm suspected. He didn't trust either one of us. It got to the point when I knew I had to do something. Miracell was too damn dangerous in Malcolm or anyone else's hands. It just had too much power. Malcolm's fears of Miracell becoming public knowledge were becoming a reality. He knew if that happened, he'd lose everything anyway. He decided to blow up the department and the people inside it to sever all ties to the formula. He counted on having the formula safeguarded beforehand though."

Margot walked over to the adjacent chair and fell against the cushions. She rubbed the back of her neck. She looked as exhausted as he felt.

He hated thinking back to that time. "Remember, I told you that I had John safeguard a copy of the formula? It was because I planned on destroying everything. The day of the blast, I was in the process of deleting every computer record I could get my hands on when Malcolm walked in on me. I know Malcolm had every intention of making copies, but I beat him to it."

"Malcolm saw what I was doing and lost it. I remember him screaming at me, but nothing of what he said." Jake swallowed and rose to his feet. He hated this part. "We fought. He had me up against the desk. There was a vial of Miracell and a syringe already prepared by my shoulder. I'd missed both earlier. Hell, I thought I'd gotten rid of the lot.

"Well, I knew I had to destroy both. I managed to toss the vial and break it against the floor, but we struggled over the syringe. All that rage made him stronger. He had me against the wall. We were both grappling with the syringe. I remember he had his elbow jammed into my throat, and I was getting dizzy and losing oxygen. It was enough to lose my grip on his other arm. He stabbed me with the syringe and injected the serum into me.

"When I managed to get him off me, I think I caught my foot on the leg of a desk. I lost my balance and hit my head. I blacked out. When I came to, I found myself on the floor. Malcolm was gone. The syringe was on the floor beside me. Empty. He left me there to die."

"I'm so sorry, Jake." Margot, with unshed tears glistening against the afternoon sunlight, seemed to stare right into his soul. "You've been through so much."

Damn. He loved her. Margot had such compassion. If only she could see how much she had to offer someone if she just gave herself a chance.

Jake cleared his throat and moved restlessly around the room. "Yes, well. Shit happens."

She frowned. "How did you get away with everyone thinking of you as dead, though? With today's technology, it's pretty hard to fake your own death. Especially if there's a missing body."

Tensing, Jake stopped by a bookcase against the wall and gripped one of the wood shelves. She was getting too close. "It's amazing what one can do when you're invisible." He tried not to sound bitter. "A visit to a certain dental office. Then of course, there's the police department and lab."

She slipped a strand of hair behind her ear. "So everyone thinks you're dead?"

"There's my sister who knows I'm alive, but little else. I couldn't let her know everything for her own safety."

"And Malcolm?"

"Well, he's not going anywhere."

"Why? You never told me what you put in his house and car to have the police arrest him."

"Invisibility has its advantages. I planted some coke in his car while he met with a business associate. Then I finished up with some at his house along with a nice supply of stolen guns."

"I can't even imagine Malcolm's reaction."

Jake laughed without humor. "It wasn't pretty."

The room fell into silence.

Margot started to speak but stopped and frowned. After a moment, her brow cleared. "There's more, isn't there?"

"Yeah."

Restless, he moved to the far corner of the room. She was far too perceptive. "There's been many a moment where I've tried to ignore the inevitable..."

"Yes?"

"It's the attacks. Every time they bring reality crashing back. They're not going away, no matter how much I'd like to pretend otherwise. With each passing day, they're more severe and frequent."

He swallowed, finding this tougher than he'd imagined. The silence lengthened as he tried to find the right words. Then he gave up and cleared his throat.

"I'm dying."

CHAPTER 17

Two words. Just two little words. But they had such overwhelming power. Margot closed her eyes against the pain they evoked. She didn't want to hear the truth, didn't want anything to do with it.

"Take it back, Jake. Please take it back."

She loved him. The reality of it hurt. She'd tried so hard to keep it from happening; the idea had terrified her to no end. She'd fought against her feelings, but they'd come anyway, slowly insinuating into her subconscious, then into her conscious.

"I wish I could."

The gentle touch of his fingers whispered across her temple and into her hair.

"I love you." She swallowed, too overcome for mere words.

"I never knew. You don't know how much I'd hoped—" Hunkered down by her chair, Jake entwined his fingers between hers and squeezed, then he brushed his lips over a tear that had slipped from her lashes and stilled on her cheek. "I've been a selfish bastard. I had no right to hurt you, no right to get you involved in my mess. I'm sorry."

"Don't apologize. I don't want your apologies. I just want you well." Opening her eyes, Margot straightened. "How close are you to finding the antidote?"

"Close. Maybe two weeks. Not enough time. My system's deteriorating too quickly."

She flinched, pulling her hand from his grasp. "What about Johnny's copy? You said he made one. It must be here somewhere. Maybe if the two of us worked together—"

"But where, Margot? I've looked everywhere. Plus, any place I might have missed, Malcolm would have found."

"We'll look harder. We'll look until we find it. It has to be somewhere." She frowned. "Didn't Johnny hint about where he planned on storing the copy?"

"No." He sighed. "At the time I didn't want to know. Then it was too late—and now. Well, now doesn't much matter."

She stiffened. "You're not giving up, are you?"

"No."

But she heard the uncertainty and doubt in his voice. She clutched the arms of her chair, digging her fingers into the thick fabric. "Don't, Jake. Don't give up on me now."

"I won't."

Anxiety knotted around her stomach. She was afraid he was lying to her. "Tomorrow we'll look. Right now, though, you need rest. Your head must be killing you."

"It's felt better."

She heard the smile in his voice and relaxed a little.

"You're right. I'll let you get back to work."

Margot felt the touch of his lips against her brow and heard the soft sigh of movement as he left the room.

But she couldn't work, she couldn't concentrate, she couldn't do anything but think of the possible places where Johnny might have hidden a disk.

She didn't move from her chair but slowly looked around the room. Could Johnny have hidden the formula in one of the books? It would be so easy to slip a disk or CD between one of the pages. No. Malcolm had torn the place apart. Then there was Jake. Between the two of them, they would have thoroughly searched every conceivable area. But what if they'd overlooked something or missed one small volume? She didn't wait and wonder but rose and started on one side of the room, paging slowly, meticulously through each book. Food had no meaning; time had no meaning—only the need to find the disk.

The light dimmed. She paused long enough to flick on the lamp on her desk and then moved onto the next shelf relentlessly. The clock chiming two above the mantel and exhaustion, weakening her shoulders and arms and blurring her vision, made her realize she needed rest. At this point, fatigue would only hinder her search. She'd miss the obvious if she wasn't careful.

She left her office, snapped on the hall light and walked down the hall to Jake's room. In the doorway, she peered into the darkened room. From the hall, the light illuminated Jake's shape beneath the comforter. He lay on his side with his back facing her. It took but a moment for her to decide. She stripped, folded her clothes on the chair and slipped under the covers behind him. Tucking her legs beneath his, she edged closer until her breasts pressed against the warm, smooth muscles of his back. Tentatively, she curved an arm around his waist.

Jake sighed, shifted and cupped her hand against his chest. Then he stilled, his breathing deep, regular and comforting in the stillness of the room. Slowly, she relaxed against his body. It felt right being in the same bed and holding him. Closing her eyes, she didn't think of the future but held onto the moment. Eventually, fatigue pulled her down into sleep.

In the pre-dawn hours, Margot woke to find they'd somehow reversed their positions with Jake spooned up against her back. For a while she lay there, savoring his heat, the feel of his hair-roughened legs entwined between her own, the hard wall of his chest pressed against her back.

Reluctantly, she left the warmth of his arms and his bed and stepped into the chill morning air. He didn't stir. She grabbed her clothes, and slipped from his room, padding against the cold, wood floor. Quickly, she showered and changed. Not bothering with breakfast other than a cup of coffee, she hurried into her office and renewed her search, starting where she'd left off the night before.

Rising up on her toes, she reached over and pulled a thick volume from the top shelf.

The sudden cry jerked the book from Margot's grasp. The volume fell from her fingers and slid across the floor to hit the leg of her desk. The loud thump didn't compare to the noise that rose up from Jake's room and smashed along the walls and into her office.

"Jake!"

She fled the office and careened around the corner into the hall. She fumbled to a stop. Panting, she stared at Jake's closed door.

Another cry vibrated against the bedroom walls. Something fell to the floor. She flinched and swallowed a sob.

He was in so much pain.

She took a step and reached for the door handle but stopped. If she walked in on Jake now, would he be able to forgive her for witnessing his frailty?

A whimper, faint but distinct, propelled her forward. She grabbed the handle and shoved the door open. On the floor, by the foot of the bed, she saw his partially clothed form.

"Jake!"

"Get out—"

Margot didn't listen.

She fell down onto her knees beside him and touched his arm. His skin, even through a shirt damp from sweat, burned into her palm. "What can I do? Can I do anything?"

"Nothing." He gasped. "The pain."

She slid awkwardly down on the hard floor beside him and held him, just held him, as she closed her eyes and prayed. She tried to project her strength into him. If he could just get through this attack—

Jake convulsed. The force of the tremors pushed them along the wood floor. He clutched her shoulders, quaking against her body, growling deep in his throat. His fingers dug through the fabric of her shirt and into her flesh. She winched but still didn't let go.

He buried his head against her throat, his hot breath dampening her skin. Then suddenly, he stilled. A long, drawn out breath rattled from his chest.

They lay on the floor, both breathing deeply, as Jake's body relaxed in her arms. Slowly, he eased from her arms and rose to a sitting position.

"I'll be okay."

She pushed herself from the floor and sat up beside him.

"Why didn't you leave?"

"My God, Jake. I couldn't sit back and let you suffer alone. What type of person do you think I am?"

He was quiet for a moment. "Thank you." On the floor, he slipped a gloved hand over her own. "For last night and now. For just being there."

Margot couldn't think of an appropriate answer so she remained silent. They sat there for a long while, holding hands. Then finally, Jake was the first to rise from the floor.

"I guess we better get to work." He helped her to her feet and then motioned with one hand. "First, I need some time to look halfway normal."

"I understand."

She returned to the office and with a trembling hand picked up the book she'd dropped earlier. Her system hadn't yet recovered from the shock of Jake's attack. She'd felt so damn powerless. It wasn't fair. Jake didn't deserve this. He had so much to offer— intelligence, warmth, empathy. She blinked back tears. They wouldn't give up. They couldn't give up.

She eyed the remaining shelves she hadn't yet searched. There were still thousands she needed to go through. Lifting her chin, she straightened her shoulder in resolve. Miracles could and did happen. She couldn't lose sight of that.

"Any luck?"

Margot jumped and whirled around. "You scared me!"

Jake, fully clothed in jeans, navy, long-sleeved shirt, gloves, wig and glasses, stood in the threshold. Makeup covered his exposed face, except for a small patch that circled his stitches.

Jake cleared his throat. "Sorry. I seem to be doing that all the time now."

She closed the book in her hands and hugged it to her chest. "Don't apologize. I'll get used to it eventually." She motioned toward the stack of shelves. "I haven't found anything yet, but I'm only halfway done in this room."

He nodded, shifting on the balls of his feet. "I'll be down at the lab." He sighed. "Let me know—"

Even with yards between them, Margot felt his restlessness and apprehension. She wanted to reach out and tell him everything would be okay, but she knew they would be only words with little comfort. Instead, she said simply, "I will."

For the next several days, Margot searched the house while Jake worked in Johnny's lab. Neither one of them said it, but Margot knew feelings of hopelessness were escalating with each passing sunrise, and with each sunset, she felt Jake withdraw further and further into himself.

By Thursday evening, nothing had changed as the sun dipped over the horizon and Jake still remained down at the lab. From the kitchen, she glanced outside to the barn. A faint light from the window illuminated the snow to silver and pressed up against the rigid trunks and limbs of the trees alongside the building.

Could today be different? Could Jake be closer to an antidote? At this point, anything would be a breakthrough. She grabbed her jacket from the closet and shrugged into it. Not bothering with boots or gloves, she hurried from the house.

Only the incandescent glow from the computer monitor softened the shadows throughout the lab. By one of the tables, Jake, hunched over something, stood with his back to her. The door snapped closed behind her as she stepped inside.

Pivoting, Jake dropped the vial in his hands. Glass shattered against the floor.

"Damn it!"

"I'm sorry!"

Hurrying over, she knelt down to pick up the pieces.

Jake grabbed her upper arms and yanked her to her feet. "Just leave it!"

She shoved at his chest. "You need to calm down."

"Calm down!" His voice rose. "How can I calm down? I'm coughing up blood. I can't hold anything with a steady hand. My mind is shot to hell and back!"

Swiveling around, he slashed his gloved hand over the table's surface. Papers, pencils and pens flew into the air.

"This is ridiculous. I'm chasing after something that isn't even here!"

Margot flinched. "You aren't any closer?"

"Yeah, but it's not enough. Not nearly enough."

Tentatively, she touched Jake's back. "Don't give up now. You're close. You just need a little more time."

Turning on his heel, Jake faced her. "Time?" He laughed harshly. "I don't have time!"

The monitor sat behind and to the right of him, throwing his silhouette into impenetrable black. He loomed over her, large, male, and filled with such unbearable pain.

"Margot, I'm scared. So damn scared—"

Before she had a chance to respond, Jake swooped down, latching both hands around her upper arms and dragging her to him. Then he kissed her, driving his fingers into her hair, bending her backward and pasting every sinew and muscle against her softer curves.

She stiffened, gasping against his mouth, then plummeted, deeply, irrevocably into the desire he'd unleashed. She scraped her palms up over the hard sinew of his arms, up over his wide shoulders to wind her hands around his neck.

She was dizzy with it. This hunger, this craving that made her loins ache and throb. Only him. Only Jake. No other man could turn her on with such astonishing power.

Margot shivered. She knocked his wig off and swept her fingers past his temple, running across the soft, spikes of his crew cut until she cupped the base of his skull.

It wasn't enough. She stroked over the column of his neck, widening the V in his shirt, snapping open the top two buttons in her hurry to feel the slope between his neck and shoulder, then down over his collarbone, all the while loving the texture and warmth of his skin against her fingers.

Margot pressed harder against his body, rolling her hips, feeling his arousal against her belly. She was weak with need, her skin feverish, her limbs and hands shaky, her heart thumping.

~~*~~

To Jake, Margot was pure heaven. He would never get enough—not until the day he died. Oh, God. Tonight could be the last time with her...

Darkness. He needed darkness. Turning slightly, he hit the button on the computer monitor and tossed the entire lab into a cloud of black. Hidden in the shadow of night, he could relax, be himself and not worry what Margot saw or perceived with his invisibility. Now he could let pure sensation take over.

Craving the feel of naked skin against her silken strands, Jake ripped the gloves impatiently from his hands and re-buried his fingers into her thick raven hair as he devoured her with his mouth. She tasted of coffee and peppermint. She smelled like sunshine, and was exactly what he'd always envisioned heaven to be.

Jake broke off, gasping. He scrapped his jaw over her cheek as he touched his brow to hers. "If I don't slow down now," he murmured against her temple. "I'm liable to have you on the floor in a second."

"So? That's where I'd like to be," she whispered by his ear, her breath and words sending shivers down his spine. "Under you, over you, around you."

"Margot..."

She didn't allow him to say more but pulled him back to her mouth, then splayed her hands against his chest before slipping the buttons of his shirt from their moorings. His stomach quivered at the way her hands glided over an invisible line above the waistband of his pants. Then she moved her fingers up over his nipples and chest to whisper across his rib cage and to the small of his back.

Jake tugged her sweater from around her waistband. He heard a rip but didn't care. He didn't care about anything but the moment, the feel of her, the taste of her. She helped him pull her shirt over her head. His palms touched skin, smooth, warm and silken.

Absolutely beautiful.

More clothes dropped to the floor, until they were naked in the middle of the lab now. He smelled the thick, musty scent of sex and desire. With one quick, sure movement, Jake swept the rest of the papers from the table. They whispered around them as they fluttered through the air and landed to the floor. He struggled to rein in his hunger, but with Margot he didn't have much self-control. Breath ragged, heart pounding, he edged her up against the table, gripped her tiny waist and lifted her up on its edge.

He nudged her legs apart with his thighs, while her hands glided across his waist to his butt where she flexed her fingers and urged him closer. For the briefest moment, his shaft shifted against her slick, wet heat. His breath caught against his throat. Then he exhaled in one quick rush. Cool air touched his damp brow. Easy. Slow.

Then one of her hands slipped along his hipbone to touch his cock with light, fleeting fingers. He ground his teeth. Damn it. When her fingers grew bolder, caressing and cupping him with both hands, his thin rope of self-control frayed and broke. Shivering, he thrust against her warm palm.

"I—" He inhaled again. "I love you."

Parting her thighs, he angled her hips higher, and with one sure stroke, he thrust into her. Her body, like a slick, hot glove contracted around him. Perfect. Not one woman would ever compare to her.

He bent over her until he pressed against her breasts, waist and hips, all soft, subtle and naked curves. As he licked and nibbled down her neck, she arched, threw her head back and shifted between the desk and his body. He loved her unabashed and passionate response and wanted to push so much higher. He lowered his mouth past her collarbone to her breast and lapped, suckled, then grazed his teeth against her nipple.

"Oh, God." She whimpered. Nails digging into his shoulders, she wrapped those incredible legs around his hips and urged him deeper, closer. "Jake, I can't think with the way—"

"Shhh. Don't think. Don't talk. Just feel. Feel the way I fill you up, move in and out of you, how you fit so tightly around me—

like you were made for me, for this moment. Perfect. Nothing else can be this perfect."

Jake groaned. She was so tight, so hot, so wet as she bucked beneath him, dragging him deeper and deeper. She was so damn good. With Margot, he could forget everything. She made him feel alive and fearless. He clasped her hips and rocked her harder, driving into her until her cry of release ripped through the lab. Only then did he come, burying deep into her, shuddering with the force of it.

After a long moment, he found his voice. "Are you all right?" he whispered. "I didn't hurt you, did I?"

"No." Her laugh sounded husky, sexy and totally satisfied.

Jake smiled and kissed the corner of her mouth. "Good."

They helped each other get dressed. When Margot slipped into her jacket, he brought the collar up to her chin and kissed her slowly, savoring the way she responded with slow, gentle kisses. He loved her femininity, her vulnerability. She made him feel invincible and so totally male.

The urge to pull her back into his arms was overwhelming, but instead, he stepped back and zipped up her jacket with hands that retained a distinct tremor.

"Let's get out of here," she urged. "I want you in my bed. I want to feel your arms around me all night."

This time it was his turn to laugh. "Try to keep me away."

When they reached the house, he opened the front door, followed her inside, and then swept her up in his arms. With the heel of his foot, he slammed the front door closed, carried her down the hall, up the stairs and into her room.

Tenderly, he eased her down on the bed. This time, when they made love, Jake savored every precious moment as if it were the last. And it could be. No. Not now. He couldn't, wouldn't think of that now. Then Margot took all thought from his mind as she straddled him and guided him into her. She bent forward, and her curtain of hair flowed over his shoulders and whispered across his face as she took his mouth in a deep, gut-wrenching kiss. She circled his wrists and pressed his hands up over his head as she moved above him with a sure, measured pace. He lost it then, giving into her and the hunger that raged inside of him.

When both were spent, she collapsed against him, and he turned to the side and pulled her back against his chest. Margot was so small against him, her hips delicate, her legs and arms smooth and shapely. He closed his eyes and cradled her tighter against his chest. He couldn't lose her. Not now.

"I love you," she whispered into the room. She touched his arm, then clasped his hand against her breast.

Closing his eyes, Jake pressed his brow against her hair. "I love you too," he said in an equally hushed voice.

He felt something wet against his cheek. Then he realized it was a tear—his tear. He'd never been so happy yet so filled with despair at the same time in his life.

~~*~~

Margot lay awake long after she heard Jake's slow, rhythmic breathing. He'd been asleep for some time now, but it wasn't a restful one. Every few minutes he would sigh and flinch in his sleep. His arm flung around her waist would tighten almost as if he feared of letting her go.

Tonight, she'd sensed Jake's desperation. It had been in his very touch, word and action. He was slipping from her grasp, both physically and emotionally, and there wasn't a damn thing she could do about it. To see this man lose the very passion for life that she loved the most about him broke her heart.

What was the point of living? What the hell was it all about? Was life some sick joke? Just when she thought it might hold meaning, learning about Jake's looming death smashed it to the ground. Margot didn't understand anything, and she didn't know if she wanted to anymore—not alone.

She couldn't lose Jake. Not now. Not when she'd just found him. She'd lost too many people in her life already—her parents, Johnny, even Malcolm or the man she'd mistaken him to be. Now there was Jake. If fate had her wish, another loved one would be ripped out of her life.

Margot closed her eyes against the tears and clamped down on the wave of panic drowning her. She couldn't lie here all night and do nothing. She'd only toss and turn, aggravating Jake's already fitful sleep.

Ever so gently, she slid Jake's arm from her waist and edged out of bed. She padded over to the chair where she'd thrown her clothes and quickly dressed. Once downstairs, she shrugged into her jacket, stuck her feet into a pair of boots and closed the front door softly behind her.

A half-moon and a thick splash of stars suspended in the night sky illuminated the path to the lab. The landscape was silent, calm and at odds with the turmoil churning through her insides. She shivered although the down jacket shielded her from the winter air.

Evening knowing Jake and Malcolm must have combed through the lab, she still felt compelled to do the same. Granted, she'd avoided searching Johnny's equipment and files until now. She hadn't had the stomach to deal with the painful reminders of his death.

Once inside the lab, Margot closed the door and snapped on the light switch by her shoulder. She avoided looking at the table where she'd made love with Jake hours before, knowing she'd just get emotional. She glanced over to the office doorway in the back and then to the cabinets lining the upper and lower right wall, but the hum of the refrigerator against the opposite wall drew her across the room.

She opened the refrigerator door and peered inside. A black case rested on the top shelf. She pulled a vial from its bed and turned the cool glass between her fingers. The clear liquid glittered against the refrigerator's interior light.

"Miracell," she whispered.

With the vial still in her hand, she closed the refrigerator just as the front door opened. Jake must have woken and seen the light coming from the barn.

"I take it you couldn't sleep either?" She turned around and froze.

"Sleep? Not a wink." Malcolm smiled. "I started to wonder if I'd ever get you alone."

He closed and locked the door.

CHAPTER 18

WHAT ARE YOU doing here?" Margot hated the way her voice quivered with fear. But then, she was afraid. He was supposed to be in jail or somewhere very far away.

Malcolm didn't answer but casually advanced toward her, the soles of his boots a menacing scrape against the linoleum floor.

She saw the very big, very threatening gun in his hand and tried not to panic. She edged backward, past the refrigerator toward the office at the back of the building. "You won't get away with it. If you shoot me, Jake will hear—"

"Exactly. He'll come running. Then I'll have to kill him. So if you don't want his death on your hands, I'd suggest you do what I ask."

His words didn't make her feel better. Actually, they magnified her panic and increased her urge to run that much more. But she couldn't get to the front door. Not with him smack in the middle of the way. And even if by some miracle she reached the office and locked the door before Malcolm shot her, she'd only get herself trapped inside four windowless walls. Then he only had to put a bullet in the lock to get at her.

But most importantly, if she acted rashly, she'd jeopardize Jake's life.

"What do you have there?" Malcolm pointed the gun at her hand as he closed the distance between them.

"Nothing." She closed a fist over the vial.

"Nice try. It's Miracell." He laughed, a harsh, guttural sound that lifted the hairs on the back of Margot's neck.

Suddenly, Malcolm lunged, grabbed her hand holding the formula, and started dragging her. Straining backward, digging her heels into the floor, Margot pried at his fingers. But all her struggles didn't seem to matter as he pulled her across the room.

She lifted her free hand to hit him in the face, but he shoved the gun barrel against her cheek and glared down at her.

"Touch me and I'll put a bullet in your face."

She stilled. His breath, smelling of fish and something harsh and acidic, washed over her face. She almost gagged.

"Do you understand?" He shoved the gun barrel harder into her skin.

"Yes," she whispered, not daring to nod or make any sudden movements as she slowly, ever so slowly lowered her hand.

"Good. We're going to walk over to the counter. That's right. You're doing good. Just a couple more feet."

Margot gritted her teeth and smothered the urge to retaliate as she docilely followed him. He let go of her hand but aimed the gun at her head the entire time he rifled through several drawers. He pulled out a packaged syringe.

Margot frowned. "What are you—"

"Shut up."

Another jab of the gun in her face.

She shut up.

"Now give me the Miracell."

She finally understood. Pure horror caught at her chest, and she reflexively tightened her hold on the vial. He planned to inject her with the formula.

"No."

"Oh, yes you will."

As he scraped the gun's barrel across her cheek and thrust it beneath her chin, he grabbed her hand with the vial, but Margot held onto the formula in a tight-fisted grip. If he thought she'd give in without a fight, he didn't know her, because she—

Margot gasped. His fingernails cut into her skin as he squeezed her wrist, slowly, relentlessly. With each ragged breath, with each frantic heartbeat, Margot doggedly held her ground and fought back the pain. Seconds now, and she knew her bones would snap with the pressure.

"You haven't changed a bit. Just as stubborn as ever." Malcolm shook his head, impatience flaring in his icy, blue eyes. "Do you want me to shoot you? Because I will if you don't give me the vial. And I won't stop until I go after Jake. Believe me, I'd enjoy killing him after the hell he's put me in."

His threats hung in the air between them. She swallowed, hating the whimper in the back of her throat, hating herself for playing the victim, and hating Malcolm.

Margot twisted her wrist, opened her hand and dropped the glass vial, but it didn't shatter against the floor as she'd intended. Malcolm caught the formula in mid-air. A smile of triumph lifted the corners of his lips, although his eyes remained as cold and ruthless as before.

She rubbed at her wrist, wincing as the blood flowed back into her hand. In minutes she'd be Malcolm's newest experiment. She thought of Jake and the torment he'd endured during his attacks. If she didn't do something, she'd find herself in the same excruciating situation. She didn't have Jake's strength. She'd never be able to endure that type of pain.

Panic bubbled up her throat. "Don't do this to me, Malcolm. You're making a big mistake. If you would just—"

"Don't bother. Nothing's going to change my mind. I want the completed formula of Miracell with its antidote. Jake needs to get motivated. Your life on the line—now that—that should get him moving in the right direction." Stepping back several feet, he placed the vial on the counter and waved the gun at her. "Okay. Now I want you to take off your jacket."

Margot took a shuddering breath and grappled for clarity. She needed her wits and a solution to get out of this nightmare.

Mind racing, unable to latch onto anything of value, she slowly shrugged out of her jacket.

As Malcolm reached for her coat, she jerked the garment back and whipped it against his gun hand. She sprang, shoving a shoulder against his chest. He stumbled back, both arms going up and outward for balance. She thought of going for the gun still in his hand, but at the last second changed her mind as the barrel swung her way. Instead, she pivoted and leaped around him toward the door and freedom.

She took two steps before Malcolm grabbed her from behind. He jerked her back against his chest by her hair. She cried out and frantically reached behind with both hands, grasping at air and little else. She heard the clatter of the gun and saw it fall only yards by her feet. Malcolm yanked harder, and tore the hair from her scalp and another cry from her lips, as he twisted her around to face him.

For several agonizing seconds, their ragged breathing filled the lab room. Blinking back tears of pain, she looked up at Malcolm's savage expression.

"I should have known you'd put up a fight. Even a gun doesn't stop you from acting up. Well, I'm done with your shit."

Malcolm pulled back his arm and smashed his fist into her face. Pain slammed across every nerve ending and vibrated through bone and muscle. Blinding white light flashed across her vision. Then nothing.

~~*~~

Malcolm swore under his breath as he dragged Margot's limp body across the floor. She was heavier than she looked, he realized in disgust. He propped her awkwardly up against one of the cabinets.

After unwrapping the syringe, he inserted the needle into the rubber cap of the vial and slowly withdrew Miracell into the syringe. When he emptied the vial, he pulled the needle from the stopper and tossed the vial on the floor. Finally, he pressed the syringe until a small, bulb formed on the needle's tip.

Hunching down on one knee by Margot's body, Malcolm

paused as he looked down into her face. Thick black lashes contrasted with the cool marble of her skin, while those lips of hers, dusty rose, thick and sensual, made a man think of hot, raunchy sex. The first time he saw her and met those huge doe eyes of hers, he'd been stunned at her beauty. He'd wanted her, and set out to get her.

At first, she hadn't disappointed him, but then she'd wanted more of him—more than he'd been willing to give.

Enough. Abruptly he thrust aside any lingering fondness for Margot and memories of their short and disastrous relationship. Sentiment would only weaken him.

He sank the needle through her skin by her inner elbow and watched as the liquid disappeared into her vein. She didn't move, but then Malcolm hadn't expected her to. He'd landed a pretty good right to her cheek. Even now the patch of broken blood vessels stained her skin into an ugly red.

She deserved it. Maybe she didn't deserve getting injected with Miracell, but oh, well. Life wasn't fair. He'd learned that even before he'd hit his teens.

When the last drop of Miracell emptied from the syringe, he withdrew the needle and watched a droplet of blood form in the hollow of her elbow. He thought about getting some gauze and taping it, but he didn't feel charitable. And anyway, he didn't have time to waste.

He'd love to hang around and watch Jake's reaction and the following drama, but Malcolm valued his life. For the next several days, he'd find a safe place to hide. But he'd be back. And when he did, if Jake hadn't figured a way to get the antidote together with Margot's life at stake, Malcolm knew even a miracle wouldn't work.

Either way, he needed to eliminate Jake and Margot and completely wipe clean any evidence of himself from the lab and house.

He tossed the syringe on the floor and gave Margot one final pat to her bruised cheek. "See you around." He chuckled at the irony. "Then again, maybe I won't."

~~*~~

The lab door slammed shut behind Jake.

He'd woken abruptly, unable to identify the cause, but something about the silence and Margot's absence drove him from bed. After seeing the lab's light from the bedroom window, he'd dressed quickly and hurried through the bitterly cold night to investigate, all the while unease following his every step.

Moving deeper into the lab, he didn't find anything odd. He took another step. That's when he saw her. Unconscious and deathly pale, Margot sat slumped against one of the cabinets against the right wall.

When he rushed to her side, Jake immediately noticed an angry welt in varying shades of red and blue across her cheek. It looked as if she'd been punched by someone. Falling to his knees, he checked her pulse by her neck and found it erratic.

What the hell had happened?

Then he saw the syringe on the floor, the vial of...Miracell.

"No—"

Jake couldn't believe it—didn't want to believe it.

With shaking hands, he brushed Margot's hair away from her cheek and brow. She didn't stir. Her brown sweater, its sleeve bunched up to her upper arm, exposing her inner elbow and the line of congealing blood snaking from a puncture wound to her skin. His stomach twisted. For a second he thought he might throw up.

Rising on unsteady legs, he fumbled around in the drawers for some antiseptic. He found a tube and several unopened packaged of square gauze. Clutching a corner of one package with his teeth, he tore off the top, spat the plastic out, and pulled the gauze from the package.

That's when he saw the taped note. Dropping the gauze, he tore the paper from a top cabinet and stared at the scrawled words.

"Like my present? Maybe now you'll get your ass in gear and finally discover the antidote."

Malcolm. The sick bastard.

Hatred rolled through Jake. Malcolm once claimed Jake didn't have it in him to kill, and Jake had agreed—until now. But now everything had changed. Jake would gladly step over that line. If they got through this alive, he'd go after Malcolm and seek total retribution.

First, he needed to focus on Margot and only Margot. He could not allow his anger to impair his judgment. She needed him.

"Where's Malcolm?"

At Margot's husky whisper, Jake swiveled on his heel. She sat on the floor against the counter, cradling her injured arm in her lap. Her brown eyes stared back at him with deep sadness, yet... her battered face held a stoic resignation. The expression cut at his heart. She knew exactly what Malcolm had done to her.

Crumpling the note in his hand, Jake found his voice. "I never saw him. You were alone when I came in."

"I'm not surprised. Malcolm's probably miles away now. He was always a coward."

When Margot struggled to rise, Jake tossed the note on the counter and hunkered down by her. He placed a gentle but restraining hand on her shoulder. "Don't get up. We need to take care of your arm."

Margot collapsed and rested her head against the cabinet. After cleaning the blood from her skin, he rummaged through the drawers and cabinets until he found some roller gauze and a pair of scissors. He gently pressed the padded dressing against her wound and wrapped the gauze three times around her elbow. Then he cut off the excess tape and placed both items on the counter.

When he turned back around, he found Margot again struggling to her feet. Dismayed, Jake caught her by the elbow. She fell against him, wrapped her arms around his waist and rested her head against his shoulder. He closed his eyes as the flowery scent of her hair washed over him, and for several minutes, he stood holding her, mired in guilt, feeling her slender frame tremble against him.

Jake wanted to tell her everything would be fine, that they'd work this out, but Margot didn't deserve his lies. She'd never asked for any of this. And because of him, she now had Miracell running through her system.

"I'm sorry." His apology sounded so useless, so hollow. "With what I now know, I would never have come here. I brought Malcolm with me. If only I'd made sure Malcolm couldn't get out from behind bars, you'd be fine. And if I'd stopped you from going to the lab—"

"Don't." Margot stepped back and out of his embrace. She frowned up at him. "Don't you dare start with 'what ifs'. No one's to blame but Malcolm."

"But why? And why you? It doesn't make sense."

"To Malcolm it does. He thought with Miracell in my system, you'd have the motivation to come up with an antidote."

"Why would he think that? I've worked day and night—every possible minute—and haven't been able to do it."

"You were getting to a point of not caring. Maybe Malcolm guessed that. I don't know. All I know is that you were giving up."

He clawed back his hair with one hand. "But I can't do any more than I already have... Don't you see that?"

"No." Margot stared up at him, her gaze unwavering. "You can do more. I know you can."

The enormity of Margot's situation hit him again. Closing his eyes, he rubbed at the bridge of his nose and took in several rapid breaths. "I need to think."

He was terrified. Until now, he really hadn't known fear, not really. One wrong decision on his part and he'd not only kill himself but he'd also kill Margot. Just the pressure of knowing her life lay in his hands could easily distort his judgment.

Jake opened his eyes. The love and trust he saw in Margot's face made him want to crawl into some dark, dank hole. He wasn't worthy of either emotion.

"Who do you think I am? Some type of god?" he asked in stunned disbelief. He shook his head. "I'm not. I'm just a man. Nothing more. I have as many strengths and weaknesses as the next one."

"Yes, you're a man. I know that. But to me you're so much more," Margot insisted. Her eyes misted with tears. "You're the man I love. And if anyone can find the answer to Miracell, it's you."

Something inside of him cracked. "You're putting too much faith in me."

"If I don't, then who will? You've lost all faith in yourself. That hope that's kept you going for so long is no longer there in your heart." She pressed her palm against his shirt and to the left of his chest. "I know that."

His throat contracted. What could he say? Everything she said was true. Every damn thing.

Suddenly, her face leached of color, and her hand dropped from his shirt. She wavered on her feet as if a violent wind had hit her blindly from the side. Then she crumbled.

"Margot!"

Jake swept an arm around her waist before she landed on the floor. The unexpectedness of her weight pulled him off balance. He stumbled, dropped to one knee but managed to hold her steady against his chest. Ever so careful, he slipped an arm around her shoulders. Her neck fell back against the crook of his elbow, exposing the long, white column of her throat. She lay in his arms, her complexion deathly pale and her thick, black lashes closed to the world.

She'd passed out.

~~*~~

Margot opened her eyes. She lay on her back in her bed with the covers pulled up to her chin. Dawn crept through the edges of the curtains and lit the room into a soft haze. For a moment she didn't know what had happened or how she'd ended up here. Then memory flooded back, painful and far too vivid in its intensity.

She must have fainted, and Jake had carried her back to her room. Oh, how she wanted to go back and erase the moments when she had walked into the lab, Malcolm had followed her inside and...what he had done. She shut her eyes against the knowledge.

Margot saw the ceiling. Impossible. Hadn't she just closed her eyes? She reopened them and saw the same ceiling. She did it two more times with no change. She could see the same thing with her eyes closed or opened.

Shock shoved her up into a sitting position. She lifted her hand. She couldn't see it. There was her sweater, the same exact garment she'd worn earlier, but now there wasn't anything at the end of the sleeve. Panic bubbled up into her chest as she looked harder for something—anything. She moved her palm back and forth.

Nothing.

Wait. There was something.

She detected movement, something indistinguishable but palpable. Almost like she saw through a pool of water or a distorted, magnifying glass where her hand should be. She brought her palm closer and extended her fingers. Yes. She wasn't mistaken. There was a distinct change in the background directly behind her hand.

Malcolm had accomplished what he had set out to do. She'd become invisible. Hard to believe, but the evidence was undeniable and right in front of her or she should say rather not in front of her.

Amazing. She could go anywhere, do anything, slip in and out of a room undetected. The power of it was mind-boggling.

"Pretty amazing, isn't it?"

Margot jerked in surprise and glanced over to where Jake's voice had come from. Even though the chair against the wall sat empty, she knew he was there.

"How did you know what I was thinking—"

"Because I did the same after the initial shock."

"Do you know what someone can do with this?" Margot asked in wonder, more to herself than anyone else.

"Oh, yeah. I know." The wood floor creaked, and the bed sank down by her hip. The aroma of coffee and Jake's scent, clean and male, drifted to her. "Miracles. But at the same time, that power holds a double-edged sword. In the wrong hands, it's deadly. Murder, theft, even war. How can you fight an enemy you can't see?"

"And Malcolm was the wrong person to have something of that magnitude in his hands. That's why you tried to stop him."

He laughed harshly. "Oh, yeah. It amplified everything

unhealthy in his psyche." He sighed and shifted on the bed. "But that's not important right now. What's important—is you. How are you feeling? You scared the hell out of me when you fainted like that."

"I'm fine—all things considered." She stared hard at where Jake sat. "You know, if I focus and concentrate, I can see your shape. It's like looking through water or curved glass. There's a faint distortion. Why is that, when I never noticed before?"

"Because you weren't looking. Remember? You were terrified. You couldn't get past that. Now you're letting your rational mind take over."

She nodded, then realized he couldn't see the movement. "That makes sense." She cleared her throat. "This is all so overwhelming. It's going to take some time to get used to."

Then Margot realized she didn't have time. Soon she'd start experiencing the same attacks as Jake. Then what? Did she have days, weeks? Clutching at the comforter, she bunched the padded fabric beneath her fingers. She'd always been afraid of living, of getting through the next day, but now she was terrified of dying.

"Don't you ever get scared?"

"Scared?" Jake sighed. "Of course. It's always in the back of my mind. Dying isn't something I expected. Not at my age anyway."

Until now, Margot had shamelessly concentrated on her own problems and failed to recognize just how traumatic Jake's own life had turned out since he left Boston. She realized he needed as much encouragement, probably even more than herself.

"It's not going to come to that." Margot's voice strengthened with conviction. "You *will* find the antidote, and both of us *will* make it. I know you can beat Malcolm at this sick game of his. I just know you will."

"How can you say that?" he asked, his words thick and husky with amazement. "I don't understand how you can have so much faith in me."

Margot reached over and found his hand against the comforter. She squeezed his fingers. "Why is it so hard for you to accept that you're up to doing this? You mentioned your parents. Is that why you don't believe in yourself?"

"My parents?" She heard his surprise. "I don't know. There's not much to say about them. They were too busy with their careers to pay attention to either Kim or me. They really didn't know what to do with either one of us.

"Looking back, I haven't a clue why they even had us other than it was the thing to do. Family, children, a house—whatever the American dream was at that time. We were both in the way. At least, I know I'd always felt that way growing up. On occasion, they'd take us out and show us off if we were well enough behaved. But only if it made them look good and fit into their plans."

"That's sad," she murmured, stroking a thumb along the back of his hand.

"What about your parents? I can't imagine them not doting on you. You must have been adorable as a child. Frilly dresses, pigtails and curls." There was a smile in his voice. "I wouldn't be surprised if you had a freckle or two."

She had to laugh at the image. "Hardly. I was a pest. I followed Johnny everywhere he went and tried to act like the typical tomboy, but I wasn't very good at it. I'd climb a tree, get stuck and ball my eyes out until my brother managed to get me down. Another time while we were on vacation on the coast, I followed Johnny without him knowing. I got lost in the process, and my parents had to call in a search party to find me. Let's just say, I was far from the perfect child."

"But they loved you anyway."

She heard the question in Jake's words but really didn't know how to answer. It didn't bring back the best of memories.

"I guess they did in their own way." She released his hand and brushed at an imaginary speck of dirt on the comforter by her knee. "I was the black sheep, while Johnny was their golden child. The minute they found out he had a head for math, they could relate to him on such a deeper level. You see, they were both scientists. My mother worked at the University for cancer research, while my father headed the department for leukemia at Phoenix's children's hospital. While me, I was just trying to fit in."

"That must have hurt—them playing favorites. It would be pretty hard not to resent your brother. At least with my sister and I, our parents treated us with the same indifference."

"Surprisingly, sibling rivalry wasn't an issue. No one could stay angry with Johnny for long, including me. He had such a giving personality." Talking about her brother brought back memories, fond but painful nonetheless.

He cupped her knee over the comforter and rubbed down to her ankle. "Sorry. I didn't mean to bring you down more than you already are."

"Don't worry about it. Maybe one day talking about Johnny won't be so hard, but right now it still—you know, hurts? But my parents—I guess I can say that I've come to terms with what little relationship I had with them."

"What about now? Do you have a lot of contact with them?"

"They died in a boating accident when I was in my late teens. Then it was Johnny and me. We were probably closer than most siblings because it was just the two of us. That is, until the last couple of years. That's when he became so deeply involved with Miltronics. He refused to talk about the company or anything involving it."

"Because he wanted to protect you."

"You're probably right." Sighing, she glanced over to the window. The sun had mounted further in the sky, spearing its golden rays between the drapes and the window frame. Minutes passed. Time was hell-bent on moving forward.

The phone started ringing.

"Do you want me to get it?"

"No. Just let it ring. It's the personal line in the kitchen. I can't imagine it would be anything important."

As they waited in silence for the phone to stop, Margot's anxiety rose, while tension pinched the muscles across her shoulders and the back of her neck. The gravity of their situation became all too apparent.

"How far along are you in finding an antidote?" she felt compelled to ask.

"I've gotten to the point where I've stopped the cells from mutating. Now I have to reverse the process."

"It sounds simple." She uttered the words with an attempt of humor.

"Sounding simple and being simple are not one and the same."

"Well, I have every confidence that you'll find the answer!" She fumbled around on the comforter until she found his hand.

"And pray to God or Fate to be benevolent." He entwined his fingers with hers and squeezed her hand briefly. The bed shifted as he rose. "I'll let you get some rest. You'll be weak for a couple of days. Eventually, your strength will bounce back. At least for a while. But after—" His voice turned harsh. "It's not going to come to that. I'll make damn sure of it. I'll find that antidote, sooner than you think. But I'm wasting time. I'll be down at the lab if you need me."

Jake's lips brushed across her brow and cheek. Then the absence of his scent—she swore it was Irish Spring soap—told her that he'd left the room.

She lay back down on the bed and stared up at the ceiling. Almost one hour later, Margot realized the pure craziness of trying to get any rest during the day. With her eyes closed, nothing changed. She still saw the dresser, the drapes, even the framed landscape against the opposite wall with the same exacting detail as if her lids were wide open. The sensation—far too odd for Margot—wasn't exactly conducive for rest.

After quickly showering, she spent an inordinately long time in the bathroom getting ready before heading downstairs to search for the disk. Things had to start changing for the better. They just had to!

But by the end of the day, Margot wanted to scream with frustration as she searched throughout her office. She rammed the last book back on the shelf. Other than tearing up the floorboards, she'd gone through every book, every piece of furniture and every centimeter of the room.

She walked over and peered out from the large bay window but couldn't see the lab from this room. The building rested on the bottom of the hill and to the west. Elongated shadows trailed from the pines and aspen and hugged the sides of the snow-covered slopes. It was getting late, near sunset.

She looked over to the clock on the mantel. Almost 5:30. Exhaling loudly, she shoved her hands on her hips and eyed the room in disgust. There were the other rooms still to go through, but for some reason she'd counted on finding something here. Obviously, it had been all wishful thinking on her part.

"This is crazy!"

"I take it you haven't found anything?"

She glanced up and saw that Jake had walked into the room. He was fully clothed, or should she say armored, with wig, gloves, sunglasses and foundation. After today, she'd come to realize he didn't use all those props for the simple reason of a disguise. It was more than that. It was vanity and the struggle to build a battered self-esteem. It was a way to hide from the overwhelming reality of a physical appearance that was both disquieting and unnatural.

That's why when she'd glanced in the bathroom mirror that morning she'd gone directly to her make-up case. A pair of sunglasses, lipstick, foundation, eyebrow pencil and a number of other cosmetic tools had helped her look somewhat human. She had some hair color tucked away in the cabinet, but hadn't bothered with it yet. The scarf wrapped around her head would have to be a temporary fix.

Granted, she would never pull it off in the bright light of day, but at night or in a dark room, she might fool someone.

She sighed. "I haven't found anything yet. But I've only touched on this room. I've still got many hours ahead of me. What about you? Are you getting any closer?"

"I might have something in several days."

"Oh, Jake! That's fantastic!" She rushed over and hugged him fiercely.

"Yeah..." he murmured above her ear.

She inched far back enough to look up at his face. "You don't sound too confident. What's wrong?"

"I have to run the antidote through a couple of tests first."

"That shouldn't be too much of a problem, should it?" She didn't like how he pulled away and shrugged. "You're not talking about testing on yourself, are you?" She paused. "But you are, aren't you?"

"Yeah. I don't have anything else to test it on, so it's going to have to be on me."

"I could always—"

"Don't even suggest it. It's too dangerous. This is my baby and my battle."

"No, Jake. It's both of ours. I am just as involved now as you are."

He grunted.

"There's really no other option but to have you test it on me."

He cut the air with a gloved hand. "Damn it! There's no way in hell that I'm going to use you as some lab rat. What do you think I am? Crazy?"

"You're going to have to. If you experiment on yourself, what happens if something goes wrong? I haven't a clue what to do. It's way out of my element. While you know every nuance of Miracell and the antidote you're working on. Don't you see? You're the key here. We both need you clear-headed and physically able. There's no other way."

Silence. She knew she had him.

"We'll see. I'm not making any promises."

Margot knew it was just a matter of time until he saw that she was absolutely right.

The doorbell chimed.

Jake swore under his breath. "Who the hell could that be?"

Frowning, Margot hurried into the kitchen with Jake right behind. She stopped at the window above the sink and looked outside. She didn't dare pull back the drapes—whoever was outside might to see.

"Do you recognize the car?" Jake asked from beside her.

Margot saw the Land Cruiser parked alongside her own.

"Joyce's," Margot whispered as she pressed up harder against the counter and craned her neck to peer down the porch to the front door. She managed to see the back edge of a beige jacket but nothing else. "It looks like she's alone."

"Do you think she'll go away?" Jake asked in a hushed tone from beside her.

The doorbell rang again.

"Maybe."

Pounding followed soon after.

Margot groaned. "Then again, maybe not."

The pounding became more insistent. Joyce's voice carried from outside. "Margot, I know you're in there. Open up. It's me. Joyce."

"She sees my car. She knows I don't go anywhere without it."

"Well, you can't open that door now. One look at you in this light and she'll flip out. That scarf around your head sure as hell isn't going to help. You look like a chemotherapy victim with it on."

"Tell me something I don't already know. And thank you for such warm encouragement." Sarcasm laced each syllable. "It does wonders for my self-confidence."

"You're welcome," Jake replied shamelessly. He shifted closer and placed a comforting hand over her shoulder. "She'll leave. Just give her some time. She doesn't know for sure if you're inside."

Several minutes later, Joyce retreated down the stairs and to her car. They both sighed with relief. After a moment, her car reversed out of the drive, and down the road to disappear behind a long stand of trees.

"Well, at least we don't have to worry about her now. You're safe."

Margot mused darkly, "Don't count on it. She's a good friend. If she thinks something's wrong, she's not likely to drop it. You have to remember this is a small town. People don't mind their own business. They stick their noses in where they don't belong."

An hour later, Margot was proven correct when the phone rang. In the kitchen, Margot picked up the receiver on the second ring.

"Oh, hi, Joyce." She watched Jake step into the room.

"Thank goodness!" Joyce said in obvious relief. "I got worried when you didn't answer the door. I saw your car and knew you had to be home. Are you all right?" Joyce asked.

"I'm fine. I guess I was in the shower when you came by. Sorry, I missed you."

Jake walked over and leaned a hip against the kitchen counter beside her.

"That's okay," Joyce said. "I'll just come back. I want to see how you're doing."

"Right now wouldn't be a good time. I'm swamped with work. How about later in the week?"

"I'd prefer to come over now. You don't sound yourself," Joyce said, doubt clearly in her voice.

"I don't think tonight's a good idea," Margot repeated in frustration as Jake, frowning, edged closer to her.

"Well, I've got this book I've been meaning to return to you."

"No, you don't want to do that. It's too late in the day. Joyce—"

At the unexpected dial tone, Margot pulled the phone from her ear and stared back at Jake in alarm.

He took the receiver from her hand and placed it in the phone's cradle. "What happened?"

"She's coming over. She said something about a book she had to return. What am I going to do? If I don't talk to her, she's going to wonder what's going on. She's already suspicious."

"Well, you're just going to have to talk to her. That's all."

"There's no way she's going to buy into my appearance. Not like this." Margot waved a hand at her head.

Jake stepped further away, his frown deepening. "Do you have any hair color?"

"I've got enough for one application."

He grabbed her hand. "Well, let's get moving. We don't have much time. If we're quick enough, we just might pull it off."

He dragged her up the stairs, and before she knew it he had her head under the sink.

Over a half hour later they were downstairs. In the kitchen,

Margot snapped on the fluorescent light above the sink and another one above the kitchen table and then turned to Jake.

"So what do you think? Will I do?"

"Turn around."

She arched a brow but complied.

"Here, you've missed a place." After rubbing a spot on the side of her throat, he brought a few strands of her hair forward. "That should do it. Just make sure you have your ears covered."

"Bossy, aren't we?"

"And, of course, you aren't."

She made a face and plopped down on a kitchen chair. "Why didn't you color your hair? I'd think it would be a lot easier than a wig."

"Survival." When she frowned, he explained. "Any time I needed to escape a situation, I'd just take off the clothes and wig and vanish. I can't with dyed hair."

Margot wondered how many times he'd had to do just that. To think of what a person could do...

Jake must have guessed her thoughts. "It's not worth it. The advantages of being invisible don't compare to the horror of it all."

The raw emotion in Jake's voice caught at her heart. Until now, Margot hadn't comprehended just how invisibility crippled one's life. Why just the thought of seeing Joyce and hiding such a secret sent her nerves flying.

She inhaled and exhaled slowly, which didn't do a thing to ease her anxiety. "I feel like I'm at an opening for a Broadway play and I haven't rehearsed a single line."

Jake joined her at the table. "You'll do fine."

She nodded sharply and drummed her fingers impatiently against the table. "I have to. If Joyce gets wind of what's going on, I don't know what she'll do. Her brother was killed because of this. She'll go to the police. She'll start screaming until someone hears her. She'll do exactly the thing you *don't* want. She'll have Miracell broadcasted to the world."

"You're speculating. Don't."

The doorbell chimed.

Margot grunted. Her stomach did a crazy flip. "How the heck am I going to pull this off?

"I'll repeat something someone told me a little while back. That someone is a person I love and admire."

"And what's that?"

"'I have every confidence in you.'"

She couldn't help but smile at how he'd repeated her own words to him. Those very words and his confidence tapped down on her spinning stomach.

"Here we go." She rose. "Any last suggestions?"

"Just keep in the shadows, and, whatever you do, don't smile. I don't have an extra set of caps for your teeth."

"Thanks," she muttered under her breath and snapped off the fluorescent light above the sink. She left the other on, hoping the low wattage would create enough shadows to hide the oddness of her appearance.

Margot walked into the hall and opened the door.

CHAPTER 19

"Hi, Joyce."

Her friend stepped into the foyer and closed the door. "I brought that book I mentioned on the phone. You know, the one I borrowed. I never realized I still had it until a couple of days ago. I think it's that cookbook you'd mentioned to Mark at the Hideaway."

Margot took the proffered book and looked down at the cover. Despite the darkness, she managed to make out the title. "Oh, yes. The dumplings. Johnny's favorite recipe."

Joyce started to shrug out of her jacket but paused. "What's with the sunglasses?"

"The glasses?"

"Yes, the glasses. Here. It's dark in here." She stepped over and flipped on the hall's light switch.

Nothing happened. Margot hadn't gotten around to changing the light.

"Well, shoot." Joyce turned back to her and frowned. "Have you been drinking? Is that why you're wearing them? Because of a hangover?"

"I might have had one or two," Margot lied. At this point, she'd say anything to keep Joyce from suspecting the truth.

"I knew something was wrong! You were acting so strange on the phone."

"Is that why you came over? To check on me?" She straightened and pointed the book at Joyce. "I'm a big girl—old enough to take care of myself."

"Well, if you ask me, you haven't been taking care of yourself for some time." She must have sensed Margot's irritation, because she backtracked. "Okay. Fine. I'll leave you alone."

"Thank you."

"Yes, well—you're wearing gloves!" She grabbed Margot's free hand and lifted it toward the kitchen light. "Why? What's going on? The glasses and now the gloves. You're scaring me."

Margot snatched back her hand. "I was getting ready to go outside to see if I'd locked up the lab."

"Since when do you start locking up around here?"

"Oh, come off it. Will you listen to yourself? You're sounding paranoid." Margot sighed. "And if you must know, I started doing it after the last time Malcolm showed up."

"Oh." Joyce's laugh sounded awkward. "I guess I'm just worried. You haven't been the same since Johnny's death. Plus, you're out here all alone."

"I seem to remember we had this conversation before. Remember? I've lived out here by myself before Johnny died. Nothing's changed."

Margot placed the cookbook on the mahogany table against the hall wall. When she turned back around, she found Joyce still frowning. "Will you stop worrying? I'm fine. Why don't you take care of yourself for a change? You've had just as bad a time as me with your own brother's death." Margot started to bite her lip but stopped just in time. "They haven't found the killer, have they?"

Joyce's shoulders dipped. "Nothing. There just doesn't seem to be any motive."

"I'm really sorry. Seriously, let me know if you ever need anything. How about we talk next week? Maybe have dinner together?" If she was still around and breathing, Margot thought darkly to herself. "It's just right now isn't a good time. This is probably the busiest time of year for me."

Placing an arm around Joyce's shoulders, she urged her friend back to the front door. Margot knew she was being grossly unfair and apathetic about her friend's loss, but she was terrified. With every passing minute together the chance of discovery escalated. One slip on her part and Joyce would have the shock of her life.

"Fine," Joyce agreed, "but only if you promise to take care of yourself?"

"Of course."

Suddenly, Joyce hugged her, brushing up against Margot's hair and face. As Joyce pulled away, Margot fought off the urge to touch her cheek, and instead, pulled her hair quickly forward and prayed her foundation hadn't smudged off.

Joyce zipped up her jacket and opened the front door. But before she left, she turned back around. "How's your renter?"

Margot's sigh of relief caught against the back of her throat. "I'm not sure," she lied. "He's been gone for the last a couple of days."

"So I don't get a chance to meet your mystery renter?"

"Maybe next time."

"Oh."

She didn't know if she'd convinced Joyce. Shadows both had their benefits and drawbacks. "I'll see you later in the week. Drive carefully."

"I will."

Then Joyce walked outside, down the steps and slipped into her Land Cruiser. When she had backed out of the drive, Margot shut and locked the door, and exhaled in relief.

Talk about nerve-wracking. Margot couldn't handle many more of these types of encounters. Not unless she wanted to end up dead from a heart attack—that is—if the formula didn't kill her first. Tonight, her meeting with Joyce might have gone in a completely different direction. She'd been lucky. But what of next time? Eventually she would need groceries or gas for her car. What if she came face to face with someone else during the day? She might not be so lucky then.

Margot pivoted and nearly screamed. A dark shadow, tall and massive, stood a little over three feet away from her.

"Jake! Geeze!" She slapped her hand against her chest. "Are you trying to scare me to death? I didn't even hear you!"

"Sorry," he said in a somewhat sheepish voice. "Habit. Keeping quiet became somewhat of a survival tactic. Half the time I don't even know I'm doing it."

For his sake, Margot didn't ask why. She knew he'd been in his own hell with no one to trust or turn to, and the last thing she wanted to do was bring those memories back for him.

So instead, she asked, "So what do you think? Did I pull it off?

"You were wonderful. I couldn't have done any better. And even if Joyce is suspicious, she's probably way off base."

"You're right." She nodded toward the cookbook on the table. "I knew she didn't come by just because of that."

Margot stared at the book that sat innocently on the glossy wood surface. She frowned. Maybe that innocent, little cookbook wasn't so harmless.

"Could it be? Do you think?" Excitement bubbled into her voice. "It makes so much sense. Johnny knew about that book. He saw me use it many a time. He could have hidden the disk between the pages. While we've been hunting everywhere in the house, I bet it's been there all along!"

She snatched the book from the table, rushed into the kitchen with Jake right behind her, and flipped on the fluorescent light above the sink. She set the book on the counter.

"Don't you think Joyce would have found it? A disk would be pretty hard to miss."

"Not if she wasn't looking for it. Plus, it might be camou-flaged in some way," she argued, not wanting to listen to reason.

Carefully, meticulously, she turned each page, mindful of the thick cardboard dividers between each food or dish category. Each separator had a front and back pocket to it for notes or loose recipes. As she checked each pocket, she felt Jake right beside her. Even though he'd sounded unconvinced, she could feel his tension just as tightly strung as her own.

"It's got to be here," she insisted. "This would be the only logical place for Johnny to hide it."

But the closer she reached the end of the cookbook, the more her excitement and hope deteriorated. She flipped over the last page and turned up nothing.

"I thought for sure—" Disappointment severed the last of her words.

"Shhh," Jake whispered against her ear, wrapped both arms around her waist and pulled her back up against his chest. "We're going to be all right. Hey, where's that optimism of yours? You've been the one pulling me through. Don't stop now. I need you right now."

Turning within his embrace, she rested a cheek against the warm, flannel of his shirt and nodded. "You're right. I'd just hoped... I guess it doesn't matter. There's always tomorrow. And you can never tell what that'll bring. After all, miracles do happen."

"Yes, they do." He slid his hand along the small of her back and brushed his lips across her temple. "We just have to remember that no matter what."

"And it just might happen real soon. You said yourself that you're only a couple of days from perfecting the antidote. Right?"

~~*~~

"That's right."

But Jake failed to mention he was ahead of schedule and would probably have everything in place by tomorrow night. Only a couple of more tests remained to ensure the accuracy of his equations. Then after that, he'd find out whether or not his hard work had paid off. But he didn't plan to tell Margot that. He knew if he said anything now, she'd be right in his face with the crazy idea of having him test the formula on her, and there was no way he'd let her be some lab rat. He couldn't—wouldn't—allow it. He wasn't about to play Russian roulette with her life.

But wasn't he?

By going ahead and testing the antidote on himself, he, in turn, jeopardized Margot's life. If his body rejected the serum and he died, he'd be leaving Margot alone to deal with her own certain death. Jake took a shuddering breath. They were screwed either way.

"It's getting late." He snapped off the fluorescent light above the kitchen counter. "We both need to get some rest. We're going to need all our wits in the next couple of days."

They left the cookbook on the kitchen counter and hand in hand slipped up the stairs to her room.

Tomorrow. Dread burrowed deep in his gut. It might be the beginning of a bright, promising future or no future at all.

The next day, several hours after the sun had lowered past the horizon, Jake injected the finished serum into his vein. In seconds it would mix into his blood stream, and then—then it would be anyone's guess as to how long it would take before he saw visible results.

He'd been praying like he'd never been praying in his entire life. Jaw clenched, he watched the last drop disappear, then retracted the needle and set the syringe on the table in front of him. He grabbed a square gauze and wrapped his arm. It was done. Now he needed to wait.

He heard the soft click of the lab door behind him. Casually, he pulled his sleeve down to his wrist, hiding the bandage and tape around his arm. Just as casually, he dropped the syringe into the wastebasket beneath the table by his feet.

He turned. Margot. She'd slipped on a jacket and gloves. Foundation covered her neck and facial features, while sunglasses hid her eyes. Times like now, he was hard pressed to imagine Miracell running through her veins beneath all that make-up and clothing.

Damn, but he loved her. His throat tightened. This wasn't something fleeting. What he felt for Margot was more than passion, more than a simple infatuation. It had substance. If things weren't so messed up, he'd have asked her to marry him. Children, a house, growing old together—he'd want it all. But only with Margot. Maybe, just maybe, it might happen if God or fate had a compassionate hand. And of course, if he could convince Margot he was worth the risk.

"So?"

Jake sensed her trepidation even from where he stood. He knew exactly what she was asking, but the lie caught on his tongue.

She took a hesitant step forward. "Have you…"

"Tomorrow. I'll know for sure tomorrow." It was the truth.

Margot hurried over and slipped her arms around his waist and rested a cheek against his chest. "That's fantastic!" She tightened her hold around his waist. "Oh, Jake. I knew you'd do it. I just knew it!"

"Whoa." He pulled back and tapped his finger lightly against her nose. Her excitement, her unbelievable faith in him, made Jake feel that much more of a jerk for deceiving her. "It's not a done deal yet."

She backed up and tugged at his hands, urging him along with her. "Well, you've more than earned a break. How about you pack it in for the night, and I give you a little something for all that hard work?"

The suggestive tone and the deep, husky throb of her voice did amazing things to his body, particular one area below his belt.

"And in exchange, how about I give you a big something?" he teased, letting her lead him from the lab.

"I'm counting on it!"

He smiled. He loved her humor; he loved everything about her.

They reached the house but not without a few delays. He hadn't been able to resist one or two deep, passionate kisses on the way. What sane man could?

Margot closed and locked the front door behind them, while Jake rubbed at his hands. He shivered. Even though he knew the house was warm, he couldn't get rid of the chill. It went too deep, seeping past his skin and muscle to scrape across the bone.

He glanced down the lit hall. Suddenly, the walls, the ceiling, the floor tilted, then wavered as if a thick, heat-wave coiled from the ground. Frowning, he blinked and found everything normal. Strange. This was nothing like his previous attacks.

"Is something wrong?"

"I'm fine."

"Are you sure?"

"Positive." Jake grinned down at her, wiping the concern from her upturned features.

He caught her hand, entwined his fingers between hers and urged her toward his bedroom. He took two steps and felt the floor buck beneath him or was it just his legs giving out beneath him? He couldn't tell. His body felt disconnected from his mind as his peripheral vision blurred, then blackened. He shook his head again, which was a mistake. Another dizzy spell, far worse than the last, crashed against his skull.

He faltered and felt Margot's clasp on his hand tighten.

"Jake?"

He glanced down at Margot. He didn't think he could pass this off as nothing. "I think I'm in trouble."

"What's wrong?"

Jake heard the alarm in her voice but couldn't respond. He felt the attack coming this time, like some huge tidal wave ready to explode against the shore. Absolutely nothing could stop it. Dropping his hand from hers, he reeled down the hall to his room.

The attack hit him sooner than he wanted. Hard. The pain, savage, all pervasive, cut through his chest, slashing into his insides and limbs. The power of it snatched the breath from his lungs.

He stumbled at the room's threshold and latched onto the doorframe before he fell flat on his face. He saw the bed just ten feet away, but somehow the distance felt like miles. If he could just get across the floor without falling...

"Jake!"

He tried to answer, tried to let Margot know he'd heard, but he couldn't open his mouth, couldn't even form a syllable. His jaw felt sutured shut.

"Jake!"

Whimpering, he pushed off the doorframe and lunged for the bed, hoping like hell he didn't crack his skull against the floor before he got there. He hit the mattress face down, twisted sideways, and curled into a ball in an effort to ward off the pain. He didn't think he'd ride through this attack. Not this time.

CHAPTER 20

MARGOT WATCHED IN horror as Jake convulsed on the bed. She rushed over and touched his shoulder. The heat of his skin seared through the fabric of his shirt and into her palm. He burned with fever. Knowing she needed to get his temperature down and quickly, she fled the bedroom and came back with several cold, wet towels.

Jake was still curled up on his side but had stopped shaking. His sudden stillness pulled her into a panic. Swallowing down a hysterical sob, she hurried over to the bed and stared down at his chest. She saw movement. Thank God. He'd passed out. At least that's what she hoped. She couldn't really tell.

This was insane. How could she help someone she couldn't even see?

After easing Jake onto his back, she unbuttoned his shirt and struggled to get his arms out of the sleeves. As she pulled the material from beneath his body, a seam ripped at the shoulder. Swearing under her breath, she crumbled the garment in one hand and tossed it on the chair against the wall. That's when she noticed the bandage. Frowning, she groped across the bed for Jake's hand and slid a palm up over his forearm until she reached the gauze at his elbow.

"No!"

Margot dropped down on the edge of the bed. She didn't want

to believe it, but the evidence was undeniable. Jake had injected himself with the antidote. The crazy fool. He'd done it without talking to her first. Tears of anger and fear welled in her eyes.

Why hadn't he talked to her? Didn't he trust her enough? Did he think she was incapable of the truth? That she couldn't handle the possibility of his death?

The idea that Jake might not live through the night shot her off the bed and onto her feet. No. She wouldn't think that way. Instead, she needed to concentrate on getting his fever down. Granted it might not do a damn thing, but doing nothing wasn't an option.

She couldn't call for an ambulance. Even if the police, the media or the general chaos Jake would cause at the hospital weren't factors enough, his condition, something beyond any doctor's scope of experience would set all records.

After she rushed to the kitchen, she came back with a bucket of ice. Stepping into the room, she almost dropped the copper pot on the floor at the high keening coming from Jake. Shivers raced up her arms and spine as she watched him wreathing on the bed. So much pain. She bit down hard on her lip. If he kept this up, he was liable to get hurt. She might have no other option but to tie him down.

Margot placed the bucket on the nightstand and dropped a handful of ice into an already damp towel. She bundled the cubes up inside and placed it across Jake's brow. She did the same with another towel and dabbed his shoulders, chest and stomach. Slipping her fingers beneath his wig, she pulled the thing off and flung it on the chair with his shirt.

She hadn't a clue when the quaking subsided. Minutes, hours all blurred into one. Searching blindly across the bed, she found Jake's wrist and a pulse, steady against her fingers, but she didn't have the medical background to read anything into it other than he was alive. Knowing she couldn't do much more than she already had, Margot, too tired to battle with her clothes, left them on and crawled in bed with Jake. She slid up behind him, rested a cheek against his naked back, and wrapped an arm around his waist.

Every person who had held any great meaning in her life was dead—except Jake. But that might change in the morning. *Oh please, God, don't take him from me, not when I just found him.*

Exhaustion forced her lids closed. Seconds later, she snapped them back open. She felt like she'd wiped her eyes against Marmaduke's fur and overdosed on cough medicine. As the clock down stairs chimed two, then three, Margot battled against falling asleep, but time and her bone-weary body were too tenacious and sleep eventually won.

Margot woke up to silence, light and warmth. She found herself still curled up behind Jake with an arm flung over his middle. For several long moments, she didn't move, too surprised to do anything but stare.

Slipping her arm from around his waist, she eased backward and placed a trembling palm across the muscle and sinew of Jake's back. The warmth of his skin seeped into her palm. The feel of his flesh against her own wasn't what amazed her, but rather the way the morning light touched his back, which illuminated the texture of his skin, the fine pores and hairs, the indentations across a strong spine. This wasn't foundation, make-up, camouflage, or what have you. It was real and undeniably visible flesh.

"Jake."

He sighed but didn't stir.

"Jake!"

Jerking up onto an elbow, she pulled on his shoulder. He grunted a response and buried his head deeper into his pillow.

"You've got to see this!"

She dug her nails into his shoulder and put all her weight into shaking him.

Jack-knifing into a sitting position, Jake grabbed his head with one hand and frowned down at her. "What?"

Margot smiled, loving the way he looked—sleepy, grumpy, but most importantly healthy.

"Look!"

She whipped the top sheet off both of them and found herself momentarily diverted at the sight of his naked chest.

He looked good. Long legs encased in low slung, faded jeans, narrow hips, a flat belly free of excess fat, and a chest thick with muscle. Nothing about him was effeminate. Especially when it came to what rested below his waist.

Jake thrust both hands in front of him, rotating his wrists back and forth as he stared at them.

"Do you know what this means?" he whispered in awe.

"A miracle."

"Yeah..."

"How are you feeling?"

He flexed his fingers and rolled his shoulders. "My joints are a little stiff, and there's a bit of tenderness to my muscles, but everything feels like it's functioning."

Abruptly, Jake swiveled and pushed her deep into the mattress with the warmth and hardness of his body. He kissed each curve and corner of her lips with his own, slowly, softly. Drawing back, he looked down at her with a crooked grin on his face. And his eyes. Oh, my. They were a beautiful blue, the color of an ocean with the morning sun shimmering across its surface. Margot thought she'd never see their color.

"It worked." He laughed, a deep rumble of pure pleasure. "Who would have thought?"

He kissed her again, this time hard and quick, and then rubbed a thumb along her lower lip. "You look a little smeared."

Margot touched her face and looked down at her palm where foundation clung to the tips of her fingers. She smiled ruefully. "I feel a little smeared."

With the flats of his hands on either side of her, Jake pushed off the bed.

"Come on!" She watched Jake's backside with interest as he rummaged in the dresser drawer.

"Why?"

"You have to ask *why*?" he asked in obvious amazement as he dashed to the closet and grabbed a shirt from the hanger. After he stuffed both arms into the sleeves, he paused and lifted his brows. "Because we have important things to do! We've got to get that antidote inside you." Grabbing her hand, Jake hauled her from the bed and playfully smacked her on her butt. "And the time isn't any better than now."

"And here I thought you were going to get a little frisky on me."

"Oh, believe me. I will. The minute you're back to your old self, I'll be on you like superglue. And that's a promise."

Margot cocked a brow and rubbed her bottom. She loved that grin of his. "Then let's get going, lazybones!"

~~*~~

That afternoon, Jake, his legs stretched out in front of him as he sat in one of the chairs, watched Margot move restlessly from one place to another in her office. She stopped at the window, and the only reason he knew that was because she'd slipped on a thick velour housecoat after her shower.

He was so proud of her. She'd been so brave, even though he suspected she must have been terrified from the moment they'd stepped into the lab. But she hadn't been the only one terrified. He'd been hovering over her since the moment he'd injected Miracell's antidote into her system.

Jake knew she was hurting. Maybe not half as bad as he'd experienced because his own system had been so tenuous, but the pain still lingered. He watched helplessly as she suffered through it silently. At first, she'd wanted to lie down, but she'd found the lack of movement only exasperated the pain. Then she'd taken a cold shower to ease the burning. While now, she'd grown restless, pacing first the kitchen and now this room.

"Why didn't you tell me?" she asked suddenly, hurt and reproach in her voice. "Why did you go ahead and test the antidote on yourself before coming to me? I thought we'd had an agreement."

"'You' had the agreement."

"And you didn't, because you couldn't trust me."

He rubbed at the bridge of his nose even though prepared for this. "That's not true. I trust you."

"Do you? Do you really?" The drape fluttered, and she moved to the other side of the window. "I don't know if that's the truth."

"Why?"

"Because you made a huge decision without talking to me first. Obviously, you didn't think my opinion had any importance."

"Damn it, Margot. I couldn't risk your life."

"It was already at risk."

"I know that, but—"

"But you still lied—by omission. Deep down, it's just as bad."

"I'll admit you have a point, but can you honestly tell me you wouldn't have down the same?" In frustration, he rubbed the heels of his palms against the chair's arms. "I knew if you found out I'd finished the antidote, you'd be right there wanting to be the first to test it out. Well, I couldn't let that happen and live with myself. There was no way in hell I was going to endanger another person. Not again. Particularly you."

"'Not again'? What do you mean by that?"

Damn his mouth. He straightened and dug his fingers into the chair's fabric. He'd let his emotions crash through any sense of caution. Guilt. He hated how it churned through his gut.

"It's just a turn of phrase," he whispered.

Silence slipped over the room as Jake tried to think of a word or thought—anything—to deflect the direction of Margot's thoughts.

"Really?" Doubt coated the one word.

She sighed and walked toward him. The hem of her housecoat fluttered, then whirled as she dropped down into an adjacent chair.

"Can you be honest with me?" she asked, her voice husky and earnest. "Can you do that? You know, you don't need to protect me. I'm stronger than you think. Stronger than I even thought." She gestured with an arm, and the empty sleeve of her housecoat wavered in the air. "I'm missing something here. I don't have any idea what it's about other than it has something to do with Miracell and Miltronics. And I guess, the reason why I brought up trust is because somewhere I've always felt in the back of mind that you don't—at least not fully. It's like you're keeping a part of yourself from me, holding back in some way.

Almost as if you're ashamed of something. I don't know. Maybe that doesn't make much sense, but that's how I feel at times."

Jake leaned his head back against the chair and stared up at the ceiling. Margot was too astute. She'd hit on something he himself had tried to deny and forget.

Yes, Jake was ashamed. At times, the feeling was so prevalent that it would wake him in the middle of the night with his heart crashing against his eardrums and sweat coating his body.

He knew she was staring at him, waiting for a response. How did he begin? How did he vocalize something he had problems formulating in his own head?

"What are you hiding? Tell me. Please. You can trust me with it. I promise."

"I—"

Jake couldn't find the right words.

"How bad can it be?"

If only she knew. Bad didn't even begin to describe his crimes, Jake realized in despair, as Margot leaned toward him. Her distinct sent of flowers and sunshine wrapped around him.

"This thing you're hiding is eating you up alive, so don't even try to lie. It's right there on your face. Absolute torment. What is it that has you so ashamed?"

Jake's eyes suddenly watered. Bowing his head, he blinked several times and tried to focus on his hands across his lap. He hated Margot seeing him like this.

"Oh, Baby. Please," she urged. "Talk to me."

The air stirred around him as Margot sat on the arm of his chair and brushed a leg up against his own. He felt the light touch of her nails as she skimmed them across his temple.

He blinked again. Finally, his vision cleared and his hands came into focus. He cleared his throat. It was time to tell his dirty, little secret and...possibly lose Margot forever.

CHAPTER 21

You know how no one suspected that I was missing, that I died in the blast at Miltronics?"

"Yes."

"Didn't you ever wonder?"

"I guess." Shrugging a shoulder, Margot shifted on the arm of his chair. "But I never thought about it in any great detail. There were so many other things I had questions about."

"It's because there was another body, another person who died in the explosion. Selfishly, I saw the opportunity and used it. Dental, police records, you name it." Jake laughed harshly, staring across Margot's office to the wall of bookshelves. "It's amazing what you can do when you're invisible."

"Who was he?"

"Henry Steward. I didn't know much else other than his general statistics—an eighteen-year-old, white male. Then again, at the time, I didn't want to know. I was too afraid to know what was going on. The guy was probably a runaway, a drug addict or some lost soul who was unfortunate enough not to have any relatives or friends who would miss him if he disappeared."

"What do you mean? Disappeared? It sounds—"

"Ominous? Oh, yeah. I know Malcolm had some type of deal with him. Money changed hands."

"You're not—you're not talking a human guinea pig, are you?"

"That's exactly what I'm saying. Experimentations didn't stop at mice or lab rats. It went much further. Steward wasn't the only one. There were others. I don't know how many. Maybe one or two. Maybe even more." Jake cleared his throat. He really hated talking about this. "I turned a blind eye to what was going on with Malcolm and Miltronics. I didn't confront Malcolm. I didn't investigate what I suspected. I'm just as bad as Malcolm. But at least with Malcolm, he never pretended to be anyone other than who he was."

"Don't. Don't categorize yourself with the likes of Malcolm. You don't compare, and never will."

Shocked at hearing compassion instead of contempt, Jake glanced up but of course couldn't see what she thought. What he wouldn't do to be able to read her expression right now.

"You don't understand," he insisted. "I suspected what was going on and I let it happen. I'm just as guilty by keeping silent."

"You can't say that. You're not positive they're dead."

"No. But they disappeared all the same, and I know what Malcolm was capable of." He shook his head and frowned. "Why? I don't get it. Why are you being so understanding? Anyone else would have turned away in disgust."

"But I'm not anyone. I'm me." She brushed his temple again with her nails. "Did you think that by revealing your worst secret that I would stop loving you? It doesn't happen that way. Love is a gift you just don't take away because of someone's mistakes. Love is knowing the worse part of that person, taking the bad along with the good, and still believing and wanting to be with them. At least that's love to me."

Jake felt truly humbled. "I don't deserve you."

"But you've got me. That is, of course, if you want me. Goodness knows I'm not the best catch. There's my drinking. I've got it under control right now. Then I tend to be a tad stubborn."

He heard the uncertainty in her voice, and quickly assured, "What fool wouldn't want you? You're beautiful."

She laughed. "Well, right now, that's pretty darn hard to tell, since you can't see me."

"Then you'd better take another look at yourself," he said in growing excitement. "The antidote is starting to work. It's only a matter of time now."

Jake pulled back the sleeve of her housecoat to reveal the ghostly image of her arm.

"Oh, my."

She wiggled her fingers in front of her face—a face slowly but undeniably materializing before Jake's eyes. In delight, he watched the clean line of her jaw, the thick sweep of her brow and how the amazement etched in her eyes sharpened and solidified. "You're an absolute genius." Wonder interlaced with sadness touched her voice. "You could have won the Nobel Prize over this. Miracell would have given you fame."

Jake shrugged, surprised at how little it mattered now. "Maybe. But I would have lost my soul in the process. Too many lives were sacrificed and, no doubt, many more would have been lost if I persisted with the project. There's no way Miracell could contribute to society as a whole, not when people continue to be motivated by greed or fear. I see that now, but at the time, I'd been blindsided by the idea of fame and my own self-centeredness. "

He saw the tenderness in her expression and felt himself melt. Strange, but that was the only way he could describe the heat flowing into his chest. Jake marveled at how one woman could touch his heart, his mind and his senses. Capturing her hand, he brushed his lips across the pulse point by her wrist. Her skin was smooth and warm against his mouth, while the scent of flowers whispered to him, entrancing him.

"Jake."

Something in her voice made him look up, and he stilled. Jake saw her clearly now, every beautiful feature—the pink flush to the gentle curve of her cheeks, the classic turn of her nose, and the full pout of her lips that screamed to be kissed. And her eyes. Desire burned in their depths, turning them almost black with it and ripping the breath from his lungs.

Hunger, hot, fierce and wild scored through his veins. With one look, she had the power to throw all logic from his mind. No woman had been able to leave him raw and open, so damn vulnerable like Margot. He'd never given the opposite sex that power.

He reached out, circled her neck with both of his hands, splaying his fingers across the vulnerable slope of her throat and gliding both thumbs across the line of her jaw. As he urged her toward him, he lifted his mouth to her own. She tasted better than anything that had crossed his lips. The soft, subtle pressure of her mouth hardened as she grew bolder and deepened the kiss, using her tongue to touch him again and again.

He groaned deep in his throat and urged her nearer. But wanted more. In frustration, he broke away and rose to his feet.

"Here."

Sweeping her up into his arms, Jake strode from her office and into the hall. To hell with the stairs and her room. His bed was closer, but not nearly close enough to his liking. The floor would be good enough for him, but he wouldn't do that to Margot.

"Wait," she murmured against his throat as he stepped into his room. "I'm tired of the dark."

He paused as she snapped on the light switch by the door. The lamp adjacent to the bed chased the darkness from the room and illuminated the bed in a warm and intimate glow.

"I want to see every inch of you," she whispered, her breath fanning lightly across his neck as she nipped at his ear lobe. "And watch your face when you climax beneath me."

His heart crashed against his ribs. "Keep talking like that and I might be coming before I get my clothes off."

Beside the bed, Jake eased her down to her feet, sliding her body, inch by glorious inch, across the length of his. Her housecoat gaped open, exposing the smooth line of her collarbone and the shadowy curve of her breasts. With one arm wrapped around her waist and the other cupping her head, he arched her backward, skimming his mouth over her long, sleek neck, then lowering to brush back the fabric with his teeth and baring one breast.

Jake heard the rapid pant of her breath, felt her hands press against his scalp, urging him on as he suckled her breast and lapped at her nipple, grazing his teeth across the hardened tip. He grew impatient, lowering his hand from the small of her back, bunching the housecoat in his hands until he felt silken skin. He cupped her bare bottom and inched lower, dipping between her legs.

She was wet, ready for him, dripping with need against his fingers. He groaned against her breast, thrusting his arousal against her belly. He wanted to tumble her onto the bed right this second and plunge into her, again and again, wrap those long legs of hers around his waist and get so deep inside her that she screamed with the pleasure of it.

Margot clutched at him, digging her fingers into his back pockets, grinding her hips against his own. "I want you, every hard inch of you. I want you bucking beneath me as I ride you."

"Jesus!" He edged back before he lost it right then and there, and dragged in a lungful of air. Patience. He needed it like he'd never needed it before in his life. "You've got me so tied up in knots."

"Are you saying you want to be tied up?" She gave him a devilish smile. "I'll be more than happy to oblige."

He wasn't fooled by the grin. The flush to her face, the heat in her eyes, the quick rise and fall of her chest beneath the housecoat, now pulled apart to the waist, told him she was just as strung up with need as he was.

"Later." He raised a brow. "Right now. I've got other things in mind."

"Sounds promising."

She helped him tug his sweater over his head. After it landed on the floor somewhere by their feet, she glided her fingers across his chest and stomach. Then she flicked his belt open. He helped her shrug out of his jeans and underwear with hands that were as unsteady as her own.

"I love the way you look, the feel of you on my hands. How your muscles tremble when I touch you like this." She slid an index finger slowly down his throat and over his chest. "Until now, I've never had the chance to see you. I missed so much."

When her finger glided past his belly to pause at his navel, Jake waited, breath drawn, but she stepped back, pulled the tie of her housecoat loose, shrugged and let the material drop to her feet.

"You're a damn tease. You know that, don't you?"

"Oh, but you love it."

"Yeah..." He slid a palm over the side of her breast, down over her waist and stilled at the gentle slope of her hip, all the while inching closer toward her. She was absolutely beautiful. "And I love you."

"I love you too."

Those words along with the look in her eyes soothed his soul like nothing ever had. It felt so right being here in this room, in this house with her.

~~*~~

Margot swallowed, sliding her gaze over every inch of him. He looked dangerous, male and hungry. With long, strong legs splayed out beneath him, he stood naked, unashamed, all silk and rock before her. It was a sin for a man to look like that. He'd inherited a thick, hairless chest, wide, powerful shoulders with arms hard and lean with muscle, a flat stomach and narrow hips. His arousal jutted out into the air. The idea of what he could do to her with that made her quiver all over.

God, she wanted him. Now. This second. She wanted to feel him atop her, beneath her, inside her. She wanted all of him— body, mind and soul.

He pressed up against her until the silken heat of him burned against her naked flesh and his chest flattened the tips of her breasts. His hair roughened legs brushed against hers as he urged her back against the bed and bowed his head to claim her lips. Easing back against the sheets, she opened her arms and wrapped them around his neck as he sank into her curves.

This time, though, she wanted to lead, to control, to push him to the edge. Pressing an elbow against the mattress, she moved, skimming across his body until she lay across the length of him, her legs cradling his hips, his penis, rigid and hot against her stomach. She inched up and across his body until she felt the tip of his shaft between her legs.

Jake gasped and jerked his hips beneath her, almost managing to thrust into her right then, but she slipped sideways. Her breasts skated across his chest as she leaned over him and bound his wrists with her hands and pulled them over his head. She nipped at his lower lip, urging his mouth open. Then she kissed him deeply, savoring the taste of him against her tongue.

He arched his head off the pillow and dipped his tongue between her parted lips, stroking, teasing, demanding a response she couldn't help but match with equal fever.

Desire burned through her flesh. So very hot.

"Oh, baby," she whispered against the corner of his mouth, "I need you. Now."

Digging her knees against the bed, Margot rose slowly, then lowered, taking his shaft inside her inch by magnificent inch, until she was completely impaled. He filled her, stretched her. The heat, the fullness of him so very deep inside her, was absolute heaven.

Jake jerked beneath her. She groaned, closed her eyes and felt the burn as she rose up and down over his shaft.

~~*~~

Jake watched her ride him. Her skin glowed, slick and flushed with desire. Her breasts swayed while wisps of raven hair clung to cheeks and shoulders, damp with her sweat. She was gorgeous, unashamed of her body, of her lust, of her beauty. He lifted the weight of her breasts beneath his palms and scraped his thumbs across her nipples. They tightened with his touch, and a whimper slipped from her throat.

When she arched above him and stiffened, he caught her hip in one hand and thrust into her, harder, faster, deeper, while he used his other hand to stroke the swollen nub between her legs, again and again, matching the rhythm with each jerk of his hips. Then she strained above him, squeezed him, and cried out his name as she came, hard and long above him.

Only then did he push off the mattress and catch her up against his chest, wrapping her beautiful long legs around his waist as he captured her mouth. He kissed her deep and hard while sliding one hand into her hair at the base of her skull and using the other to hold her hips steady as he plunged into her. He'd thought he'd been deep before, but now—now she had all of him as she tightened her legs around his waist and crashed against him, over and over until he felt his climax build, higher, tighter, harder. Then he was spilling his seed into her, jerking uncontrollably and shivering in her arms. He was falling...drowning.

Slowly, he became aware of Margot wrapped around him, of the evening behind the drawn curtains, of the cool air against his skin. The flannel sheets had been flung off the bed.

"Jesus." Jake eased back and looked at her. He saw the wonder in her eyes and knew the same expression reflected from his own. With a knuckle, he caressed her cheek and found her skin, still damp and flushed from their lovemaking, incredibly soft. "That was beyond words. Beyond anything. You're beautiful. Do you know that?"

"No." She shook her head and kissed him lightly, tenderly. "You're beautiful. Inside and out. I fell for you even before I knew what you looked like. I fell for the man you are and the man you can be."

"You know, I don't think—no, I know—I've never been this happy in my life. There was always something I wanted, something I always felt I was missing. I didn't realize until this moment that it was love."

He reclined against the pillows, and Margot nestled up against his side and rested a cheek against his chest. He reached over for the bedside lamp, but she caught his wrist.

"No. If I wake up during the night, I want to make sure you're there. Flesh and blood and not some phantom shadow."

He left the light and pulled her closer. The touch of her lips against his chest was so faint that for a moment he thought he'd imagined it. He glanced down at the crown of her head and then smiled up at the ceiling.

Happy. That didn't even begin to describe the feeling inside of Jake. Tightening his arm around Margot's waist, he rubbed his chin against the glossy waves of her hair and drank in the scent of her. He'd never get tired of her distinct fragrance—not in this lifetime or the next.

Jake thought of one thing that would make it perfect. He opened his mouth to ask her to marry him but stopped.

No. Not yet. The timing was way off.

Earlier today, he'd gotten ahead of himself and placed an order on the net while she'd been in the shower. He should get the package tomorrow. But it didn't matter. Not now, at least.

Because there was Malcolm. For a while, he'd forgotten about Margot's ex-husband. Somewhere out there, Malcolm, a constant threat, waited and planned his next move...until Jake stopped him. Tomorrow, after Jake destroyed Miracell and insured Margot's safety, he'd finish this thing with Malcolm, one way or another.

~~*~~

Reaching over, Malcolm pulled the 38 out of the glove compartment. He checked the safety before placing it on the car seat beside him and kept his hand wrapped around the cold metal. He glanced back up at the road and saw the sharp curve. Too late. He hit the brakes hard and sped around the turn. Too fast. The tires lost traction and started skidding.

"Son of a bitch!"

He pumped the brakes. The tires gripped the road again and some miracle stopped the car from nose-diving over the shoulder and into one of the pines that lined the side of the road. When he pulled back in his lane again, he exhaled loudly.

Shit. That was a close one. He might have ended up like John. Dead. He laughed harshly.

Margot would have loved that.

At the thought of her, Malcolm wrung the steering wheel with fisted hands. What the hell had happened to them? There was a time, which seemed more like decades ago right now, when he'd loved her and he knew she'd felt the same about him. But then she'd become this woman he didn't know. Someone that wouldn't listen to him, wouldn't take his suggestions, wouldn't agree with him. She'd become someone separate with her own thoughts and ideals.

And those damn questions of hers about Miltronics and his work. She hadn't been able to leave it alone. She'd started harping, digging into dangerous territory. Why hadn't she been able to understand that work and his personal life were separate and completely different from each other?

Then the fights started. She wanted to know every stupid detail of his life. Intimidation, threats, nothing had worked to shut her up. The last time they'd had a row, she'd ended up in the hospital. It hadn't been his fault. She was the one who fell down the stairs. It wasn't like he'd pushed her.

He blinked back watery eyes and wiped at his nose with the back of his hand. She'd walked out on him and filed for divorce. Just remembering being served brought rage to the forefront. Yes. He needed to focus on that emotion. He didn't love her anymore. He wouldn't. She'd betrayed him. Just as Jake and John had betrayed him.

He'd left Pinetop almost an hour ago, and was about twenty-minute from Greyson. He hated the mountain town. He hated everything about the two-bit little clapboard, stinking town.

Malcolm exhaled, his breath fanning clouds into the car's interior. He cranked up the heat. He hadn't been able to get warm since he'd left the airport in Flagstaff. But he was almost there. Another fifteen minutes and he'd hit the road that led to Margot's place.

His jaw clenched. Soon. Real soon. The gun wouldn't be cold metal in his hand. It would be hot, so damn hot from putting a couple of bullets in Jake's head.

To hell with the formula. If Jake hadn't figured it out by now, he never would. He'd used Margot to push Jake harder, knowing how much of a sucker Jake was for a lost cause. But now, Malcolm wanted revenge. He craved it.

As for Margot. If the formula hadn't killed her, he'd have to do something. He didn't see her keeping quiet. Her principles wouldn't allow it. Surprisingly, she had that in common with Jake. There'd been a time that he'd thought Jake hadn't had any. That was a gross miscalculation on Malcolm's part. Well, he'd eliminate that problem real quick.

CHAPTER 22

HEY, SLEEPY HEAD."

The next morning, Margot placed a breakfast tray with orange juice, waffles, scrambled eggs and a banana across Jake's lap and sank down on the edge of the bed beside him. He lay flat on his back with only a flannel sheet draped across his hips. When he didn't stir, she sat in silence and watched him with a silly grin on her face. God, he looked good.

This was the first time she'd had the chance to really sit back and take in Jake's appearance. He had such a masculine face—a strong jaw, thick brows and high, prominent cheekbones. Lines bracketed his mouth. A mouth with a full, sensual bottom lip that knew exactly what to do with her body. She shivered in remembrance. Reddish gold hair, thick and cut close to the scalp, capped and accented his strong, square face. There was nothing feminine about him, except maybe his dark lashes and sun-kissed complexion. Not one scar marred his body. It was shameful to have such beautiful skin.

He also had the most incredible baby-blue eyes. Eyes now open and smiling at her.

She smiled back. "How are you feeling this morning?"

"Tired and thoroughly used."

She gave him a cocky grin. "Oh, really? And I wonder how that happened?"

"This incredibly gorgeous woman decided to jump my bones last night. The way she moved that body of hers had me doing the most amazing contortions."

"Oooh, reeeally?" Unable to resist, she took the banana from his tray, started to peel it and looked for a reaction.

~~*~~

Jake watched her slip her mouth over the fruit's tip and take a slow but deliberate bite. Wow. Then she licked her lips in the most suggestive manner. He swallowed audibly. "You better watch it. If you keep that up, I'll be wanting you to do something equally suggestive on me."

"Is that so..." She took another slow nibble from her banana, all the while holding his gaze.

"Oh yeah..."

He curled a hand around the back of her neck and urged her over his lap. He kissed her, tasting the banana on her lips, loving the way she quivered against his hand and her little intake of breath that told him she was just as moved as he was with a simple, little kiss.

He pulled her closer. The glass of orange juice on the breakfast tray shot sideways and spilled onto his lap.

"Damn!"

Margot pulled away and made a face. "Now look what you did. You made me spill your juice!"

"Me?"

"You better believe it. If you'd kept your hands to yourself..."

As she took the glass from beside his hip and placed it back on the tray, he shifted and winced as more liquid seeped through the sheet and right into his crotch. A cold shower couldn't have been better.

"I guess that's just as well. I need to get up and get going. After a shower, I want to go down to the lab and clear out the formula and antidote from the computer files." He placed the tray to the side, pulled back the sheet and stood. "You want to join me in the shower?"

He watched her look boldly over his naked body and tried not to grin.

She glanced at the bed and wrinkled her nose before she retrieved the tray. "I better clean this up before it soaks into the mattress."

Jake watched her go, then shook himself mentally. If he weren't careful, every minute of his day would be consumed by thoughts of her. But then again, that wouldn't be so bad.

He showered and dressed. Fifteen minutes later he headed down to the lab. The second the door closed behind him, he walked over to the desk and booted up the computer. Systematically, he went through each file and deleted it from the system. While he waited for the large files to purge, he pulled out two thumb drives from the desk drawer. He didn't bother erasing the data through the computer, but took each one and broke them apart. He tossed the plastic and metal pieces into the garbage.

With the files almost purged and the backups in the trash, the suffocating burden strapped around Jake's shoulders lifted.

The lab door opened from behind Jake.

"My, God!"

Jake stiffened, tension cracking through his limbs as he turned around.

Malcolm, gun in hand, stood five feet from the lab's entrance. Excitement glittered in his eyes. "You pulled it off! I knew if anyone could do it, you'd be the one. You just needed a little more incentive with Margot."

Right this second, Jake wanted to launch himself at Malcolm and pound a fist into his face. "You're sick. I can't believe you involved Margot. She had nothing to do with this."

"Oh, please. Save me the bullshit. It's called opportunity. Margot just happened to be in the wrong place at the right time." His face hardened as he advanced toward Jake. "And don't think you're any better than me. You've played just as dirty—what with that number you pulled back in Boston."

"That doesn't compare. But it stopped you for a while. I just don't understand how you managed to get out of jail so quickly."

"Money and a good lawyer. What else? Did you really think

framing me would stop me? Life's not that simple. Haven't you learned that yet?"

He hated Malcolm's confidence, his holier-than-thou attitude. "Money can only last so long. Even you can't pull from a bottomless well."

"I don't particularly care what you think. But I do care about Miracell." He lifted the gun and waved it to one side. "Move away from the computer. I want those copies."

"You're too late."

Malcolm frowned. "What do you mean?"

"They're gone." He edged away from the computer. "They don't exist. Got it?"

"You're lying. Only a fool would destroy them."

Jake watched cautiously as Malcolm rushed over to the desk and attempted to pull one empty file after another from the computer. He backed away from Malcolm. Maybe, just maybe he might get out of the lab without getting shot at.

Swearing loudly, Malcolm whipped around. His eyes flared with hatred. "You stupid idiot! How could you?"

Jake tensed. For a second, he thought the gun would go off then and there.

"We're talking millions. Do you know what a person can do with that type of money? Do you!"

"I really don't give a shit." Jake lifted a brow and rammed Malcolm's words right back at him. "Life's not that simple. Haven't you learned that yet?"

Face mottled an ugly red, Malcolm swore again and kicked viciously at the garbage can. The contents inside spewed into the air and onto the floor.

Malcolm lifted the gun suddenly. Jake saw the flash. No time to react. A shot blasted, whizzing by but missing him. Too damn close. Inches if that. He aimed a shoulder and dove into Malcolm's gut. The gun spun into the air. It clattered to the floor and skidded across the tile to butt up against a cabinet door to his right.

They both went for the gun. He grabbed onto Malcolm's jacket to keep him from getting there first. The corner of the desk slammed into Jake's hip. He blinked and struggled with the pain, desperately keeping his grip on Malcolm's jacket. Malcolm rammed an elbow into his throat, tore from his grasp and shoved him aside. Choking, Jake landed hard on his stomach and saw Malcolm scramble for the gun.

No, damn it.

Swiveling, Jake kicked out. His toe connected with the handle and the gun darted across the floor, parallel to his shoulder. He lunged for it. His fingers closed over the warm handle. With the other hand, he struggled to his feet with the help of the desk while Malcolm raced around the chair toward the front door.

Before Jake had a chance to use the gun, Malcolm had opened the door and escaped outside.

~~*~~

The sound of a gunshot shattered the quiet, morning air. Margot dropped the bag of trash she'd carried outside. With a cry, she sprinted around the corner of the veranda toward the lab. Jake was down there!

Just as she reached the side of the house...someone came rushing from the lab. For one second she thought it was Jake. But the runner didn't have the easy, smooth gate of Jake. No, this man was thinner, shorter and—

Malcolm!

He plunged to his left and through the knee-deep snow butted up against the building. Rounding the corner, he stumbled to a stop and pivoted until he stood half hidden from the open lab door. He stood hunched as if waiting to strike. An instant later Jake barreled out of the door. The snow and sun reflected off something in Jake's hand. Metallic silver blinked, once, twice.

A gun.

Hunched over, Jake edged toward the corner where Malcolm waited. At the same time, she saw Malcolm pick something up from the ground. Frowning, she hurried down the steps. She couldn't see—Oh, God. A shovel. Malcolm hefted it up in both hands as if to weigh it.

Margot jumped down the last two steps. "Jake! Look out!"

At her voice, both men looked up, but Malcolm moved first. He lifted the shovel, leaped forward and swung it at Jake. The metal hit the side of Jake's head. She recoiled. Even from this far away she heard the sickening thud of metal against flesh and bone. The force of the shovel sent Jake sprawling to the ground. He didn't move, didn't do anything. Just lay there like some broken and abused doll. He was probably unconscious. He could even be—

"No!"

Her cry of pain and anguish exploded from her lungs as she stumbled forward.

Malcolm turned in her direction and threw the shovel aside. It landed against a snowdrift. Once deadly, now harmless on its own. But Malcolm was far from harmless. She stilled, feeling his threat even with the distance between them. A sudden fear, not for Jake, but for her own safety crawled across her skin. She edged backward.

Then Malcolm was running, running right toward her.

Margot whipped around and raced up the stairs to the front door. She opened, slammed and locked it behind her. The phone. She needed to call for help. She grabbed the receiver from the one in the hall. No dial tone.

No. No. This couldn't be happening. It was a nightmare. Things like this just didn't happen.

Her breathing became more ragged, labored and hard to grasp. She dropped the receiver just as Malcolm started twisting the knob and banging against the door.

"Margot!" Malcolm's voice, hard and urgent, penetrated into the house. "Let me in! I'm not going to hurt you."

Full-blown hysterical laughter peeled past her lips. Margot backed along the wall toward the kitchen. She needed to get a grip, push back the fear if she wanted to survive—

Think. Think. If Malcolm had the gun, it wouldn't take him long to use it on the lock and blow it open. Her cell phone. Yes. In her purse. The kitchen. With her gaze fixed on the front door, she edged to the threshold of the kitchen, then rushed to the counter and her purse.

She dove into her purse, rifling through the mess, flinging wallet, receipts and pens wildly out onto the counter and floor but couldn't find her cell.

Glass shattered from the back door's window right beside her. Shards bounced off her arm and caught in her hair. She jumped back and screamed. Malcolm's arm appeared from outside as he reached inside for the deadbolt.

Lurching to the door, she punched his hand with a fist. Once, twice. It didn't do a thing. Stupid. So stupid. She needed a knife, not her stupid hand. He managed to grasp the lock.

"Damn it, Margot. Calm down. I just want to come in and talk to you."

"Liar. You sick liar!"

She ran to the drawer where she kept the knives. Just as she opened the drawer, the lock snapped open with a loud clink. She glanced back to the door. In one second, Malcolm would have that door open and be inside. No, time. No, time. Even if she did get a knife in her hands, the thing would probably end up being used against her.

Her boot heel squealed against the linoleum floor as she twisted around and dashed across the floor and out of the room. Just as the kitchen door banged open, she grabbed the baluster. Margot tumbled up the stairs, using one hand on the railing to pull herself up faster. If she could just get into the bathroom. It was the only place on the upper floor with a lock. But that wasn't going to stop Malcolm. Not if he had a gun. Or did he? She'd just assumed—

Margot couldn't remember. Think. She couldn't think. Did Malcolm get the gun from the ground by the lab? She hadn't seen him pick it up.

Then she realized the bathroom was out of the question. There was no window, no other exit other than the one door. It had to be her bedroom. Maybe if she could get through the window and up on the porch roof, she could backtrack to the kitchen and get the car keys.

She hit the landing and turned sharply right and into her room just as she heard footsteps, heavy and rapid in the hall below. It wouldn't take but moments for him to come charging in here. She looked around the room in indecision. She didn't have a gun; she didn't have anything to stop him from walking through that door and killing her. She glanced around. The dresser. It was big, heavy, and wouldn't hold long. There was no carpet to lock the dresser legs against the floor. But it could delay Malcolm and give her a couple more minutes to plan, to think, to live.

She rushed over to the dresser and shoved her shoulder against the side, grunting and digging her heels into the floor. The dresser's legs squealed a protest as she pushed it across the hardwood floor and up against the door.

Something slammed against the door, shaking the dresser. Malcolm. He hit the door again. The dresser gave several inches. She didn't know how long it would keep Malcolm at bay.

Panicked, she glanced around and saw the window. She raced over, snapped the locks and slid the window open.

The bedroom door shuddered again. She looked over her shoulder with dread. The dresser had inched further across the floor and the door had opened a crack. She could hear Malcolm's heavy breathing from the other side. He shoved at the door. The dresser legs slide even more across the floor. Malcolm's hand appeared in the widening gap. No gun. But he could have it hidden in his other hand.

She banged on the screen until it snapped off at one corner. Then she pushed the remainder of the frame off with her shoulder. The screen fell to the roof of the veranda and skidded across the sloped overhang for several feet. Cold air slapped at her skin as she ducked her head outside and looked around. She stood directly above the veranda.

The roof from here was probably a fifteen-foot drop. But further down, on the other side of the house, it sloped downward several feet. From there, she could hang from the side and hope to hell the shorter drop and layer of snow cushioned her fall. Then she could sneak back in the kitchen and get her keys to the car and get help.

Jake.

She couldn't get a clear view of the lab area from here. She wondered if he was unconscious, mortally wounded or already dead. No. She couldn't, wouldn't think of him in that light. Otherwise, she might just give up.

What to do? What to do? A gun really stacked the deck against her. She also needed to consider Malcolm's strength. He might be thin, but he was still pounds heavier than her and had more muscle and power in that frame of his.

For several terrifying seconds, she stood in complete uncertainty, but the widening gap between the door and the frame spurred her into action. Taking a deep breath, she flexed her fingers, gripped the window seal and lifted a leg over the ledge to the outside. She straddled the ledge and tried not to think of losing her footing and sliding off the roof.

Malcolm grabbed her arm and yanked her backward and into the room. "Oh, no you don't."

Grunting, she twisted away and stumbled. She caught a palm against the wall and pushed, launching herself away from Malcolm and across the bed. He caught her ankle and pulled. Crying out in fear, Margot clawed at the mattress. The comforter bunched between her fingers. She slid backward, losing ground. She grabbed the edge of the mattress and pulled frantically at its edge. Her muscles screamed in protest as she tried to gain ground, but she found it impossible. Malcolm was just too strong! It would be only a matter of minutes before he had his hand wrapped around her throat instead of her leg. She kicked back with both feet, trying to shake free of Malcolm's vice-like grip. Her foot connected with something solid.

Malcolm grunted. "Damn it!"

Panting, Margot twisted back and forth, jerking her ankle, again and again. He wouldn't let go! She rolled on her side and glanced back. Face flushed, teeth gritted into a savage grimace, Malcolm hunched over her and now had both hands bolted around her ankle. This time she aimed with her free leg, snapping her heel back into Malcolm's groin.

He cried out but somehow managed to keep his hands glued to her ankle.

A loud bang crashed into the room.

A gunshot? Margot stiffened. That couldn't be. She twisted around, but Malcolm's hand on her back shoved her against the mattress.

"What the hell are you doing?" he asked from above her, his fingers digging into the flesh of her back as Margot squirmed and bucked.

"What I should have done months ago." Anger and rage dripped from the person's voice.

"For God's sake, don't—"

Another blast resounded inside the four walls—a gunshot. A new burst of terror gripped Margot's mind and jerked her body into motion.

Frantic, she clawed at the bedding as Malcolm landed on top of her. His full weight crushed her against the mattress and shoved her face into the comforter. Struggling for air, she turned her head to the side and inhaled sharply, smelling linen, dust and something else she couldn't define. She wiggled and twisted from beneath him until she turned to her side. Her hip hit his stomach and she stared at his face. Malcolm grabbed at her shoulders. His dull nails bruised her skin as disbelief and fear flashed in his blue eyes. Then he stilled, his hands limp on her arms, his body once heavy, now unbearable.

Sightless eyes stared at her, while blood from a wound in his cheek dripped onto her brow. She shoved at the suffocating pressure of his body with the flats of her hands. Using her knees as added leverage, she pushed out from under Malcolm. Blessed air scraped into her lungs.

She scrambled off the edge of the bed. Joyce stood in front of the doorway to the hall. A gun rested in her right hand.

Rising to her full height, Margot clutched at the bed's footboard to keep herself from falling. Her entire body shook in reaction.

"Y—you saved my life," Margot managed to get out.

Joyce stared back, an unfamiliar expression on her face.

"He was going to kill me." Margot's voice strengthened. "If you hadn't come when you had…" Feeling her legs start to buckle, Margot lowered herself to the bed but froze. Blood stained the daisy comforter. Malcolm, his face buried, his hair matted with blood, lay motionless on the bed.

Dead.

Margot's stomach rolled with nausea and she quickly turned away and faced Joyce once again.

Joyce blinked rapidly, but tears welled from her eyes and trailed down a red, blotchy face. "The bastard. He deserves to die. He killed my brother."

"Why did he murder Carl? Do you know?" Margot took in a deep, shuddering breath. Her heart still hammered like crazy inside her chest.

"It all started with your brother's death. Carl began asking questions after that. I know he was hiding something about the car accident. I found this strange guy's wallet in Carl's desk drawer. It took me the longest time to try to figure out why my brother would hold onto something like that. I uncovered a couple other things to where I think someone else died in that crash—was even murdered—and John's alive somewhere. I think Carl covered it all up to protect John either from Malcolm or from being arrested for murder. I never could figure out which one, but I do know he did it because of you. He loved you, you know. He would have done anything for you. And you didn't give a shit."

Margot balled her hands into fists. "Johnny's alive?"

Joyce's gaze narrowed. "I don't care if he's alive or dead. It doesn't change a thing for me. *My* brother is dead. I tried to stop it. I told Carl, again and again, to keep out of our business. I never thought Malcolm would go that far."

"What do you mean by 'our business'?"

Joyce's lip curled. "You're so self-centered. You never look beyond your own problems."

"What are you saying?"

"I was seeing Malcolm. Carl hated the idea. He started digging into things no matter how much I told him to stop. All I wanted to do was get out of this hell-hole of a place. I thought Malcolm was the key. I was wrong. But I still have a chance with the formula. Where is it?"

Margot swallowed. Tension snapped into her muscles. Oh, God, all this time Joyce was in on this. "Formula?"

"Come off it, Margot. I'm not buying the stupid act. I know everything. Malcolm told me. I want it. I didn't save you just because of our 'friendship'."

Betrayal tasted bitter against Margot's throat. "I don't know where it is."

"You have to know!" Joyce stepped deeper into the room. Her eyes glittered, but not from tears. Rage shone from their depths. "Carl was never supposed to die. I begged him. You don't know how many times I told him to keep his nose out of it. I knew Malcolm was getting nervous. But I never thought— Malcolm promised me he wouldn't do anything, but he lied. It was supposed to be so simple. Get the formula and get out of town."

"Nothing's ever simple," Margot whispered. She glanced at the gun in Joyce's hand. At least she didn't have it pointed at her. Yet. "How about you put the gun down and we can talk this out? I'm sure between the two of us, we can find the formula."

"Liar. You're just like Malcolm." New tears spilled from her eyes as her face curled up in fury. "You lie. Everyone lies. You're all the same. Do you think I'm that stupid? You'll turn me in the second you get the chance."

Oh, God. Rationalizing wasn't going to work. Margot eased backward. One step. Two. Four more and she might get to the open window before Joyce decided to plug her with holes.

Joyce lifted the gun in a tight-fisted hand. In horror, Margot jumped to the side. The gun went off in a loud boom. The bullet hit the wall to her right. Plaster and paint sprayed Margot's face. Margot clambered over the window ledge to the roof.

She slipped against the slick tile but regained her footing. Patches of snow and ice covered a good part of the roof. Joyce appeared from the window, straddling the ledge with the gun in her hand. Two seconds and she'd pull the trigger again.

Damn it. Blood pounding in her ears, using a hand against the brick for balance, Margot lunged and kicked out. Her boot connected with Joyce's wrist. Crying out, Joyce jerked back. The gun tumbled from her grasp and skidded across the veranda's sloped roof to bunt up against the easement.

Margot could try to scramble down and get it or escape along the veranda's roof. Deciding on the later, she edged slowly across the tile and along the perimeter of the second story wall, trailing a hand across the brick for support. On this side of the house, the ground had several outcroppings of rock hidden beneath the snow. Last summer, she'd pulled them from the dirt to prepare for a flower garden. She didn't want to take a chance on landing on one of them.

Around ten feet more and the veranda sloped downward several feet. It would be easier to drop down to the ground from there without getting hurt. There were several low-lying bushes that could break her fall. She moved quicker, using both hands now along the wall.

Joyce followed. Margot heard the scrape of her shoe against the tile, her labored breath growing louder with each passing second. She didn't dare look back. It would only slow her down and frighten her that much more.

Suddenly, Joyce grasped her upper arm. Margot choked back a scream of surprise. The pressure of her fingers deepened as she tugged Margot back toward her. She tried to shrug off Joyce's hold. Shifting sideways, she rammed her nails into the brick, scraping her fingers, then her cheek against the unyielding wall as she struggled to latch onto any crevice.

Joyce pulled harder at her arm, digging and bruising her skin with vicious fingers. The woman's rage was giving her a strength Margot never imagined possible. Margot lost her grip against the brick, skidding up against Joyce's chest.

"Bitch." Joyce's breath crawled across her ear. "You had everything. Everything and you tossed it away."

Margot jabbed an elbow into Joyce's stomach. Grunting, Joyce staggered back and pulled Margot along with her. The sudden jarring movement and the snow beneath Margot's feet thrust her off balance. She landed hard on her back with Joyce half on top of her. The action slid them toward the edge of the roof. Margot caught the eaves with the heel of her shoe, saving her from tumbling closer to the edge but dislodging the gun. The weapon tumbled over the roof's edge.

One wrong move and Joyce could push her over the side. She'd hit one of those rocks and die from a bashed in head. It wouldn't take much with the way she was losing her strength. She was winded and weakening with each passing second.

She needed to somehow get past Joyce to the window. If she could get into the house, maybe lock the window after her, she might get the car keys and get behind the wheel. Then she'd be able to get help. But she had to get to the window first.

Pushing off the eaves with one foot, Margot lunged to the left of Joyce. On hands and knees, she scrambled over the tile, hell-bent on getting to the window. Joyce grabbed at her waist, hooking her fingers around her waistband, then landing on her back. Margot went down in a loud gasp, the air knocked completely out of her lungs.

Margot managed to get enough room between them to drive an elbow into Joyce's ribs. She heard a groan as she rolled sideways. Joyce was to her right when she lifted her knees up against her chest and thrust her feet out and connected with Joyce's stomach. Joyce growled, skidding down across the tile, her feet, ankles, then calves sliding off the roof's edge.

Panic flared in Joyce's face as she continued to slip over the ledge. She clawed forward frantically, seizing Margot's leg, then her waist. Her weight pulled Margot along with her.

Margot dug into the tile and snow with her hands. Her fingers, nails torn and bloodied, came up empty. She slid toward the roof's edge, inch by torturous inch, unable to kick out, unable to do anything while Joyce grappled over her, trying to drag herself up as she continued to slither across the snow. Joyce's weight, too heavy for the both of them, drew Margot relentlessly toward the eaves.

Margot didn't have time to pray. She didn't have time to do anything but close her eyes as she plummeted from the roof and followed Joyce into the air.

CHAPTER 23

A PIERCING CRY CUT through the mournful sigh of the wind as Jake ran up the embankment toward the house. With knife-like pain stabbing his temple where Malcolm had hit him with the shovel, he glanced up to the roof and saw Margot and another woman up there, both fighting and locked in some obscene shuffle.

He quickened his pace, kicking up snow, pushing his arms and legs until they screamed from the abuse. Frigid air cut into his lungs. Sweat broke on his brow and chilled his already cold skin as he raced toward the house.

Suddenly, they rolled off the roof. He heard the sickening thump as both bodies hit the ground. Nothing but stillness and silence carried over the wind.

"No!"

He stumbled, caught his balance by grabbing onto a tree branch, and charged out into the clearing and over to Margot's motionless body.

"For the love of God, don't do this—"

Jake collapsed onto his hands and knees beside Margot, uncaring of the snow's bitter cold against his bare palms. She lay face up, both arms flung out at her sides, her eyes closed, her skin almost as white as the snow around her.

Quickly, he checked for a pulse and found one, strong and steady against his fingers.

"Margot?" His words scraped against his throat. "Can you hear me?"

Her lashes flickered but remained shut. He glanced over at the other woman several yards from her side. Joyce. The short blonde hair gave her away. Her body rested face down in the snow, unmoving. Knowing Joyce wasn't going to be much of a threat any time soon, he turned back to Margot.

She hadn't stirred. Scared of the seriousness of her injuries, he didn't attempt to move her. He didn't have the equipment or know-how to work with a possible spinal injury. He wasn't that type of doctor. He rose on one knee with the intention of calling for an ambulance but paused when a sigh whispered past Margot's lips.

Her lids flickered open, and she squinted up at him. "My head. What—"

"Can you move? How are your limbs? Do they have feeling?"

She wiggled her fingers in the snow beside her. "Okay, I think."

He helped her struggle into a sitting position.

She winced and placed a hand to her brow. "Oh, yeah. I have feeling. It feels like a semi-truck flattened me."

"I wouldn't make any sudden moves. You're bound to have hurt something with that fall."

Panic flared into her eyes, and the rest of her face leached of color. "Where's Joyce?" She pivoted at the waist and stiffened. "Oh, God. She shot and killed Malcolm and tried to do the same with me."

She backpedaled, flinging snow with the heels of her shoes as she slid away from Joyce and into Jake's arms. He caught her head against the crook of his arm and chest.

"Is she..."

"I don't know."

He held her in his arms and ran a soothing hand over the silk of her hair. She was shaking in shock. Her body felt like a damn block of ice. He needed to get her in the house and soon before she went into hypothermia.

He also had to check on Joyce. Easing his arms from around

Margot, he rose to his feet and stepped over to Joyce's prone body. He rolled her onto her back. Snow clung to her lashes and hair and an ugly gash cut across her temple. Blood had congealed in thick patches over her brow, temple and cheek. More blood stained the snow where she'd lain, while her eyes, unblinking and blind, stared up to the sky. He felt for a pulse to double-check.

"She's dead."

Jake glanced up at the second story of the house and the open window. Malcolm must be up there. Dead. Jake didn't know what he felt. There was no relief, no exhilaration, absolutely nothing but indifference right now. Maybe that would change.

"We need to call the deputy on duty," Margot said from behind him. "The house phone is dead. I have my cell somewhere. Probably in the kitchen. They haven't filled Carl's old position yet. I don't know how in the world I'm going to be able to explain this."

He glanced over his shoulder and found Margot standing behind him. She was looking at Joyce with a mixture of horror and disbelief. If at all possible, the pallor to her face had worsened. Jake needed to get her away from here.

"When it comes to Joyce, I guess it would be self-defense. It's not like I murdered her or for that matter Malcolm. They're not going to think I tried to kill him. He did force his way in." She let Jake lead her across the yard, up the stairs and into the house. "The police will see how dangerous Malcolm really was. They just have to look into his history. There's the police report filed when the house was vandalized, and his arrest. And of course, there's the restraining order back in Boston. That should clear any suspicion of foul play."

He stiffened, alarm crawling across his flesh. He shut the door behind them and turned to face her. "What are you talking about?"

She shrugged. "Nothing."

"No, it's something." He frowned down at her. "I want to know. What happened in Boston?"

She blinked and looked up at him now with clear, focused eyes. "After the divorce, I'd put a restraining order against

Malcolm. I'd since had it revoked, but at the time I was afraid of him."

"Why?"

"His temper."

Margot sensed the immediate change in Jake's body. It fairly oozed with tension, while the planes of his face had grown rigid. She placed a reassuring hand on the corded muscles of his forearm. "It was an accident. He caught me in the parking lot of the apartment where I'd moved after filing for the divorce. I didn't want to talk. I didn't want him anywhere near me. He wouldn't listen but followed me up the stairs to my place on the second floor. He wouldn't leave me alone. We argued. I don't remember the particulars—probably subconsciously blocked most from my mind. I do remember being on the landing and thinking that he was going to hit me. I stumbled, tripped over something I think. I'm not sure. The cement stairs were closer than either one of us thought. I fell down them and ended up in the hospital with a broken hip."

He pulled her gently into his arms and cradled her head against his shoulder with a trembling hand. "I'm so sorry. Life's hit you below the belt too many times." He kissed her lightly against her temple. "You're one strong lady. Any other person would have cracked."

"You don't understand. I almost did. I was so close to being hospitalized. I had to get on anti-depressants for a while." She pulled back and gazed up at him. "As for today, if not for you, I'd still be drinking, hiding behind some drunken fog. Don't get me wrong, I still have that craving—probably always will—but I can beat it. You gave me the insight and will to climb out of the hell-hole I dug myself into."

"Well, you're not alone now. I want you to know that you can count on me. Always. I'll do whatever it takes. Remember that."

His words touched her heart like nothing else could. "Thank you. I needed to hear that." Reluctantly she drew away. "I guess it can't be delayed any longer. I'll make the call to the police. You need to disappear for a couple of hours."

"Oh, no. I don't think so. I'm not about to let you do this alone."

"Oh yes, you are." She straightened her shoulders. "I'm not budging on that. Having you in the picture is going to raise questions. Questions neither one of us want to answer. We haven't gone through all this just to have Miracell become public knowledge. You've been dead against it from the beginning. And I'd be the first one to agree that it's just too dangerous. You know it." When he looked like he might argue, she lifted her chin and shook her head. "I don't need to be coddled. Do you understand?"

His lips firmed, but when she continued to argue her point, he finally nodded to her relief.

"You're too damn stubborn."

She lifted a brow. "And of course, you aren't?"

After Jake disappeared from the house, she found her cell phone and made the call to the authorities. It didn't take long for the coroner and police to get to the house and do their thing. The questions were direct and to the point along with her answers. She didn't have anything to hide. Not really. As to any suspicion directed toward her, there was none. Only sympathy.

As she watched them carry Malcolm and Joyce away in body bags, it really hit her how final and real everything had become.

Several hours later, she stood in front of the window above the kitchen sink and watched the last police car drive down and disappear behind the trees. The coroner had left an hour earlier. Several minutes later, she heard Jake enter the kitchen and join her at the counter, but she continued to stare out the window.

"Well, it's finally over," she said.

But was it? Margot wondered. Joyce's words came back to whisper inside her head. Was her brother still alive? Could he be out there somewhere and not tell her?

Never. Johnny would never be that cruel. Still…

Tomorrow she'd mention to Jake what Joyce had said. But not this moment. This moment she needed to heal her shattered body and mind from the day's events before she had the needed strength to investigate further.

"Yeah, it's over," Jake said softly beside her.

She grabbed the edge of the counter with tight-fisted hands. "I killed someone today. And not just a stranger—someone I considered a friend at one point."

He eased up from behind and wrapped both arms around her waist. "Don't say that," he whispered thickly against the crown of her head. "It was an accident."

She sighed hard. Closing her eyes, she leaned against his chest. "I know."

But even knowing Jake spoke the truth, she still felt tainted. Today, she'd lost her innocence, but at the same time, she'd gained something more important—the knowledge that she was a survivor. She could take life's blows and come up for more. She'd always had little self-confidence. First, it had been her parents, and then it had been Malcolm who had brought her down. When she'd taken those baby-steps to gain that inner strength, Malcolm had rebelled against it. But she was strong. Stronger then she could have ever imagined. Yes. She'd become a survivor.

She searched and found Jake's hand across her stomach. It felt strange yet wonderful to touch warm skin instead of the cool leather of his glove.

"I love this—having you here with me."

"The feelings mutual." His hold tightened around her.

She smiled, feeling the brush of his lips against her hair as she turned in the circle of his arms. Looking up, Margot caught her breath at the expression in Jake's eyes. She realized she'd stumbled on something far more profound than the will to survive.

Love. Simple and honest. The emotion softened the rugged lines of Jake's face and darkened his eyes to indigo.

Who would have thought? When Jake came into her life, she'd been drowning in despair and self-pity, but somehow she'd managed to claw her way out. She wouldn't have done it without Jake. And now with him in her life, the future held so much promise.

"It all feels too good," she whispered. "What if something—"

"Don't." Rubbing a thumb over her lower lip, he slowly searched her face. "I'm not about to question anything. Not anymore. Because you know what? When I ran from Boston, I'd been so terrified of dying that I missed out on what really mattered. And that's the journey, not the end. So don't start doubting the future. Instead, when something good comes along, take it and savor the moment."

And Margot did exactly what Jake suggested as he bent down and brushed his lips against her mouth. She savored the taste, the feel and the heat of Jake's kiss.

THANK YOU!

T HANK YOU FOR reading all six episodes of Anxiety. I hope you enjoyed it, and if you did, don't forget to leave a review.

For news on latest releases, contests and other news, you can signup for my newsletter (http://www.hdthomson.com). Also, if you feel like contacting me, you can always catch me on Facebook (https://www.facebook.com/authorhdthomson).

COMPLETE LIST OF TITLES

ROMANTIC SUSPENSE

SMOKE & MIRRORS SERIES

ANXIETY #1
DUPLICITY #2
IDENTITY #3

PARANORMAL ROMANCE

ONYX & MERCURY SERIES

A KISS BEFORE DYING

SHADES SERIES

DEADLY SHADES #1
SHADES OF HOLLY #2
KILLER SHADES #3
KILLER SHADES BOX SET - BOOKS 1 THROUGH 3

CONTEMPORARY ROMANCE

THE LONG ROAD HOME
PROTECTING KATIE

ABOUT THE AUTHOR

H. D. Thomson moved from Ontario, Canada as a teenager to the heat of Arizona where she graduated from the University of Arizona with a B.S. in Business Administration with a major in accounting. After working in the corporate world as an accountant, H. D. changed her focus to one of her passions-books. She owned and operated an online bookstore for several years and then started the company, Bella Media Management. The company specializes in web sites, video trailers, ebook conversion and promotional resources for authors and small businesses. When she is not heading her company, she is following her first love-writing. You can read more about her and her books at HDThomson.com.

What they're saying about H. D. Thomson's books:

"My applause to the author on an entertaining read." – *Romance Novel Junkies*
"Author H.D. Thomson does a great job of keeping the reader guessing." – *Paranormal Romance Party*
"Bravo H. D. Thomson!" – *Writer's and Reader's of Distinct Fiction's Top Read.*
"Thomson's writing is spot on…" – *Confessions of a Bibliophile.*